W9-BCX-500

Rumor of Evil

Also by Gary Braver

Choose Me, with Tess Gerritsen

Tunnel Visionary

Skin Deep

Flashback

Gray Matter

Elixir

Writing as Gary Goshgarian

The Stone Circle

Rough Beast

Atlantis Fire

Rumor of Evil

A NOVEL

GARY BRAVER

OCEANVIEW PUBLISHING
SARASOTA, FLORIDA

ISBN 978-1-60809-593-3

Published in the United States of America by Oceanview Publishing

Sarasota, Florida

www.oceanviewpub.com

10 9 8 7 6 5 4 3 2 1

PRINTED IN THE UNITED STATES OF AMERICA

For Kathy, Nathan, David, and, now, Jessica

One must have a mind of winter
To regard the frost and the boughs
Of the pine-trees crusted with snow; . . .

For the listener, who listens in the snow,
And, nothing himself, beholds
Nothing that is not there and the nothing that is.

FROM "THE SNOWMAN," WALLACE STEVENS

Rumor of Evil

PART I

CHAPTER 1

THE DEAD WOMAN was suspended by the neck from a rope tied to a low branch of a flaming sugar maple in her backyard. Her head was upright to the slant of her body, which angled forward from bent knees, and the toes of her boots just grazed the ground as if she were in the middle of a balletic leap. Her neck looked hyper-stretched against the polyvinyl noose; and not only was her skin void of the flush of life, but over the hours it had turned blue-gray. Her eyes were slits of red jelly, and her tongue protruded through her teeth like a slug. She was dressed in sage-green jeans, a black sweater over a white shirt, argyle socks, and a new-looking pair of New Balance shoes. A scent of perfume lingered as he studied the ligature.

Detective Kirk Lucian had seen too many ugly scenes in his twenty-one years as a Cambridge homicide detective. At times he wondered why he didn't apply for a teaching job in the police academy or at some school with a criminal justice department as his wife, Olivia, had urged. Murders were always unsettling because they were mostly about some disturbed creep exacting revenge. But suicides bothered him more because they were about despair and hopelessness of victims who could no longer endure the one life they had been given. And the forever message: Look how I've suffered.

But there was something obscene about hangings, especially this one since Kirk could not stop looking at the woman's distended neck, as if her head would rip off from her torso at any moment.

The woman's house was a yellow Victorian with white trim and black shutters, with a mansard roof and slate tiles—like so many of the august and pricey homes on side streets off Brattle, within a mile of Harvard Square.

Evidence of autumn was everywhere as cold winds had scattered leaves luxuriously across the lawn. And although the house needed a new paint job, new shutters and chimney work, the backyard, walled in by trees, was meticulously groomed, with an expanse of still-lush yard grass around a brick patio lined with potted yellow chrysanthemums, purple asters, rose bushes, all still in bloom on this bright November day. Puffs of clouds floated across a delft blue sky and birds chirped through the air. A large calico cat snuffled at something in the grass. But for the clutch of uniformed officers, ME techs, and Cambridge PD personnel, the hanging woman looked so grossly out of place that the scene could have been a detail from Hieronymus Bosch.

But something else about the scene pecked at Kirk's mind.

"It looks like she's been dead for two to three hours," said Dr. Chad Davidson, Chief Medical Examiner, who was studying the ligatures of the dead woman's neck through a magnifying glass. Behind him was an assistant taking photographs.

Kirk nodded. "Who is she?"

"Her name is Sylvie Cox Thornton, age thirty-six," said Mandy Wing, Kirk's partner of two weeks. "Her ex resides in Belmont with their son, Aaron, age eighteen, freshman at Dartmouth. She lost another son, Devon, three years ago to cancer."

"Who found her?"

"The guy who cuts the lawn. He's in the squad car and not holding up well."

There was a Tot Finder sticker in a second-floor bedroom window. "Anyone else in the house?"

"No."

Kirk nodded in relief. "Did anyone touch the body?"

"Not according to the uniforms," Mandy said.

Kirk turned something over in his mind as he did a half circle around the dead woman. "Mandy, how would you dress for suicide?"

"Come again?"

"If you planned to kill yourself, would you dress up or down?"

Mandy shrugged. "I don't know. It's not something I've given a lot of thought to. I guess probably on impulse—whatever I'd thrown on."

"Right, except this doesn't look like impulse," Kirk said. "More like she's dressed for a luncheon and not her hanging. She's too well put together—color coordinated, carefully made up, perfumed."

"Maybe this is how she wanted to be remembered." Then she added, "And, by the way, I think that's Magie Noire by Lancôme. My cousin wears that."

Kirk made a smile of approval. Mandy was smart and intuitive, and she had aced an academy exam. Ten years his junior, she was recently promoted to detective, and his captain tapped Kirk to mentor her through investigations because, as he had said, she was still "rough and raw."

While his assistant took more photos, Davidson with gloved hands showed Kirk the purple ligatures on the woman's neck. "I'll know when I get her to the lab, but I suspect her hyoid bone is broken—what holds the tongue in place."

Kirk slipped on surgical gloves. "She's wearing a chain of some sort." With a Q-tip, he carefully pulled it out of her blouse. It was a locket containing a tiny photo of a child. "Strange she didn't remove it first."

"Unless she'd forgotten or didn't care."

Losing a child, you don't have any care left, Kirk thought. *Been there.* "Maybe," he said.

"If she wanted to die, why not OD in bed?" Mandy said. "I mean, why such a dramatic way to go? And a nasty scene for survivors?"

"That might just be the message," Kirk said. "Look where my suffering brought me." *Got close myself when Megan died.*

Davidson turned to Mandy. "You might be right, you know," he said. "This may be how she wanted to be remembered. Sometimes how suicide victims end their lives is their last statement for those left behind. She dresses herself with care and ends things. Remember Mitchell Heisman?"

"Yeah, the Harvard Yard guy," Kirk said.

"What Harvard Yard guy?" Mandy had joined the force long after that case.

"About fifteen years ago," Davidson said, "a Mitchell Heisman, mid-thirties, dressed himself in a white tuxedo, white shirt, and matching shoes and shot himself in the head on the steps of Memorial Hall in front of a group of tourists. He left quite a mess."

"Jesus!"

"For some suicides, death is a staged performance," Davidson said almost cheerily.

Kirk nodded at the house. "Did she leave a note?"

"Nothing yet, but we haven't done a thorough inside."

If there was one, it could be sitting visibly. But they would also check any electronic devices—cellphone, computer, tablet—and social network posts.

With gloved hands, Mandy pulled up the sleeve of the woman's left arm. "Some kind of tattoo. A shamrock, or whatever."

Kirk was about to inspect it when a uniformed officer entered the yard, leading three EMTs with a gurney to take the body to the morgue. "Not yet," Kirk said. "And keep your distance." The men stopped in their tracks.

"But we got a call of a suicide," the officer said.

Kirk walked up to him. "Who said it was a suicide?"

"I got here after the call came in and found her like this. It's what I assumed."

"Assumed suicide," Kirk said.

The officer's face darkened. "Yeah. I mean, look at her."

"Officer Sherwood, how do you spell *assume*?"

"Huh?"

"Ass u me," Kirk said—the old joke. "We don't yet know what we have here." The Officer's face fell. "Thank you, officer, and please go around front and keep anyone else from entering."

Sherwood made an incredulous face and left.

"What are you thinking?" Mandy said.

What had nagged Kirk from the moment he had laid eyes on the deceased. "This looks staged."

Mandy looked at him as if reading his mind. "Oh shit! The place has been overrun by us, uniforms, EMTs, maybe even some neighbors. I mean, it's totally corrupted."

"Maybe not."

Davidson called them over. "What do you make of this?" He was on his knees at the dead woman's feet. "Her boots."

Kirk got down and looked where Davidson was pointing with a magnifying glass. Grass stains and a few blades bunched on the tips of her boots. "The toes are clumped and stained, but the rest of her boots are clean."

"What if she started hanging and in the last few seconds decided she didn't want to die? You know, toed the ground to right herself up."

"Right, and ran out of air." Davidson waved for the photographer for close-ups.

Or was dragged.

Kirk moved to the other officers standing in the driveway. "I want the whole backyard and front gridded off. Touch nothing, put on shoe bags, watch where you step, and clear everyone out. I want forensics all over the place, inside and out." Mandy was right, the scene was already compromised.

She was instantly on her phone. "They're on their way."

Before following Mandy to the gardener, Kirk caught movement out of the corner of his eye. The cat was now pawing something in the grass—a half-eaten chipmunk. It reared its head to take Kirk's hand. A safety collar said *Callie Thornton* with a telephone number.

He gave the cat a tickle under the chin before she returned to her kill. "What happened here, Callie?"

And who let you out?

CHAPTER 2

THE LANDSCAPER WAS waiting in a squad car with two uniformed officers. Kirk called him outside to talk.

His name was Matteo Cabral, age twenty-two, and he was dressed in a gray Patriots hoodie over a green John's Landscaping t-shirt. His eyes were red, making his face all the more pale. According to Mandy, he had called the 911 dispatcher who sent Cambridge PD officers within four minutes.

"Mr. Cabral, what time did you arrive here?"

"A little after ten," he said, his fingers fidgeting with the string of his hoodie.

"Is that the usual time?"

"Yeah, unless there's weather."

Mandy had said that jibed with the call to the dispatcher. "Tell me how you found Mrs. Thornton."

"We come every Tuesday if the weather's good and cut the grass, do the trimming, you know."

"And did you come alone or with coworkers?"

"Alone. We bring the other guys when it's cleanup," Cabral said, still looking ashen, and still fidgety. "But like always, I do the front first, then go 'round the back because that's got a lot of trimming with the weed wacker. So I went around the back—and that's when I saw her." He winced at the image in his head.

"And how long did it take you to trim and cut the lawn out front?"

"Maybe fifteen minutes. I got other jobs, so the faster the better."

"Right. What exactly did you see?"

Cabral hesitated. "At first, I didn't know what to make of it, you know, if it was even real . . . like maybe some Halloween thing. Then I got closer and seen it was her, Mrs. Thornton hanging from the tree, her neck . . . you know, stretched on the rope. It was freaky. She looked like she was trying to kneel, but this rope held her up, not like you see pictures of people hanging." He began to choke up and rubbed his face as if to erase the image.

"Did you touch the body?"

"Touch? . . . God, no!"

"And you called nine-one-one."

"Yeah, right away."

"Did you see Mrs. Thornton before you discovered the body?"

"No. I figured she was in the house or out."

In the garage sat a Volkswagen EcoSport, which seemed out of place in a neighborhood of high-end wheels. "In the past, did you talk to her much?"

"If she was around, just to say hello or wave, you know. We just do our job and leave for the next one. Sometimes never even see our clients."

"The last time you talked, said hello, how did she seem—you know, upset or angry or depressed."

He shook his head. "She always seemed fine."

"How about the way she dressed?"

"Normal, but I really didn't notice."

"Did you see anybody else on the property today or nearby, or anything unusual?"

He shook his head. "No, nobody or nothing," he said.

The questioning continued for a while until it was clear that Cabral had seen nothing suspicious. They took down his information and let him go. Mandy said he had no prior criminal record or complaints.

If he discovered the body at ten and she was dead for two or three hours, she had died a couple of hours before Matteo arrived.

They made their way to the front as the crime scene team arrived with their equipment. Kirk gave the investigators approval to do their work in the backyard and then went inside the house with three others, led by Sergeant Annette Volpe, a meticulous, sharp-eyed investigator on Kirk's team.

They entered a large foyer with a living room on the left, a dining room on the right, a hallway leading to the kitchen, and a staircase to the second floor. The living room was traditionally appointed in a floral couch and Queen Ann upholstered chairs, a dark wood desk, and a marble fireplace. The furniture was old, worn, and cat-scratched in places, even though a scratch pole with a cat nest sat in the middle of the room. It was a great old house that appeared shabby now with lack of any upkeep.

The kitchen looked better—recently modernized in polished gray granite, brushed steel, and black-and-white subway tiles. In the sink sat a cereal bowl with milk and granola, and a partly filled coffee mug. Those and the contents of the dishwasher would be scanned for prints and DNA if someone other than Sylvie Thornton had been in there that day. On the floor was a two-bowl wooden holder of cat kibble and water.

On a small table beside a reading chair sat a cellphone. If it was the victim's, she had ended up outside without it. Sergeant Volpe bagged it to be brought to the lab where, even if passcode protected, they had tools to retrieve emails, texts, and other data like recent communications with individuals who would prove useful to the investigation.

A small pile of mail, probably a few days' worth, sat on a counter—bills, magazines, supermarket circulars, and a lot of junk, plus the last two days' *Boston Globe* unopened. Those too would be bagged and sent to the lab.

They continued up the stairs to the various bedrooms. The wallpaper was peeling in places, and there were water stains on the ceiling, which meant some roofing work was needed.

They moved into the master bedroom. The window treatment had been pulled back to let in the sunlight, which fell on dark wood furniture and a double bed that had been neatly made.

"Doesn't look like she got out of bed intent on hanging herself," Mandy said.

"Why not?"

Mandy shrugged. "Well, I don't know."

"Maybe like you said, this is how she wanted to be remembered—well dressed and everything in place."

On the wall over the bed hung a gold crucifix. And on a bureau sat a statue of the Infant of Prague. The discoloration of the white gown and red cape suggested that it was a childhood artifact. Beside it was a small photo of four girls with St. Bonaventure cheerleading outfits, arms embraced, and beaming happily at the camera. With his cellphone, Kirk took a picture of that. Also framed photos of two smiling handsome boys, one a young teenager and the other looking about six years old. Her college kid and the boy who died of cancer.

In a night table beside the bed, they found a vial of Ambien. That too would be bagged.

He stepped into the bathroom, and for a flash saw theirs after his wife, Olivia, had gotten ready for her day. On the sink counter stood an electric toothbrush, a soap dish, fingernail brush, a round of rose-colored soap. A hair dryer lay on the sink counter with the cord curled neatly around the nozzle. Also a rack of hair rollers.

A large towel hung from a hook behind the door. It was still damp.

The inside of the glass shower stall had leftover drops of water and a small puddle around the drain. On a shelf stood containers of shampoo, conditioner, and body wash. Also a can of pomegranate raspberry shaving cream and a pink-handled razor. With a gloved hand he inspected it under the light and could see traces of soap. If she had staged her own death, she had done so with sadly firm conviction—having shaved her legs, blow-dried her hair, brushed her teeth, and dressed smartly. He clicked off more photos.

Inside the medicine cabinets were two vials of medications. Those would be bagged also.

Outside on the landing Annette waved him into the other bedroom, which appeared to be the deceased son's room with dinosaur posters and baskets of toys on the floor. The bed was made, but the blue bedspread with cartoon figures was wrinkled. "I think she either slept on it or lay on it," Annette said.

Mandy held up her cellphone. "There's an online obit from the local funeral home. The boy died three years ago today, age seven."

"My, my," Kirk said. "So then she kills herself on the anniversary." It would be three years next May when his daughter, Megan, had died.

They moved into the adjacent room, which was the woman's office. An old wooden table served as a desk beside a window overlooking the backyard, and on it a closed laptop, cellphone charger, pencils and pens in a mug, and a ream of paper beside a printer. Annette lay a plastic bag on the laptop to be taken to the lab.

On a file cabinet sat an array of photos of her and her two children over the years, including a blowup of the child's photo in the woman's locket.

They went through the other rooms but found nothing that caught their attention. But the full forensic team would go through the place in great detail.

Unlike the kitchen, these rooms needed work and updating—fresh paint jobs, resurfaced oak wood floors, and new window casements. But the interiors were nonetheless neat and orderly, whispering *I still have control.*

Before they left, Kirk met the head CSI tech who confirmed that her team would collect any electronic devices—cellphones, tablets, laptops, computers, et cetera—anyplace Sylvie Thornton could have left a suicide note. Or any recent calls, texts, emails sent or received that could bring light to her death.

Kirk and Mandy left through the front door to notify the next of kin. As they drove away, they spotted a woman on the front porch three houses down taking in the police commotion. They pulled over and got out.

Her name was MaryAnn Liczek. She looked to be about fifty and was visibly shaken by the news that Sylvie Thornton had been found hanging in her backyard.

"How well did you know Mrs. Thornton?" Kirk asked.

"We weren't terribly close, but we took walks on occasion at Fresh Pond and played tennis a few times."

"When was the last time you saw her?"

"I think maybe two weeks ago, in passing. I was out raking and she stopped by in her car to say hello."

"How did she seem?"

"Fine, you know, normal, friendly."

"Did you detect anything unusual?"

"Like what?"

"Her mood, her manner."

"No."

"You know she lost her son to cancer a few years ago," Mandy announced.

Kirk wished she hadn't said that. You didn't feed a potential witness suggestive information.

"Yes, and that was awful, but I think she had slowly adjusted as well as a mother could who lost a child. I mean, no matter what people say, no one ever heals. You just get harder around the loss and try as best you can to move on. And she did, especially with community work and charities." She hesitated a moment then added, "Are you saying that may have been the reason she took her life?"

"The investigation has just begun, so we're not guessing."

"Well, she'd been through hell with Devon's death, then the divorce a year later, and her other child moving in with his father."

That would be something they'd look into. "Can you tell us anything about Mr. Thornton?"

"Not much. I haven't seen him for years, and she almost never spoke of him. He seemed like a nice guy, but I really didn't know him."

"The last time you saw her, did she say anything revealing?"

"No. She was going food shopping. She did say that we had to get in one more game before the courts iced over. But that was it."

"Okay. In the times you did communicate with her, any signs of trouble with her ex-husband or her son or any other relative or friends?"

"No, not really. I know she was crazy about Aaron and wished she saw him more, but nothing that suggested any trouble." She shook her head with sadness. "I can't believe this. It's so horrible. She seemed to have come a long way in recovery and all. But you never know what's going on inside, the private suffering and all."

They talked some more, but Ms. Liczek wasn't able to add anything new. Sylvie Thornton seemed settled in her losses, with evidence that she had managed to move on, joining community projects, and apparently keeping physically active with walks and tennis. Kirk said they would probably be back to talk to her again.

"By the way, we spotted a large orange cat in Mrs. Thornton's backyard."

"Yes, that's Callie, Sylvie's cat. She's a house cat and shouldn't have been let out."

Someone did.

Before they drove away, Kirk said, "You mentioned tennis. Was Sylvie right-handed or left?"

Liczek thought for a moment. "Same as me, right-handed. Why do you ask?"

"Just wondering."

CHAPTER 3

MORGAN

Nineteen years ago, August 15

LOOKING BACK, I remember the day she came into our lives, so pretty, so polite, so meek—the innocent little exchange student from Slovakia with the coffee skin, black eyes, funky braids, cute accent, and dynamite body. She had come to spend half a school year with us during the fall term.

When my parents had announced that they wanted to host her, I thought it was kind of cool, like having a part-time sister that I never had, and possibly someone I could hang out with at home since my brother, Richie, was six years younger than me, and in his own pre-pubescent world of video games, skateboards, and Slime.

We were told that exchange students were here as guests to continue their schooling and learn about American culture, American ways, to improve their English, and to share some aspects of their homeland for better understanding. My dad explained that the ultimate idea was to "help make the world a more peaceful place" by recognizing and celebrating cultural differences. Being good middle-class liberals, my parents thought that it would also be great for me and my brother to become familiar with someone from a country with different customs and beliefs, and that her stay here would be life-changing not only for her but for us too. Little did I know how true that was, and how things would change forever.

Our house was a central-entrance Colonial with four rooms upstairs—mine, Richie's, my parents' master bedroom, and the guest room where Vadima Lupescu would stay. Because my mom was a real estate agent, she knew where to get furniture to stage a "girl's room." So before Vadima arrived, my mother had prepared the room in totally feminine cheerfulness, repainted white with fluffy pink curtains and a matching white duvet and pink pillows, faux-Tiffany stain-glass lamps, flowering plants, and scenic pictures my mother took on Cape Cod. I wished she had done that to my room. Oh well.

Understandably, Vadima was initially quite shy, which meant that I had to take the lead in making her feel at home and connecting her to school and other kids. It also meant making some adjustments to help her catch up to things American. We couldn't do much with her accent, which some kids at St. B's thought was cool, but she needed serious help with her wardrobe, which looked like hand-me-downs. But the first thing we did was to Americanize her name: from Vadima Lupescu to Lulu—which she liked.

Part of the program was for her to attend St. Bonaventure Academy with me. Because she wanted to fit in, I introduced her to my three best friends—Krista, Riley, and Sylvie. Even before school started, we made our first outing to the mall, which was like Disneyland for her, given she was from a small Slovakian farming village. Because they had television, she knew how American kids dressed. But her clothes had no style or coordination. So we brought her to Aeropostale, Old Navy, and, of course, Lululemon—all on my dad's Amex card. By the time we were done, she had half a dozen great tops and two pairs of shoes, which gave off sporty casual vibes, plus three different colored jeans, although she could not understand why we wore them with slash-holes in the knees. Because she was slender and long-legged, she looked trendy in them. Like a model, which I must admit I envied. Yes, I was tall but had a bigger frame, like my father.

Over the first few weeks, we introduced her to peanut butter and jelly sandwiches, baseball, backyard BBQs, Mexican food, and American TV. My dad owned Fitness You, a popular health club in town, so he brought us in there on occasion to let us work out. I must admit Lulu looked great in the yoga leggings and workout tops. My father thought so too, since he couldn't take his eyes off her. He said he liked having us around to attract a younger clientele.

He also owned a power boat and took us all for a cruise around Boston Harbor. Lulu had never been on a motorboat before, so she was wicked excited. He even promised to take her fishing someday. But the big surprise was that he got us tickets for a Pearl Jam concert at Gillette Stadium. Lulu was out of her mind, yelling and bouncing in place like the rest of us kids.

Mom and Dad liked her, especially Dad who for her sixteenth birthday bought her a new camera to document her visit. Even though it had the latest camera technology, she wasn't that interested in taking pictures. Instead, she would go off by herself and do sketches in pen and pastels in small notebooks she'd carry with her. I must admit she was really good at it. In fact, Mrs. Griffin, the art teacher, said she was gifted. I even brought her to my favorite place on earth, a bench at Horn Pond in Woburn where we used to picnic and fish with my dad. And because swans and ducks hung out there, I thought it would be a great place for her to be inspired.

Lulu didn't have a bicycle, but my mom had one she no longer used, so we would often ride to Horn Pond and my favorite spot under a spreading willow tree near the water's edge. I remember one Saturday morning we were out there gazing at the water and the geese bobbing up and down for water grass. "When I die, this is where I want my ashes scattered," I said to her.

"What? I don't understand."

"Maybe it's a custom you don't have back home, but around here when some people die, they're cremated instead of being buried in a cemetery, and the family scatters their ashes in a favorite spot."

I explained that sometimes they would want their ashes to be scattered in the wind on a mountaintop where they had hiked a lot or in the waters of a favorite beach. Then I told her how when my grandmother died last year my parents scattered her ashes at a lake near where she grew up in Springfield.

"This is something I don't know," she said. "Were you close to her?"

"Yeah, she was a nice woman," I said, but in reality, she was a sour, officious old bitch who would never stop complaining about her aches and pains and asking me to do things for her. She also nagged my mother about not being aggressive enough in her real estate business and about her need to lose weight—which only encouraged my father to join in. My mother also had suffered from vertigo and her doctor had said it was because tiny crystals in her ear were out of place to which Grandma would snicker that it wasn't the crystals in her ears but rocks in her head. At her funeral, I faked crying because that was what was expected of me. But I could not wait to get out of the church.

"That must have made you sad when your grandmother died."

"Mmm."

From the saddlebag on her bike, she removed her sketch pad and showed me a drawing she made of her grandmother. I remember even then being impressed with the lifelike rendering of an elderly woman sitting in front of a small wooden cottage with flowering bushes behind her and smiling at a small dog in her lap.

"She taught me how to draw," Lulu said, with tears in her eyes.

That didn't surprise me. Lulu wore her heart on her sleeve, showing her emotional needs and yearnings—wanting to be accepted, to be loved, to belong. I supposed that was enviable, but I had always thought that such displays made one weak and vulnerable.

CHAPTER 4

SHORT OF BEING SHOT, notifying the next of kin about a loved one's death was the worst part of the job. And the one task no cop was trained for.

"Why not just call to let them know we're on the way?" Mandy said. "I mean, it might just soften the blow."

"Like: Hi, this is Detective Amanda Wing, and I'm calling to let you know your sister was found hanging from a tree in her backyard. We'll be right there with details. Have a nice day."

Her face flushed. "Okay, point made."

"Also, what if the person who answers is elderly with a heart condition or is unstable? Or a kid? No. You do it in person. In pairs and in plain language. And with compassion," Kirk said. "And it still sucks."

"And if nobody's home?"

"Then we call and leave a message to contact us, hopefully for an in-person visit."

Mandy nodded. After several moments, she said, "By the way, why did you ask if Sylvie Thornton was right-handed or left?"

"Did you examine the knot around her neck?"

"Yeah, of course."

"She was right-handed, and it was a left-handed knot."

After a few seconds, she nodded. "Oh yeah. Shit! I missed that."

"You're looking but not seeing. The story is in the details." Mandy was bright and expressive in report writing. But she was hasty, impulsive, and lacking in people skills, which the chief hoped would come in time and by example. Kirk glanced at her and could see she was crestfallen. "Look, you're new at this, but you'll catch on."

Mandy thought for a moment. "I mean, she could have been ambidextrous."

"True, but we don't know that."

"Do you think that suggests anything?"

"I don't know. We'll have to wait for the autopsy."

She nodded and remained silent until they arrived.

Erin Cox Delmonico lived in Winchester in a brick Tudor set on a neatly groomed lawn, fringed by a bank of rhododendrons and azaleas. Unlike Sylvie Thornton's house, this did not appear to need exterior work. A white Lexus SUV sat in the driveway with a bumper sticker that said: "All you need is love."

As they approached the front door, Kirk felt his chest tighten. He had done this dozens of times, and he still felt the clamping, knowing that in a few seconds their news would bring unimaginable pain to a family of strangers.

Why do I do this?

Because if you didn't you might be braiding your own noose.

He rang the bell, and a pleasant looking woman opened the door. "Mrs. Delmonico?" From the photographs at the Thornton woman's home, the resemblance to her sister was evident.

"Yes."

Kirk introduced themselves, flashing their badges, triggering the familiar fright-freeze.

"What happened?"

"May we come in?"

She did not move. "What happened?"

"I think it would be better if we spoke inside."

The woman put her hand to her mouth in anticipation and let them inside. Kirk nodded to the living room on the left. "Maybe we should sit down."

"Oh God," she whispered, but still did not move, as if to forestall the inevitable.

"It's about your sister, Sylvie. We're very sorry to report that she died."

"What? What? No." She let out a long wail of horror.

"I'm so sorry," Kirk said, feeling the sadness come over him and thinking how at times like these, language failed utterly.

They walked her to the couch and pulled up two chairs. Barely able to speak, she gasped, "What happened?"

Kirk took a deep breath, knowing that the next words would fester in this woman's mind for the rest of her life. "She was found in her backyard hanging from a tree."

For a split second she did not seem to process the words. Then she screamed in her hands. "Nooo! Oh God, nooo!"

Kirk knelt beside her with his hand on her shoulder and nodded for Mandy to get a glass of water from the kitchen down the hall. "I cannot tell you how sorry I am."

He let her cry for a long moment, feeling his own eyes fill up. "I know how horrible this is."

Through her gasps she said, "I knew something was wrong."

"What do you mean?"

"She didn't answer my calls and texts," Erin finally said, her voice thick with grief. "We were supposed to meet a friend at the MFA and have lunch. I thought she may have overslept. But she didn't call back. And our friend was at the museum and hadn't heard from her either."

"What time were you supposed to leave?"

"Around nine because we were to meet at ten." She got up. "Please, I have to call my husband."

"Of course."

She left the room and made the call from the kitchen. They could hear her sobbing while telling her husband the news.

Unlike that of the Thornton home, the Delmonicos' living room was a bright open space with gray sectionals floating on a blue-gray Oriental carpet with large photographs of woodland scenes on the walls. Green plants and glass *objets d'art* color-splashed the otherwise monochromatic space. In one corner sat a baby grand piano covered with a large array of family photos, including her children.

It was a room that projected light, unity, family togetherness, and joy. And in the five minutes since their arrival, they had cast a pall of darkness over it all.

Before Erin returned, Mandy muttered, "Yes, this sucks."

"And never gets easier," Kirk said.

"He'll be here soon," Erin said when she returned.

"Mrs. Delmonico, you said that you and Sylvie were planning on going into Boston today. Is that something you did often?"

She nodded. "I wanted her to get out today." There was a suspended moment, as Erin took in a deep breath to catch herself. "Today's the third anniversary of her son's death. And I didn't want her stuck in that house."

"Of course. How old was he?"

"Devon was five. He had been in the hospital for weeks, but sadly he didn't make it. Non-Hodgkin's lymphoma." Erin made a little sob and shook her head. "She'd gotten over the worst part as much as a mother could and still go on. But she suffered depression and health problems. I know she was seeing a therapist."

"Do you know the name of her therapist?"

"I can give that to you."

"Fine. So as far as you know, was she taking medication?"

"I believe so."

"Do you know what she was taking."

"Not exactly, but something for anxiety and to help her sleep. Ambien maybe."

"I understand Sylvie and her husband got divorced."

"Yes, like a lot of marriages when a child has died."

About 19 percent, he thought. "Right. So how long ago was that?"

"Two years ago. Things were falling apart, and then their older son, Aaron, moved in with his father, which was such a blow to her."

"Understandably. What is the father's name?"

"Harry. Harry Thornton. He owns a restaurant in Arlington and lives in Belmont."

Mandy was poised with her pencil and pad, but Kirk gave her a fast headshake and handed Erin his notepad and pen. "His name, address, and number if you know it." He watched her write down what she knew. She said she'd have to check her phone for his cell number. "We can get that later," he said as she handed back the pad and pen. "Is Aaron close to his father?"

"I suppose, but he was also close to Sylvie."

"Mrs. Delmonico, when was the last time you talked to your sister?"

"We talked yesterday about going into town today."

"And how did she seem?"

"Fine. She was looking forward to the MFA and lunch later with me and her friend Diane."

"And the last time you saw her?"

"Last week. We went for a walk together along the Charles."

"And how did she seem then?"

Before Erin could answer, Mandy cut in. "You know, did she seem depressed or down in spirits or distracted in any way? I mean, did she give any indication that something was bothering her? Something that made her want to take her own life?"

"No, nothing like that. She was fine." Then she added, "The death of Devon was devastating and had permanently scarred her. But in time, she did as well as she could. I mean, she had Aaron still, and she survived the divorce. But she was not so depressed that she would take her own life. And even if she had such thoughts, she would have told me. We were very close." Her voice cracked, and she began to sob again. "I can't believe this. I can't believe I'm talking in the past about my own sister."

After she again regained control, Kirk said, "So you saw no reoccurrence of that darkness?"

"No, not really. I mean, she would sometimes becoming sad, more inward, as can be expected."

"How do you mean?"

"I don't know, less forthcoming about her feelings. Actually, she was always a little like that."

"Like what?"

Erin thought for a moment. "There was always a private part of Sylvie that never came out, like she lived with secrets. You could feel it at times, you know, sudden mood shifts. Maybe it was that grief she carried inside. I guess it never leaves you."

"You mentioned secrets. Did she ever let on what those secrets might have been or been related to?"

"Not really."

"I see. Did she see other friends?"

"Yes, she said she did, maybe an occasional lunch. She even talked about going to her twentieth high school reunion in a week or two. But I think she had second thoughts and decided to cancel."

"Did she say why?"

"No, but I imagine seeing old friends would bring back feelings of loss."

After a moment of silence, Kirk said, "It's a necessary formality, but we'll need a family member to identify Sylvie. We can wait until Mr. Delmonico arrives, or we can ask you to identify photos we took of her. I understand how traumatic that would be, but for some relatives of victims it's a way to come to terms with the reality of their loved one's death. And a moment to be alone with her."

She nodded that she understood and wiped her eyes.

"If the moment is too much, you can always defer until tomorrow at the Medical Examiner's office."

"The Medical Examiner? You mean there's going to be an autopsy?"

"In Massachusetts, the Medical Examiner is required to perform an autopsy in the event of a suicide."

"I see."

"Mrs. Delmonico, was you sister right-handed or left?"

"Right-handed, why?"

"Just curious."

CHAPTER 5

Paul Delmonico arrived about twenty minutes later. He was in his forties and dressed in business attire. Kirk pulled him into another room and told him about Sylvie. When he had settled into the awful news, Kirk asked him to identify the photos of the woman, with the warning that the images were grotesque. His face in a rictus of horror, he confirmed that the victim was Sylvie Thornton.

"What did she do for a living?" Kirk asked when they returned to the living room.

"She was a biology teacher at the Prentiss School in Watertown," Erin said. "But sadly, she left that after Devon died."

"Of course," Kirk said. That meant she was living on a retirement pension and Social Security, which might explain why she couldn't afford the upkeep of her house. "Do you know if she had any issues? Medical, financial, or personal ones—anything that may have beset her or pulled her down?"

"Not really," Erin said. "She kept in touch with past colleagues and friends. And she had us. And that's what I can't understand—how she could have taken her own life and how she didn't open up . . . and how I missed signs that she suffered so much. I had thought we had made her happy." She started to cry again. "I feel like a failure to my own sister."

Paul put his arms around her in comfort. "You weren't a failure," he said. "You were always there for her. We both were."

Kirk had seen this before in family members of suicide victims—shocking disbelief, confusion, and guilt. In time, before a numbness set in, Erin would even feel anger that her sister had rejected their closeness, even abandoned her and leaving her and the rest of their family a legacy of despair. But was this a suicide?

Mandy cleared her throat. "Erin, how would you say she got along with her ex-husband, Harry Thornton?"

Erin took a deep breath to center herself. "They got along on a practical level, but they were emotionally estranged, of course. Divorce does that."

"Was it a contentious divorce?"

"Yes. As I said, when Devon died, Sylvie was in no condition to continue working, so she left Prentiss, which meant she no longer had an income. Harry helped her a little, as did we. But things were unstable for her. And then Aaron, who needed support himself, turned to his father, Harry."

"So, Aaron moved in with him?"

"Yes, until he went to college."

"How did she take that?" Mandy asked.

"Badly, of course. Plus she had financial issues, which exacerbated matters."

"But she got the house," Mandy said.

"Yes, because that's where we grew up," Erin said. "But she had a tough time emotionally, but the good news was that she agreed to get psychiatric help. But I guess it wasn't enough."

"Do you know how often she and Harry saw each other?"

"I'm not really sure, but I suppose only when it involved Aaron, such as school functions."

"So he still had a key to the house."

"I suppose."

"How would you characterize her relationship with Aaron of late?"

"I'd say transactional."

Kirk checked his notes. "You said earlier that there was a private part of Sylvie that never came out. That she may have lived with secrets that could have explained her mood shifts."

Erin and Paul looked at each other and nodded. "Yes."

"Siblings sometimes don't open up about matters that bother them, but maybe they're more comfortable with close friends. Although it's a formality, can you give us the names of Sylvie's close friends and associates—business, civic, old college friends—anyone she may have confided in?"

"Yes, as best I could."

Kirk handed them paper and pens for them to write down names and contact info from their phones. Both Erin and Paul were right-handed.

"Which friend would you say she was closest to?"

They made a short list that included Evie Schultz and Diane Ruffy. They talked some more but got no other pertinent information. Before they left, Kirk said, "Two more questions. Was your sister a religious woman?"

"Well, we were brought up Catholic, and she went to Catholic schools, but she wasn't a regular churchgoer. Why do you ask?"

"There are a few religious objects in her house—a crucifix and an Infant of Prague." As far as Kirk knew, suicide to Roman Catholics was considered a mortal sin against God. His concern was whether or not her particular church would make a pastoral judgment to grant Sylvie Thornton a Catholic funeral and burial.

Erin teared up. "Yes, that was a gift from our grandmother, which Sylvie adored."

"We also found some muffins and a magnum of beer from the Brothers of Saint Julian's Monastery in Smithfield, Mass."

"Oh, yes, that's from a childhood friend of hers who's a monk in that order. They brew beer and bake breads and muffins and other things for tourists."

"One more question," Kirk said before they headed for their car. "Your sister had a tattoo on the inside of her right arm in the shape of a four-leaf clover. Do you know anything about that?"

"Yes, she got that in high school."

"Just curious if there's anything significant about that."

"I think it was something she did with other girls she was friends with. They each had the same tattoo, but a different leaf filled in red, I believe—a best-friends-forever thing."

Later on their way to Harry Thornton's restaurant, Mandy said, "I wonder how many people stay best friends forever from high school."

"I suspect not a lot. When you're in grade school, you're sharing growing-up intensely, so everything is exaggerated including belief that things are forever. Like friendships."

"Like these women."

"Right."

"I've got a couple carryover friends from high school. What about you?"

"I did," Kirk said. "My wife." *And she left me.*

CHAPTER 6

MORGAN

Nineteen years ago, August 29

As we were told, getting to know Vadima meant recognizing some strange customs and beliefs. For one, she always took her shoes off when entering the house. We told her she didn't have to do that since we all wore our shoes inside. Then on the first day of classes, she stood up when the teacher entered the classroom—apparently a show of respect back in Slovakia. The kids laughed and Mr. D'Amato smiled, thanked her, and said she didn't have to do that. She was also shocked by how everybody hugged each other whenever they met. Instead of Coke or milk whenever we ate, she always asked for herbal teas. In fact, she brought her own, which smelled like roses.

Instead of regular tattoos, her hands and wrists were covered with reddish brown designs that she explained were done with henna, a dye made from plants and used for thousands of years by her people, called the Romany. When I more closely inspected the design, I could make out tiny intricate vines surrounding concentric circles that looked like a string of all-staring eyes. She said that certain designs were for good luck and happiness, such as birds and flowers. Others like the eyes were meant to grant the person powers over adversities, as if they had magic powers.

She said that if I was interested, she'd do some for me, assuring me that I could wash them off if I didn't like them. I declined because I already had a real tattoo, which I showed her—a four-leafed clover with three leaves blanked and one filled in with red. I explained that my three closest friends each had the same tattoo, but with a different leaf filled for each, making the four of us a permanent whole.

Things went smoothly for the first month. We all got along, and she was doing well in school and was adjusting to us and to being away from home. She said she lived on a farm in Bolavec, Slovakia, which I assumed was pretty basic, but she really appreciated the comfort and conveniences of our home, especially instant hot water and the microwave.

She also was a welcome buffer for my parents scrapping over my mom's weight. Looking at their wedding pictures, she was once slender and built like a fashion model. But after the birth of Richie, she could not take off the pounds, probably tipping the scales at a hundred and fifty or more. And my father kept reminding her of that whenever she ate ice cream or watched TV with a bowl of buttered popcorn or when she'd breakfast on eggs with bacon and toast slathered with butter. In fact, he'd mutter stuff like "Just layer that on your hips instead." Or refer to her as Mama Marshmallow. He was also constantly on her for not spending time at our gym since she could go anytime and spend an hour on a StairMaster. Lulu's presence helped a bit, as Dad cut down on embarrassing her in front of us. And Mom did make an effort to diet and return to aerobic classes, probably motivated by Lulu's figure and the way Dad was taken by it,

In those days, our backyard had a treehouse, built by my father for Richie and me. Lulu loved to go up there. We'd climb up and spend hours talking or doing schoolwork. She even asked if we could overnight there because she loved to do that at home, sleep outside and watch for shooting stars, or study the constellations before falling asleep. We couldn't see the stars because the structure had a roof, but we hung out there, listening to cicadas and watching the night close in. But I really preferred my bed.

Then things began to change.

It started at a pizza party at Sylvie Cox's house. Her parents were home, of course, but they left us to ourselves in the downstairs rec room while they retreated to their bedroom to watch TV, occasionally coming down to check that everything was going well and that the music wasn't too loud. Between their "visits" we managed to pass around a few nips of vodka and gin, which Riley's older brother got us.

We did some dancing and singing and a little making out in the corners. We got Lulu to rock dance American style, whatever that was. Her moves were weird and a little sexy, which we assumed were what Slovakians did to their own music, probably because they weren't so uptight about sexual matters. It was fun as Sylvie and I joined in mimicking her. Riley also got Grayson "Gee Gee" Gallagher to join in, knowing that Lulu had a crush on him.

I should mention that from early on Riley didn't take to Lulu and always referred to her as *Vadima*, as if the nickname Lulu suggested she was closer to us than Riley liked. She said she didn't trust her. Riley claimed that even though she attended St. B's, Vadima wasn't really religious but only faked being Catholic. That she was really a pagan Gypsy. She also asked if anything of value was missing from our house since Lulu came from a country famous for thieves. She said she read that online. I didn't know of anything missing, but that set me on guard.

Later that evening when some of us took to the couches, Gee Gee asked Lulu what her family life was like, her schooling and activities, et cetera. She said that she walked to school about three kilometers each day—almost two miles—and when she came home, she would help with chores. She was raised on a farm in the eastern part of Slovakia near the Ukrainian border. Her family raised pigs.

Pig farmers!

That raised a bunch of eyebrows and snickers from Riley and others, who no doubt imagined a fallen-down two-room shack connected to mud-filled barn with pigs wallowing in their shit.

"So you're a pig girl," Gee Gee said. "I never met one before."

More giggles, and Lulu's face turned red. But she forced a smile. If she was offended, she did not let on. It was clear that she was interested in him, hoping that he wouldn't make more disparaging quips. "Yes, I feed them and help my uncles get them ready for slaughter."

"Do you slaughter them yourself?" Riley said, barely able to hide her sourness.

"I have, but we now have a man who comes to do this."

"Wow—that's something. I never killed a pig," Gee Gee said and winked at Justine Zajac who stood next to him with other girls pressing in. "How do you do it?"

Without changing her expression, she slashed her fingers across her throat.

A few "Ooos" and "Awesomes" rose from the group, and from Gee Gee, "That must be pretty gross."

"Yes, lots of blood. But very quick. They don't suffer."

The image of her doing that clearly impressed everyone.

"God, I couldn't do that," Gee Gee said. "That must take a lot of guts."

"That comes next," someone quipped. And several people groaned.

"My uncle does that. But this is what you must do to eat, no?" Lulu said, seeming to enjoy all the attention, especially from Gee Gee.

"And what do you do for entertainment on cold lonely nights when you're not killing pigs?" he said.

Gee Gee was something of a flirt and had put little hits on Lulu in English class, winking at her and passing her notes, nodding her on when she answered questions. And last week when she aced a test, he gave her a high-five. Something about that bothered me. Not to mention Justine who was Gee Gee's girlfriend.

"I tell you," she said, smiling. She made him sit next to her on the couch, and then took one of his hands in a surprise moment and turned it up. He stared at her, chuckling nervously as we all watched her spread out his palm, run her own hand across it, then trace the lines in his hand with her index finger.

"Oh wow! You tell fortunes?"

That created a buzz. "Give me a break," Riley muttered.

Gee Gee grinned. "Is that what you're gonna do?"

Without answering, Lulu licked her lips and slowly traced his lifeline with the tip of her finger.

"Oooh, I like that," Gee Gee said, and more snickers rose up.

"You gotta be kidding," Riley said with a sneer. But others were chanting "Do it, do it."

When the kids quieted down, Lulu said, "You have big, strong hands." And someone said, "Ooh la la," and the place broke up in hoots and raucous laughter.

But Lulu did not react and just stared at Gee Gee's palm intensely. Someone else said, "Tell him what college he'll go to." Another kid said, "Or what seminary," because Gee Gee was very religious. Then Markie Coburn slipped in, "When he'll pop his cherry," which got more cheers.

The whole scene was annoying me, with Lulu sitting there holding his hand in all seriousness like some carnival fortune teller. "You can't predict the future," I slipped in. "It hasn't happened yet. Besides, like Mr. D'Amato says, there'd be no free will."

Gee Gee nudged me with his elbow. "Don't interrupt, Smarty Pants." Then to Lulu, "So, can you tell me if I'll be rich and famous?"

Still playing some kind of swami psychic, Lulu said, "No, but maybe how you do in relationships." She then traced more lines with her finger and muttered something to herself, probably in Slovakian or whatever. She drew her finger the full length of the line crossing his palm. "You are very popular and open with your emotions. Maybe too much."

Riley whispered in my ear, "Such bullshit. Like freaking fortune cookies."

I nodded in exasperation as Lulu continued.

"You are very kind to people and make many friends," she said. "You know what people to let into your heart."

"Okay, to the chase," Gee Gee said. "Can you tell me about my love life?"

"There goes seminary," Markie said, which got more laughs, as the circle pressed more tightly around them.

"I see a girl who will be a woman in a few years," Lulu continued. "The girl loves you and wants you to feel the same for her."

That raised a loud "Whoa" from Gee Gee and cheers from the others.

After the crowd calmed down, Gee Gee said, "Can you tell me the name of the girl?" With that he grabbed Justine Zajac's hand. Everyone knew that they were boyfriend-girlfriend. "Shut up," Justine said good-naturedly.

Lulu was not ready for that and actually flinched. To regain herself, she dropped her eyes to his hand again, studying the lines as her finger traced a fork in his palm.

She then reached for Justine's hand. "Go ahead," Gee Gee said, and Justine scoffed but held out her hand to Lulu.

For a long moment she studied Justine's hand, tracing the lines with her fingers. She looked up at Justine with a startled look and said something I couldn't make out, perhaps another foreign phrase. Then suddenly Lulu dropped her hand. "No more," she said and shot to her feet. "I must go."

"What?" Gee Gee said in disbelief. "No, keep going."

But Lulu shook her head and started cutting her way through the crowd toward the door, muttering to herself. I caught up to her. "Hey, Lulu, what's the problem?"

All she said was, "Sorry," and she looked pale and on the verge of tears.

"Hey, it's only nine thirty. We have until eleven."

"Sorry, no," she said. "You stay. I can walk back."

We lived twenty minutes away. "That's nuts. It's cold and dark." I really didn't want to leave, and we didn't have cash or a credit card for her to take a taxi. So, I called my father.

He showed up in a few minutes. "What happened?"

"Sorry, I just don't feel good," she said, her eyes huge and glassy.

I shrugged to say I didn't know what happened, although I suspected it had to do with Gee Gee's feelings toward Justine, which may have explained all the annoying "sorrys" she muttered. Or maybe she really was psychic and saw something in her palm that said she had no chance with him and took it pretty hard. Whatever, I was just pissed because my dad made me go home too.

The next day I pressed her about what had happened, what she saw in Justine's palm, if anything, but she shook her head and walked away.

So I let it go and chalked it up to a lot of self-drama. She had the hots for Gee Gee who had the hots for Justine. End of story.

Or so I had thought.

CHAPTER 7

"YOU HAVE A REPUTATION."

Mandy humphed. "I can't wait to hear."

"The official term is 'unorthodox,' which is administration-talk for pain in the ass."

"And proud of it."

Kirk snickered. "That you're impulsive, that you feed answers to witnesses instead of letting them respond on their own or squirm. That you have a tendency to overreact. That you have the people skills of a warthog. And you don't trust men."

"So, you want to trade me in?"

"That or reform you."

"I trust you."

"Good start."

According to the lieutenant who had assigned Mandy to Kirk, she was at an Antifa protest some weeks ago in Boston with another officer and got cornered by counter-toughs. She and her partner, Sean Concanon, separated when she recognized one guy who had pummeled a female protestor. When he bolted, she went after him, leaving Officer Concanon on his own. She nabbed the thug and held him at gunpoint. Unfortunately, Concanon was stabbed in an ambush and ended up in the ICU. He survived, forgave her by saying she had to do what was necessary. But Mandy was reprimanded, leaving her twisting with guilt. But she was eventually promoted to detective and assigned to Kirk to keep her on the rails.

"You've been at this for twenty-something years. I think I can learn a few things from you." Then she added, "And for your information, I don't distrust all men, only those who've abused women."

"Sounds like you've seen a lot of it."

"Yes, but that's for another day," she said.

They drove in silence for several moments. "I feel sorry for the surviving kid," she said. "His younger brother dies of cancer, his parents divorce, and his mother is found hanging in their backyard. Jesus! The kid's in his first year trying to adjust to college life. Imagine what that'll do to his head." Kirk heard a hitch in her voice. "May my child never see that kind of horror."

"You have a child? I didn't know you were married."

"I am and my son is nine years old, and my wife, thankfully, works from home."

Kirk knew she was gay and wore a ring, but not the rest. "If you don't mind me asking, did you adopt?"

"No, Sally delivered. And I'll do the next one."

She may be a headstrong screwup, but he suddenly had more respect for her. Nothing more humanizing than parenting. "Good for you, Mandy."

"His name is Brett. Brett Wing Sherman, Sally's last name."

"Brett Wing Sherman. Nice name," Kirk said. "That must make your parents happy."

"Grandparents. My parents are dead," she said but did not elaborate. "Happy is a little strong. My grandmother's from a large Irish family and was expecting a big, fat Irish wedding and a lot of grandchildren. But she eventually came around. But not my grandfather. He never even came to our wedding."

"Maybe he'll come around when you have your own child."

"Doubtful. He was a cop himself but never accepted my lifestyle. He tried to discourage me from joining the academy, claiming that gays and lesbians would turn the Pittsburgh PD into a bunch of *pansies*. Worse, I'd experience a lot of abuse—you know, harassment, being shunned and never promoted."

"Did you?"

"Not at first because I played the Don't-Ask-Don't-Tell game until I came out. Then things became uncomfortable—some taunts and threats, and a gift-wrapped dildo for my birthday. But I wasn't alone. And a class-action suit by LGBTQ cops pretty much put an end to that. Three years later, I transferred up here, and it's a whole different experience. A couple of harmless homophobes, but they all came around because it's a lot more inclusive now."

"And not your grandfather."

"Not really. He says Brett is not his grandchild, just a stranger's artificial kid."

"Sorry to hear that."

"The thing is—he wasn't a good cop."

"In what ways?"

"He was bigoted, disinterested in contradictory evidence, and overly aggressive in nailing perps. He may have even planted evidence. I just want to be better. I want to make a difference."

He smiled at her sunny earnestness. "You're on your way."

CHAPTER 8

KIRK HAD DROPPED Mandy off at the station to check with techs on Sylvie Thornton's cellphone while he headed to Mount Auburn Cemetery.

"Hi, honey."

He got down on his knees, removing fallen leaves, and laid a vase of calla lilies beside the gravestone. Although they wouldn't make it through the next frost, they were Megan's favorites, and a florist in Harvard Square always carried them.

Eighteen months ago, on May 14, she was walking her bike across the street at a stoplight heading for the bike path along the Charles when she was struck by a car running the lights. She died later that night at Mass General Hospital, and the driver was never caught. A witness remembered the car, but it turned out to have been stolen and impossible to determine its driver. And no surveillance cameras were at that intersection. Unlike cop shows, some crimes never got solved, and families suffered the injustice, and bad people got away with the wrongs. Megan was fourteen years old. Three months ago, he and his wife separated—like a double-death.

"You'd probably remember Mom and me bringing you here with your first bike. A bright pink Schwinn with the training wheels removed. Yeah, it was against regulations, but you learned here, which was a lot better than the Star Market parking lot. And you did great, going along the winding paths, me trotting beside you. And a good workout at the same time."

Three weeks ago, when he was last here, the place was bright with fall color. Now most trees were stripped bare, looking like X-rays of themselves, and the ground was hard and covered with leaves brown and curled. In a distant tree a red-tailed hawk sat on a limb picking apart a squirrel.

"Did I tell you Mom and I used to date here? She lived in an apartment down the street, and we'd pack a picnic and sit under a towering redwood by Halcyon Lake near the mausoleum of Mary Baker Eddy. We brought you there as a toddler. It's where you learned how to quack and thought you were a duck."

For a second Kirk got lost in the memory of Olivia laughing with joy at watching Megan waddle after the birds.

"God! I miss you, girl." His voice cracked. "I miss her. I miss us."

Megan would have been sixteen years old. He felt himself begin to fill up as he always did.

"I've got a new partner. She's still a little rough around the edges, but I like her. She's gay and married to another woman, and they have a child. We're on a new case, and it's the kind of distraction I need."

A few months following Megan's death, his marriage to Olivia began to crumble as Kirk fell into dysfunction and depression. He barely talked and had to take a leave of absence.

He was by profession a protector, and Megan's death left him feeling impotent, a failure. He had blamed himself, and in his trough of grief he felt so lost that he could not muster enough comfort for Olivia who suffered Megan's death in her own way. As much as he had tried, he was unable to lessen Olivia's pain or meet her needs as he always had. Their grief over Megan's death had strangely isolated them. And then anger and resentment set in, filling the void with petty arguments. Because Kirk had a tendency to internalize his emotions, to cry in private, Olivia had accused him of not grieving enough while she broke down constantly. She also passed through a spell of blaming him—for letting Megan go off on her own with the bike and not arriving home in time to accompany her. He had gotten held up by traffic as he headed home to change and join her, texting her to wait. But she returned a text to meet on the path.

Olivia never accepted that explanation—as if he blamed their daughter for her own death because she had headed off to the bike path without him.

That irrationality led each of them to seek grief counseling, but after a few weeks, that failed to mend them. She still in part needed to blame him.

Soon they agreed to a trial separation, but Kirk insisted that since they still cared for each other they would have regular dates—maybe once a week. They had also agreed to be free to see others, although he had no interest in dating other women. He also feared that her seeing other men could lead her to divorce court. But he did concede that his freedom to socialize would lessen the pain of living without her.

After a few weeks of separation, Kirk discovered that Olivia was seeing Ted Rizzo, the wealthy owner of a contracting company that restored homes and who once oversaw the rebuilding of their own kitchen. When he confronted her, Olivia reminded him that she and Kirk had been exclusive since high school, had dated throughout college, married two years later, and two years after that had become parents. The reality was that Olivia had never been with another man but Kirk. And in her most vulnerable state of despair, he was not there. But Ted Rizzo was.

"Mom's doing well. Still teaching psychology at Pilgrim State University. She has her own condo in Newton. I saw her last week. We had dinner at Lucia's in the North End, and she looked great as always. I felt like I was dating her all over again. I wish I were."

Kirk could still grieve the loss of his only child and the love of his life, but he needed to keep working so he wouldn't slip into a hole of annihilating self-pity or take his own life. Despite the fact that he was constantly exposed to violent crimes, abuse of children, torture, and all manners of cruelty and death, he kept telling himself that what he did mattered, that he helped make a difference, as Mandy had said.

The sun had set behind the canopy of trees, and the cemetery closed at five. He had to leave to meet Mandy.

"I'll be back in a couple of weeks. Before I go, I'm thinking about dating. It's probably a good idea, and Mom's encouraging me. But deep down I'm not interested. I want Mom back. Life without her is like breathing on one lung—"

The moment was interrupted by the chime of his cellphone. Mandy calling to report on Sylvie Thornton's cellphone content. She read him texts and calls from her sister, Erin, as well as a friend, Diane Ruffy—who waited for Sylvie at the Museum of Fine Art—wondering where Sylvie was.

By then Sylvie Thornton was dead.

CHAPTER 9

THORNTON'S RESTAURANT WAS located in Arlington center at the intersection of Mass. Avenue and Mystic Street. Because it was late afternoon, the place was still closed as the kitchen crew prepped for dinner.

Kirk tapped on the window and the hostess came to the door to say they wouldn't open for another twenty minutes. They identified themselves, showing their credentials. "We'd like to speak with Harry Thornton."

The woman's face stiffened. "He's in the back, but I'll get him."

The same look police always get. Show your badges, and expressions freeze, heart rates kick up, the worst fears arise. And almost always for good reasons.

Out of the kitchen stepped Harry Thornton, a big partridge-shaped guy who looked as if he spent too much time sampling his own menu. He dismissed the woman.

Thornton's face was stretched with concern. "Is my son all right?"

"We're not here about your son, Mr. Thornton. Can we find a corner to talk?"

"Sure," he said and led them to a booth at the rear of the dining area. "What happened?"

"It's about your former wife, Sylvie."

"Oh no, what did she do?"

"*What did she do*?" Mandy snapped.

"Yeah, well . . ." He caught himself. "What happened?"

"We're very sorry to say that she was found dead earlier today at her home," Mandy said, contempt grating her words.

"Oh, sweet Jesus! What happened?"

"We're not yet sure of the circumstances, but she was found hanging from a rope in her backyard."

"Oh God! Jesus! How awful." He rubbed his face and gestured with his hands, looking shocked, but it was hard to determine if that was genuine or prepared. "I was afraid of something like this," he said, shaking his head. "Ever since our son Devon died, she's not been the same."

Kirk nodded, but what he heard was unconscious self-defense—that he had no part in her suicide, that it was rooted in the death of their son. "Why do you say that?"

"I'm sure you've heard that the death of a child is not something a parent ever gets over, believe me. I'm still dealing with it and it's been three years."

Kirk nodded. *Tell me about it.*

"But, you know," Thornton continued, "somehow you find the strength to go on, especially when there's another child . . . our son Aaron."

"Maybe you could fill us in on that," Kirk said.

"When Devon died, we were overwhelmed with grief, of course. But Sylvie barely survived it. She stopped eating and cut off all social ties. She barely got out of bed in the morning. Like she just couldn't face the day. Many days she couldn't. It was horrible. She had lost her will to go on. Know what I mean?"

Kirk nodded. "Did you seek counseling?"

"Yes, of course—psychiatrists, grief counselors, marriage counselors, occupational therapists to deal with daily functions. You name it. The thing is, she had receded into herself, left her job, cut herself off from friends, associates, neighbors, and, of course, Aaron and me."

Mandy looked up from her notepad. "Mr. Thornton, when was the last time you saw Sylvie?"

"A few weeks ago. I stopped by to pick up some winter clothes for Aaron."

"Did you do that often, stop by for things?" she asked.

"Yeah, when he needed stuff."

"Did you notice any changes in her mood or general condition?"

"When she was there, she seemed okay. Usually it was a cool reception, you know, she seemed flat, dispirited I guess you'd call it."

Mandy flashed Kirk a supplicating look and he nodded her on. "Mr. Thornton, your carrier's records show that you texted Sylvie at eight forty-seven the night before she died that you were going to stop by the next morning for some items for Aaron. What time did you stop by?"

"Yeah, that was for a pair of boots. My son's an avid hiker and needed his water-resistant boots," Thornton said. "The thing is, he called me back to say never mind because he'd already ordered a pair online. So I never showed up."

"And what did you do instead this morning?"

"Actually, I slept in."

The hostess came by with a check ledger. "Do we have to do this now?" Thornton said. "We're busy." He flashed the woman a withering look.

She reddened and apologized for interrupting but said she needed Thornton's signature for a vendor who was waiting out back. Thornton muttered under his breath and scribbled his name on a check and voucher, and the woman left, again apologizing.

Mandy shook her head as she watched the woman walk away embarrassed. And Kirk noted that Thornton had signed with his left hand. "Would you say that Sylvie got along with her sister, Erin, and her family?"

"Yeah, she was pretty close to Erin. They talked often and did things together, which helped Sylvie, especially when she was in a funk."

Mandy asked, "Do you know any of Sylvie's close friends or business associates who might shed some light on her death?"

He gave her a puzzled look. "You mean if they would suggest something other than grief over Devon?"

"Erin did say that she was also affected by your divorce and estrangement from Aaron."

"Yeah, well, I had Aaron, and he needed me . . . us. But Sylvie was barely there, so after months of counseling and support groups, things just fell apart." He made a what-are-you-going-to-do shrug.

"Would you say it was a contentious divorce?"

He scowled at her. "It wasn't high amicable . . . but it was what it was."

"But you remarried less than a year later," Mandy said. "And Aaron lived with you before going to college."

Thornton's expression hardened. "Why does that sound like an accusation?"

"Given the timing, you seem to have known the new Mrs. Thornton for a while."

He glared at Mandy. "I don't like what you're suggesting, Detective."

"What's that?"

"That my marriage to Amy is somehow responsible for Sylvie's death."

Mandy was about to push on when Kirk cut her off. "Mr. Thornton, we didn't come here to question you about your second marriage. We're wondering what might have triggered Mrs. Thornton to have taken her own life this morning."

"Well, it is the third anniversary of Devon's death."

"According to Erin she was scheduled to go to the MFA today with her and a friend, just to get out of the house and get her mind off the day. But something held her back."

"Like what?"

"If she had a recent run-in with anyone—you or your son—some emotionally disturbing conflict."

Feeling the barbs of Mandy's words, he turned his response to Kirk. "Look, I haven't spoken to Sylvie in a few weeks, and the only communication was that text about Aaron's boots. As for Aaron, he's away at school at Dartmouth, and I don't think they have an issue that would push her over the edge. Also, ask anyone, Sylvie was very active in the community and had a lot of support from her friends. So I can't think of anything that would lead to this . . . this tragedy."

That assessment jibed with what they had learned from neighbors, her sister, and what they had found on the internet—that Sylvie Thornton was a warm and giving person who raised money for local charities and who started a clothing drive for the underprivileged and unemployed. And that she had come to live with her grief.

But something went very wrong.

CHAPTER 10

Kirk arrived at home a little after eight. The place was dark except for the outdoor lights and a solo lamp in the kitchen. He reminded himself that he needed to get timers for lights and the radio, so he'd come home to some semblance of life.

Daisy met him at the back door and curled around his feet meowing the way she did. It wasn't that she was happy to see him. She'd do the same for the FedEx guy. She was hungry, so he led her into the kitchen and dumped some kibble into her bowl and changed the water. He watched her crunch the stuff, envying her basic animal needs, unfettered by human consciousness. Give her food, a litter box, and a window near the birdfeeder, and she's in cat heaven.

He poured himself a glass of chardonnay and headed into the living room. He wasn't crazy about chardonnay, but it was an oaky vintage that Olivia liked, and the half-empty bottle was still the only wine in the fridge. And any wine in the fridge when you were too tired to drive to the nearest package store was a good wine.

Most of the place had been decorated by Olivia—white sofa, floated on a pale blue and beige Oriental, with pale blue chairs and color accents—constant reminders of the way they were—their space, her art. A friend had suggested that he do a clean sweep from top to bottom. Maybe even turn it into a man cave with beer signs and sports posters. Right!

He moved to his chair across from its mate where Olivia would join him before a cozy fire and tally up their days. One of the hundred rituals now on hold. Dead log ends sat in the hearth.

Or gone.

Please, God, not forever.

That thought set off hot eddies in his gut. He took a sip, thinking that his life was losing meaning and purpose. He and Olivia were supposed to grow old together, maybe even have another child. Women still had babies in their early forties, and as a college professor, she could get a maternity leave.

But now he was peering down the long dim corridor of the rest of his life on his own.

Olivia had been a fundamental condition of his life. He was who he was with her, a composite being—KirkandOlivia. And now he felt like a stranger to himself, unsure how to create a redefinition, or if he wanted to.

It had occurred to him that he had in their separation even suffered a language loss: a secret patois that they had developed over twenty years of marriage—code words, nicknames, insider jokes, references, silly nothings, verbal shortcuts that didn't exist in the lingua franca that they used with others, that made no sense to anyone else but perfectly communicated to themselves. Theirs was a dialect rooted in shared history, shared memories, and a shared mind.

He turned out the lights, dumped the wine into the kitchen sink, and headed up to the bathroom off their bedroom. Olivia's hairdryer was gone—so was her electric toothbrush, which had stood next to his like close friends.

Her closet was half empty, with just spring and summer blouses and dresses hanging. He gathered the material of a mint-green linen shirt she wore on summer nights. He could still smell Light Blue by Dolce & Gabbana—which he had gotten for her last birthday.

Come back, Olivia. Please.

He was still not used to sleeping alone in that big king-size bed, cooking for one, learning to be alone with his own company, to be who he was before Olivia. But after all those years, he had been defined by his life with her, not cruelty and grief.

* * *

He had set his alarm for six o'clock, and out of habit the next morning, he patted her side of the bed only to feel cold empty sheets. There was a time when Olivia would wake up to make love before she took off for her day. Now only the cat snuffled against his legs purring like a small machine and pawing him for kibble.

He gave her a few scratches under her chin and went down to feed her. A few minutes later, he headed back upstairs to take a shower. But on the way he suddenly began to hate the place. Some of their best memories had been made here, together, then with Megan, but now his own house felt empty, utterly empty—and alien.

He reentered the bedroom and sat at the edge of the bed and for a long moment stared at Olivia's pillow. He lowered his face to it, taking in the scent of her hair, her apricot shampoo, her essence. And then it came to him full force, from some deep bottomless cavern; and he lowered himself into the pillow and gave in to wave after wave of deep wracking sobs until his chest hurt and there was no more left in him. *I can't go on much longer without you.*

When it was over, and feeling hollowed out, he took a long hot shower, got dressed, and headed for the autopsy of Sylvie Cox Thornton.

CHAPTER 11

MORGAN

Nineteen years ago, September 5

SHE NEVER EXPLAINED why she had bolted out of Sylvie's party that night last week, and I didn't bring it up. But I was still humming with curiosity.

It was a warm Indian summer afternoon, and because we had been studying the American Revolution in history class, I took her to the Visitor's Center in the Lexington Green just a short bike ride from my house. A few tourists walked around taking photos and people picnicked on blankets under the sun. We locked our bikes, and because I had been on guided tours a few times when friends of my parents came to town, I took her to the key stops—the Minuteman Statue of Captain John Parker who led the Lexington militia against the British soldiers, the gravesite of the Minutemen who lost their lives, and various key stops on the Battle Green.

When that got boring, we settled at a table under a large beech tree not too far from a couple of Lexington High School kids on a blanket maybe fifty feet away, in a world of their own making out. Nearby there was a small gaggle of Canada geese nibbling on the grass.

As usual Lulu had brought her sketch pad and pens and pastels in her saddlebag and insisted on drawing me. At first I hesitated, not wanting to pose, but she chuckled and disregarded me as her fingers sketched out my face with a thin black pen. I was amazed at how in a matter of seconds she had turned squiggles into an image of me. Mrs. Griffin the art teacher was right—Lulu had natural talent. So I sat quietly as she filled in the lines with pastels.

"Wow! That's awesome," I said, looking at the finished product, which I had to admit made me look prettier than I am. As I took in the drawing, I noticed other sketches on pages beneath mine, and in a fast flipping of pages, I caught a glimpse of a sketch of my brother, Richie; my mother; and Gee Gee Gallagher. Before I could riffle through others, she snatched the book away and returned it to her saddlebag, leaving me curious about what she didn't want me to see.

The couple on the blanket nearby were now pressed against each other making subtle humping motions. "You should draw them," I whispered. She looked over her shoulder and made an expression of disapproval, even embarrassment. That had got me wondering.

"So, do you have a boyfriend back home?"

"No, not really."

But I could see some giveaway in her eyes. "Come on, someone as hot as you has got to have a bunch of boys honking after you."

"Honking?"

I made elbows and flapped them like a goose, making honking sounds. "You know, like those bull geese out there, when they get horny for a gander."

She made a nervous chuckle. "No . . ."

"But . . . ?"

"Well, there was a nice boy at my school I liked, but he was not interested, I don't think. He liked his football more than girls."

We chuckled. I nodded at the couple going at it on the blanket. "Did you ever make out, you know, do a lot of kissing?"

She glanced at the couple, as the boy had moved his knee between his girlfriend's legs. She shook her head, clearly uncomfortable at their blatancy. The girl was now moving against his knee.

"Sometimes, but not like they do."

"Did you ever do, you know, *it?*" I then filled in the blankness of her expression and cupped my hands. "Did you ever have sex?"

She made a pained expression and shook her head as if warding off a foul thought. "No! no. I did not do that."

"So, you're still a virgin?"

Her face actually flushed and she looked away. I could see her struggling, and at the time I couldn't determine if she was just shy about sexual matters, embarrassed, or offended by my forwardness. Or maybe it was something darker that rose up in her. Whatever the reason, sex was not a topic she wanted to discuss. It was only later that I learned why.

I let a few moments pass for her to get settled again. But I was determined. "Okay, so of all the boys you've met so far, who is your favorite?"

She shrugged and looked away, probably wishing I'd change the subject. "All the boys are very nice," she said, in a feeble effort to deflect me.

"Come on, Lulu. You know what I mean. There's got to be one boy who's special."

"Why do you want to know this?"

I cocked my head and gave her a sly glance. "What about Gee Gee?"

Again she blushed. "Yes, he's very nice and very cute."

"So you like him, no?"

"Yes, but he has a girlfriend."

"Justine."

"Yes, of course. Everybody knows." She made a shrug of resignation.

"So, what happened the other night at Sylvie's house? You took her hand to do a palm reading, and suddenly you freaked out and left. What was that all about?"

"Nothing."

"Nothing, my ass. You looked at her right hand for a long time, you mumbled something nobody got, and suddenly you said, 'No more.' What did you see that made you want to go home all of a sudden?"

Another shrug. "I saw he was in love with her and she was in love with him. That's all."

She made a move to get up again, but I grabbed her arm, knowing I couldn't hold back. "You're saying you have a crush on him, right? You saw he was smiling and holding her left hand, and you couldn't take it because you were jealous that she was his girl, right? I mean, admit it, it's no problem. But everybody's wondering what the fuck happened."

She didn't like my harsh persistence. "I don't understand."

"You don't understand? Well, let me explain because everybody figures that you and Gee Gee have secretly hooked up—that you have been having sex with him, and when you saw him at the party holding her hand and making kissy-face you just couldn't take it anymore. Admit it. You and Gee Gee are fucking each other."

Her face suddenly drained of blood and her eyes widened with disbelief. "No," she rasped. "We are not having sex." And she glared at me as if seeing a demon. "How can you say these things?"

"Then what the fuck was going on?"

"It was the other hand."

And in my head, I saw her glaring at the palm of Justine's right hand. "Huh? What about the other hand? What did you see?"

She shook her head. And without another word she bolted for her bike, jumped on it, and peddled away, leaving me wondering what had just happened.

CHAPTER 12

"SHE DID NOT DIE from hanging," Chad Davidson said.

It was around nine thirty that Sunday morning when Kirk and Mandy met with Davidson in his autopsy room, a garishly lighted chamber in porcelain and stainless steel, lined with shelves containing glass jars of human organs—labeled *brain, liver, stomach, uterus* with case numbers—and a butcher scale hanging at one end of the table and at the other a rolling tray of shiny tools for cutting, shearing, and sawing.

Sylvie Thornton's body was laid out on a table under a bank of fluorescent tubes. A crudely stitched Y incision ran from her clavicle to her pubis while under her chin was a gaping hole where the skin of her neck had been peeled back revealing the insides of her larynx. Her skin looked like gray vinyl, and her face was puffy and bluish.

Mandy had witnessed only a handful of autopsies as an officer and was spared today the actual procedure of slicing down her midsection, cracking open her chest cavity, and removing her internal organs. Nonetheless, Kirk could see that her face was a mask of revulsion.

"As first suspected, she suffered a hyoid fracture," Davidson said.

He had sliced two pieces of the once horseshoe-shaped bone out of Sylvie Thornton's neck and placed it on a towel.

"You can see how the bone was snapped in two. But this is not consistent with hangings. The bone did not break from the noose, which exerted stress elsewhere in her neck. Given that and the angle of the ligature and the abrasion, the only conclusion is that she died from manual strangulation."

"She was murdered?" Mandy said.

"Yes," Davidson said. He turned to Kirk. "You did say something about her death looking staged, and you were on the mark. She appears to have been choked by hand and then somehow set into the noose."

From a folder he retrieved photos taken of the woman's footwear. "Given how the grass and discoloration are restricted to the front of the boots, my guess is that she was drugged then dragged to the rope and strung up, the toe ends scuffing across the ground."

"And by someone strong enough to haul her and lift her body to the noose," Kirk said.

"That would be my guess. And as we discussed, she was tied by a left-handed person."

Kirk looked down on the sorry remains of Sylvie Cox Thornton. Just yesterday morning she had showered, done her hair, put on makeup, sprayed herself with perfume, and dressed in a pricey casual outfit, projecting an image of a woman about to celebrate another day on the calendar of the American Dream—spend the bright sunny morning with friends at the Museum of Fine Arts after which enjoy a lovely lunch at the elegant restaurant on the second floor. And here she lay sliced, bone-sawed, stitched, and looking like a prop from a zombie movie.

"We also had a tox screen done, and she had a substantial amount of TCAs in her system."

"Antidepressants."

"Yes, tricyclic class, most likely Norpramin, the brand name for desipramine—and the same drug found in her medicine cabinet. It's a common drug to treat depression and anxiety. It also comes with a black box warning that high dosages can lead to thoughts of suicide."

"An antidepressant that may lead to suicide. Nice side effects," Mandy muttered.

"Well, that's the devil's bargain," Davidson said with a chilled grin. "But any such thoughts should send patients to alert their doctor."

"No suicide note has been found anywhere including her electronics," Kirk said.

"As expected," Davidson said. "What's interesting is that we also found a concentration of atropine, which is used to treat bradycardia or slow heart rate. We're waiting for confirmation from her primary on this."

Mandy checked her notes. "That's not on the list of meds in her medicine cabinet."

"Quite suggestive, isn't it?" Davidson said with a flash grin.

"Given the concentration, what would have been the effects on her?" Kirk asked.

"In combination with the others, probably disorientation and drowsiness." Then he added, "We found a good amount in her stomach as well as some kind of fruit bread and coffee."

"Fruit bread?"

"Maybe a berry muffin or fruitcake with raisins, candied cranberries, apricots, and a dairy spread like cream cheese."

That explained the sour odor in the air. Her stomach contents sat in a cloth-draped silver basin. "Why's that interesting?" Kirk asked.

"Well, most of the coffee in her stomach was regular coffee with some traces of sugar. But the lab report says that what was left in the mug in her sink was hazelnut sweetened with honey, not sugar. And there was also hazelnut still in the Bunn carafe and the same grounds in the filter sitting on the counter in her kitchen. But no Norpramin or atropine were found in her mug, just hazelnut and honey."

"So possibly the killer brought her coffee from the outside and spiked that with the Norpramin and/or atropine."

"Possibly," Davidson said.

"But no report of any other used cup or mug in the dishwasher or paper cup in her trash," Mandy said.

"Unless the perp took that after killing her," Kirk said. "And no prints in the kitchen since it was cold and gave the killer an excuse for wearing gloves."

"Which means the killer most likely drugged her first, then strangled her, and dragged her out to the tree," Mandy said.

"And all before the neighborhood was fully awake."

"And before the landscaper showed up."

Since they had found no signs of forced entry, it was possible a person—or persons—Sylvie Thornton knew drove or walked up to the house, was let inside, where he killed her, and then took her body out back to stage her death.

"There was nothing on the security videos from other houses—no strange car or pedestrian dropping in—just the vehicles of the construction people, and they all checked out."

"That meant the killer probably left by the woods in back," Mandy said.

Kirk nodded, thinking they would have to check with the neighbors on the far side of the trees.

"Another clue of foul intent," Davidson continued. "In a suicide victim who isn't completely pendant and resting on her feet as she was, the reduction of oxygen to the brain would cause unconsciousness in a matter of seconds. However, there was no way that self-hanging could account for snapped vertebrae."

"Meaning what?" Mandy asked.

"Meaning the killer probably exerted a large tug to her head against the rope."

A disgusting video played inside of Kirk's skull of the woman hanging from the rope, her feet scuffing the ground in torment for air and the killer grabbing her from behind and lying on her full weight until her neck made a hideous snap.

"I mean, her neck looked like something out of a Modigliani painting," Davidson said. "It's nearly two inches too long. In fact, it's amazing her head did not get torn off her body."

"Jesus!" Mandy muttered under her breath. "So why the hell do that?"

"She may have still been alive when the killer put her head in the noose," said Davidson. "So he used his own weight to finish her off. From the length of the rope, the killer wouldn't have had to lift her too high."

"What's her weight?"

"One hundred forty-one."

"So the killer could be a male or strong female."

"Right."

"God, what kind of person would do this?" Mandy whispered.

"A snow man," Kirk said. "Someone with 'a mind of winter.'"

Davidson looked at Kirk. "How does a homicide cop know a poem by Wallace Stevens?"

"I minored in English. How does a medical examiner know a poem by Wallace Stevens?" Kirk said.

"I was born and raised in Hartford where he was an insurance executive, and I did residency at Saint Francis Hospital just down the street from where he'd lived. His house was a tour stop.

"As an English minor you may know the closing lines," Davidson continued. "'*For the listener, who listens in the snow / And, nothing himself, beholds / Nothing that is not there and the nothing that is.*'"

"Pardon me, but I was a straight CJ major," Mandy said. "So what are you two saying?"

"The poem is called 'The Snow Man,' and applied here, we're saying that the killer was someone so used to the cold that they regard human life with chilled objectivity and detachment, hardened to his own humanity and to that of others. In short, a heart and mind of snow."

"Your basic psychopath," Mandy said.

"In a word."

Mandy nodded at the remains of Sylvie Thornton. "We see enough of these, and we may all be snowmen someday."

I'm on my way, Kirk thought.

"Any signs of struggle?" Kirk said.

"No, which suggests she was well drugged and not fighting. But she does have that odd tattoo on her forearm." He lifted her arm to show him. "It's not something I've seen before," Davidson added. "But it doesn't look recent, so she might have gotten it when she was a lot younger. Like she discovered she was quarter Irish. Something a kid would do."

"Her sister said it was some kind of friendship thing she got with other girls."

Later, as they left the M.E.'s office, Kirk said, "You did well."

"We were spared the worst part," Mandy said, "but I still thought I was going to run out of the room."

Kirk nodded, still remembering his first autopsy. The victim was killed by a bullet to the chest and one to his face. Although he had prepared himself with police photos, autopsy videos, and all the cool patter that it was scientific inquiry just like tenth-grade biology lab when he dissected frogs, it was the sound and spray of the bone saw on what remained of the victim's skull that sent him flying to the men's room to puke.

"So you've been to a few."

"Yeah, and I have to remind myself that it's a necessary part of investigations, to help the pathologist determine the exact cause of death. But it's still disturbing. I mean, after a day of cutting up cadavers, Davidson goes home to his wife and kids around the dinner table. And probably has a good night's sleep."

"Probably because he went to medical school and views those on his table not as people recently alive but as specimens crying for answers," Kirk said.

"Right," Mandy said. "I just kept telling myself that that's not about me but for Sylvie and catching the bastard who did this to her."

"You're already ten steps beyond your grandfather."

CHAPTER 13

MORGAN

Nineteen years ago, October 12

I CAN'T SAY that over the weeks of her living with us that we had become close. I never did discover what she saw in Justine's palm and just dismissed that little show and her sudden exit as a lot of Romany self-drama.

But it was obvious that Lulu wanted to be my friend and a member of my inner circle of best best friends—Sylvie Cox, Riley Malone, and Krista Barber. But she was a little too needy, a little too desperate to belong. Besides, she was an outsider who would return to Slovakia at the end of the year.

Yes, she was smart and pretty—maybe a little too pretty for me, since the boys at St. B's snuffled around her like pathetic puppies. She really didn't seem all that interested, probably because Gee Gee Gallagher was not available and hooked on Justine. But she had wanted to be good buds with us, even becoming a member of our little sisterhood.

Over the weeks, she showed little acts of kindness such as asking me the mailing addresses of my BBFs and then sent miniature drawings of them in friendship cards. And about a week before

Halloween, Riley's mother got into an accident on the highway. Conditions were clear, but she swerved off the road and slid into a tree and ended up in the hospital with a few broken bones. While we all got together and sent flowers, Lulu sent her a beautiful pen-and-ink portrait she had made of Riley, which won a few points with her.

She also went out of her way to ingratiate herself to me, helping with my homework. I always made the honor roll, but math was not my strong suit. I guess she had good training in schools back home. When I asked her, she said that even though her father was a farmer, he was very smart and helped her with mathematics and science. I appreciated her help even though on some level I resented being beholding to her. She also did me little favors, like fold my laundry if it was in the dryer and buy me Gummy Bears and put them on my pillow, or surprise me with drawings of me.

Once while we were doing homework together, she asked about my four-leaf clover tattoo and why three of the leaves were blank and one was filled in red. I explained that this was a symbol of my best friendship with Sylvie, Riley, and Krista, and that a different leaf of the four is filled in red on each of our tattoos, signifying our forever bonding. Lulu ran her finger across the tattoo and said she wished she had best best friends. It was then I noticed her eyes fill up. But I was sure she had friends back home.

Then something happened that altered my feelings.

It was a warm Indian summer day and my father had dropped us off at Walden Pond as a last fling of the season before the leaves changed and the days turned cool. The water was still warm, and while the rest of us bounded into it, Lulu sat on her blanket wearing a long-sleeve top. We tried to get her to come in, but she resisted for a while until she came in up to her knees. We tried to convince her to take off her top and get wet with the rest of us since this might be the last swimming day of the year. She finally removed her top, and there on her arm was a tattoo of a five-leaf clover.

We didn't know what to think because we were so stunned. For a lack of anything else to say, Sylvie said in a flat voice, "Oh, five leaves," as if we couldn't count. Riley, her voiced edged with dismay, blurted out, "That's our symbol." In disbelief, I said, "Where did you get that?" And she said, "At the same place in Waltham, Ink Inc." So stunned by her presumptuousness, Riley said, "But that's our special emblem." She must have picked up the resentment because she said in all innocence, "I asked your dad, and he said he didn't think you'd mind."

"My dad? He did?"

"Yes, and he drove me."

"He had no fucking right to give you permission."

Lulu's face went blank. "He said you wouldn't mind."

"Well, I do mind. We all mind. That's *our* symbol. You had no right to get that."

Her face fell and eyes began to water. "Sorry," she said and went back to her towel.

I followed her. "Sorry nothing. You knew that was just for us, our own private symbols. Why didn't you ask me instead of him?" I hated her at that moment.

"I didn't know," she said, starting to cry.

"You're not one of us!"

Later, when I confronted my father, he said he thought it would be a nice gesture since she wanted to be friends with us all. "So what's the big deal?"

"The big deal is that I don't need you to tell me who my friends should be."

"It would mean a lot to her to be best friends. Besides, she'll be returning home in a few months, so what difference does it make?"

"That's not the point. She's not part of my inner circle, *our* inner circle. We're special and best best friends forever. And she's *not*."

For the better part of a week, I did not speak to my father, plus I was really cool to Lulu and avoided her, except when I couldn't, like in school. But I had made it clear that she had no right to go ahead with my father's encouragement and get that fucking tattoo, especially without our permission, which we would never have given.

I guess my father was right about me when in a heated moment he said that I never forgave or forgot an offense. This was a betrayal, and I could not forgive either of them.

Lulu got the point and kept to herself, retreating to her room after school and following dinners. My mother said she understood how I felt, saying that she didn't realize how special our tattoos were to us. But my father told me to suck it up—that I should get over it. Lulu was a fine young woman who just wanted to belong, to have American friends, to simply fit in. Besides, after she was gone, we could go on with our "little sisterhood bondage club"—his words snickering with sarcasm. So to reduce her guilt, he took Lulu for a spin in the Boston Harbor in his boat. Alone.

I remember how I had resented his siding with her. He knew I was pissed and carried on about how the program of hosting foreign exchange students was all about making global friends and about encouraging global peace and that it began with individual people like us—that world peace begins at home, or some shit like that. I pretended to understand and took comfort in the fact that in four months she'd be back at her pig farm and never to be heard from again.

I also remember how I hated the way he'd glare at her—that secret gleam in his eye, his saying how she looked *hot* and *model-y* in skinny jeans with high showy slashes and tight cheeky buns. It wasn't just that I felt big and horsy by comparison. It was like he was undressing the leggy bitch in his head.

CHAPTER 14

THEY WERE BACK at Sylvie Thornton's Cambridge home later that Sunday morning.

The property abutted an area thick with scrub and trees with no discernible pathways, giving the backyard a screen between it and the nearest neighbors.

Those woods would have to be searched thoroughly for clues, Kirk reminded himself.

As they stood in the driveway looking over the backyard and the killing tree, Mandy groaned. "But it's been so corrupted."

"Yes, but no," Kirk said. "Are you familiar with Locard's Principle from your CJ courses?"

"Yeah. Edmond Locard, the Sherlock Holmes of forensic science. Something about how a perpetrator will leave a crime scene with something that will affect forensic evidence. That's my point. It's already been compromised."

"Right, but the other half of Locard's Principle is that a perpetrator will also bring something to a crime scene, and that's what we have to find."

Already a second team of investigators had made the rounds to the nearby homes, asking residents if they heard or saw anything or anyone that might shed light on the murder of Sylvie Thornton. That drew a lot of blanks. Nobody had seen anything unusual or any unknown persons but for the contractors working across the street. And nobody knew anyone who had issues with Sylvie Thornton.

Because one of the homes nearby was having interior work done, several contractor vehicles had moved in and out all Saturday beginning at seven a.m. But no one had taken notice of anyone entering the Thornton property. Unfortunately, the house had no security cameras, but the few others on the street showed nothing since the Thornton house was out of range.

Crime scene techs had confirmed that there were no signs of forced entry or physical evidence that another party had entered the house but for the coffee found in Sylvie Thornton's stomach. Also, no rope matching that used for the hanging in either the house or garage. That meant the killer had brought his own and must have worn gloves since no prints were found on the hanging cord. All cunning calculations on the killer's part.

"So what do you think?" Mandy asked Kirk, as they headed back to the Delmonicos' house.

"Given the amount of drugs in Thornton's system, she might have been just functioning enough for the killer to walk her outside to the tree and tie her up."

"But she had grass on her shoes like she was dragged."

"But that could have been from shuffling against the noose. Think of it, you're fighting for air and your feet start dancing by reflex. Then seeing she's not dead, the killer takes to finishing her off manually."

"With the rope still on her neck?"

"Yeah, strangles her then pulls her body down full weight to make it look like suicide."

They arrived at the Delmonicos' where several other cars filled the driveway, belonging to friends who had stopped by to offer comfort.

They rang the bell, and Paul Delmonico answered.

"Sorry to intrude, but we have a few more questions," Mandy said.

Paul led them into the living room where several people were gathered quietly with Erin. Kirk apologized and asked for a private space to speak with Erin. She directed them into the family room.

When they were seated, Kirk explained that there were new developments in the investigation. "We just returned from the autopsy on your sister. We can't go into details, but we're sorry to report that the Medical Examiner has determined that Sylvie did not die by suicide but was killed by someone."

"What? Murdered? Oh good God! Why would someone want to kill her?" Erin said, choking out her words. "And who?"

"That's what we're hoping to find out. Can you think of anyone who would want to harm Sylvie?"

"No. She was a warm, friendly person everybody liked," Erin said between sobs.

"You said you were very close to Sylvie, so you would know if she had any medical issues, correct?"

"Yes."

"Then would you know if Sylvie had any heart conditions."

"Heart conditions? Not that I knew of."

"According to the lab, traces of atropine were found in her system. It's a prescription medication that treats low heart rates."

"Low heart rate? That's nothing she ever told me. Did you check with her primary or the doctor's name on the vial?"

"We will."

Erin's expression sharpened. "Are you saying you found a pharmacy container in her house?"

"The investigation is ongoing, so we can't talk about it."

"Well, I can assure you that if she had heart problems, she would have told me."

"Verizon provided us a log of recent calls to Sylvie." Mandy handed Erin a sheet of names. "Do any of these look familiar to you?"

Some were vendors, contractors to clean the gutters, some from Erin, Sylvie's son Aaron, Diane Ruffy, Harry Thornton, and Morgan Cassidy.

"Morgan Cassidy. Yes, she was friends with Morgan when they were younger. They went to grade school together. I think she was on the planning committee for a high school reunion at the end of the month. But I don't think they were particularly close."

"So she might have called about the reunion."

"That's my guess. But I think they went their separate ways after graduation."

"What do you know about her today?"

"Not much. I know her parents got divorced, and that her mother died a few years ago. I think she's married and is an English teacher somewhere on the Cape, but I don't know where exactly."

"Please don't be offended, but it's a question we ask of all people involved with the investigation. Can you tell us your whereabouts yesterday morning between seven and eleven o'clock?"

"I was here waiting for Sylvie to pick me up and drive to the MFA. I had called her a few times wondering where she was. I also called Diane Ruffy who was meeting us at the museum. When she didn't show or answer the phone, I figured she overslept or just didn't want to get out of bed. And given the day—you know, the anniversary of Devon's passing—I understood. Then you showed up."

"Right. And your husband?"

"He was here with me."

"Thank you. One more question," Kirk said. "Was Sylvie a coffee drinker?"

"Yes."

"And a morning coffee drinker?"

"Yes. She once joked that coffee was the only way to make her feel human."

"I know that feeling," Mandy said.

"So you're saying she had regular caffeinated coffee each morning."

"Yes."

"As far as you know, did she prefer any particular roast or flavor—you know, French, Kona, pumpkin, whatever?"

"I know she liked hazelnut. In fact, I stored a package just for her." She said that, and she filled up.

"Black or with cream. . . ?"

"With milk and honey."

"Honey, not sugar."

"Yes. She said she preferred honey because it had a flavor and sugar was just sweet." Erin Thornton wiped her eyes. "Please, find the monster who did this."

Kirk nodded, thinking that they were dealing with a killer of malignant rationality. Unlike domestic violence done in a moment of rage or home invasions, Kirk sensed he was facing a cunningly methodical killer who made a logical decision to end the life of Sylvie Thornton because she had posed a threat to the killer's well-being and, thus, staged her murder on the anniversary of her child's death. As hideous as that scene was in Sylvie Thornton's backyard, the killer concluded that hanging was the best option for solving the problem while appearing to be the only logical choice for the victim to end her own problem—her own tormenting grief. In short, the end justified the means. And the killer staged a perpetrator-less crime.

"We'll do our best," he said and handed Erin his card. "Anything you can tell us about Sylvie or anything relevant to the investigation, please let us know."

She nodded.

"We'll get him."

CHAPTER 15

THEY LEFT THE Delmonicos' and Kirk dropped Mandy off at the station while he stopped at an Armenian deli in Watertown for a fast lunch on lamejuns. Halfway through, he got a call from Mandy.

"Hey, guess what? Nineteen months ago, Sylvie Thornton was arrested for attempted blackmail of Harry Thornton for income tax evasion."

"What?"

"She wanted spousal maintenance money when she left her job and got caught in a sting when Belmont PD nabbed her outside the bank with twenty grand in cash she got from Harry."

"You mean she tried to extort him?"

"Right. She knew he hid a lot of income and squeezed him for the cash to keep quiet, but she got caught. A slick lawyer got her a suspended sentence. Then a few months later, Harry married wife number two, Amy, and Sylvie sends Thornton videos of Sylvie having sex with her ex, Harry, while divorced and threatened to send them to Amy."

"Huh?"

"Yeah, and another extortion attempt. He notified authorities, but never pressed charges. But the threat of sending the vids to Amy still hung over him."

"So why would he have sex with her after their divorce and his remarrying?"

"Maybe out of pity, you know—comfort her given her messed-up emotional state. Whatever, she made it known she was available and probably desperate, and he was armed and compliant. By the way, pretty amazing video."

"I'm sure." Suddenly images of Olivia in bed with Ted Rizzo lit up his mind. He shook them away.

"The point is she threatens extortion Round-Two, and he puts an end to it from a tree."

"At least we're not jumping to conclusions."

"Well, he had a clear motive—stop her from draining his bank account and from a possible breakdown of his marriage to Amy."

"But that doesn't mean he went over and killed her."

"Except techs checked with her cell carrier and found that Harry had sent Sylvie a text the night before she died that he was going to stop by the next morning to pick up boots for Aaron. Yeah, he claimed he never did because Aaron ordered a new pair, but that doesn't clear him."

With no signs of forced entry, the killer was a friend, acquaintance, or a family member whom she had let inside. "My, my," Kirk said.

"Yeah, he's climbing the perp charts."

"It'll be interesting to hear his alibi."

"Whatever, see you at the bastard's place."

* * *

Kirk steadied his gaze on "the bastard" as they again sat in a booth in his restaurant. "We have reason to believe that your former wife did not kill herself. That she was murdered."

Thornton looked as if he'd been electrically shocked. "What? I don't believe this. Who would do that?"

The expected response, although Kirk could not determine if he was playacting. His mouth had gaped in disbelief, and his eyes had saucered. "Do you know anyone who had a grudge or felt ill-will toward Sylvie—even someone from her past?"

"No. I mean, we've not been close since our separation, but she was liked by everyone."

Mandy nodded. "So can you tell us where you were yesterday between the hours of seven and ten?"

He flashed Mandy a hot look. "You gotta be kidding."

"It's a routine question we ask everybody, including family."

Thornton nodded and re-centered himself. "Like I said, I was home in bed. When Aaron said to forget the boots, I went back to sleep."

"And when did you get up?"

"I don't know. Around ten."

"Can your wife confirm that?" Mandy said.

His face clouded over. "Well, not actually. She's visiting her parents in San Diego. She left three days ago."

Mandy let out a scoffing puff of air. She'd had her claws out for Thornton. "And when is she planning to return?"

"Sunday."

"Do you recall which airline?"

He glared at her and then checked his cellphone. He named a Jet Blue flight number.

"We're going to want to question her also," Kirk said. "So maybe you can give us her contact information."

He held Kirk's eyes then conceded. "Yeah, okay." Then he added, "If she was found like you said, you know, hanging, how would someone do that?"

Kirk locked eyes on Thornton's face for any telltale hints that belied his words. "Let's just say the investigation is ongoing."

Thornton nodded and wrote down the email address and cell number for his wife as well as the telephone number of her parents. Again, left-handed. "While you're at it, we'd like the names of Sylvie's friends, people who knew her—old friends, from school or college or place of business. Anyone to help in the investigation."

He named off five women, including Diane Ruffy and the tennis partner MaryAnn Liczek.

"Do you know if she had any issues with any of these people?"

"Not really. But remember I haven't seen them in a few years." Then he recalled, "I think she had a falling-out with Morgan Cassidy. I don't know the circumstance, but they used to be close in school."

"I'm sorry to bring this up, but a year and a half ago Sylvie was arrested by the Belmont police for attempting to extort you over income tax evasion. Can you tell us about that?"

His face became hectic with red blotches. "I'm not sure how relevant that is."

"We're looking for motives behind your former wife's murder, so we're exploring all possibilities."

"Well, I didn't kill her," Thornton snapped. "And you can check the damn records—that all that was resolved. I declined to press charges, and the matter was settled out of court."

Kirk nodded. "Right." He handed Thornton his card. "Even the smallest detail could help."

"Yeah, sure. I just can't imagine anyone having a reason to kill her."

Someone had one.

Later in the car as they headed back to the station, Kirk said, "Mandy, are you all right?"

She knew what he meant. "I was doing all I could not to tear his face off."

"Yeah, and I think he got the drift."

"So why didn't you bring up the sex tape?"

"First, that was settled out of court. Second, no point of rubbing his nose in that until we know if his alibi stands up. Which means we contact his wife and go from there."

"He claims he was sleeping, so how do we disprove that?"

"We disprove that if he was seen at or on his way to and from Sylvie's Cambridge place."

"I'm sorry but I think he just inched up on my list."

"Based on what?"

"Is this a test?"

"Yes."

"For one, he seemed to have answers on tap. Like he'd rehearsed what he'd say. Like he wanted to appear shocked and saddened. Like he's either lying or omitting important information. Plus, he has no real alibi for sleeping in with his wife away."

"Check on that."

Mandy called their IT guy, Sergeant Greg Lainas, at the station. By the time they arrived at her car, Greg confirmed that an Amy Thornton was on the manifest of the Jet Blue flight to San Diego with a return flight this Sunday.

"Granted it's a short list, but he's still on top. He left his wife for another woman when she was at her lowest and fought for custody of the other son. Plus, he still has the house key. And maybe she was still pressing him for money," she said and got out of the car.

"Anything else?"

"Yeah, he's got a penis."

CHAPTER 16

IT WAS DATE NIGHT, and Kirk phoned Olivia to say he'd pick her up.

She lived in a condo in Newton Upper Falls, a handsome mid-rise brick town house with two spacious floors. On the first was a large living room, a dining room, an office, and hardwood floors and oversize windows. The second floor had two bedrooms with skylights, a full bathroom, a guest room, and a walk-in closet. Unfortunately, it was a very attractive place and one into which she had comfortably settled.

As on the past date night, Olivia had said that she'd meet him at the restaurant—her way of discouraging the possibility of his staying over, if even to sleep on the couch. She had made a clean cut and wanted it to remain that way.

So they met at Vinotta on Moody Street in Waltham. As expected, she was smartly dressed in a beige skirt, an auburn turtleneck sweater that accented the highlights of her hair, and brown leather boots.

It was the first time in three weeks since he had last seen her, and she was as beautiful as ever. "You cut your hair and had it highlighted."

"Yes, a little something new."

"I like it," he said, but really thinking that this is what women do when they are in the process of seeking a divorce—getting a makeover. Rebirth as an unmarried woman again.

But all else was as he knew her—full fleshy mouth, high cheekbones, small sharp chin, and wide eyes, *lovely, dark, and deep*. Yet he felt his heart gulp to think that Ted Rizzo was now enjoying the pleasure of her.

"How's work?" she asked.

"I've got a new partner. As you know, Artie retired."

Artie Stamos, who was sixty-two, and Kirk's partner for twelve years, was wounded in a shoot-out while investigating a home invasion four months ago. After being released from the hospital, he announced that he was retiring. He had had enough of dangerous people. Having made a full recovery, he and his wife moved to Florida where he now spent his days bonefishing.

"I've also got a new case, and it's quite interesting," Kirk said. "Looks like a homicide that was staged as a suicide. I'll spare you the details, but it's going to be challenging. The victim was apparently well liked and devoted to community services and charities."

"I still wish you had a job that didn't center on murder."

"It's what I do."

"I know. You see yourself as bringing justice to the world. That's important and honorable," she said. "But I wish you'd consider teaching criminal justice instead. Given your experience, any college or university would love to hire you. In fact, I can give you CJ contacts at Pilgrim State."

It was a familiar conversation that went back even before Megan's death, especially after the news of a local police officer being killed in the line of duty. "I appreciate that but being in a classroom—that's just not me."

"But it would be safer and less stressful, and you wouldn't be dealing with horrible people and dead bodies. Or threats of retaliation."

"Granted, but I can handle the stress. Plus the challenge of getting some horrible people off the street means fewer dead bodies we have to contend with."

"But you'd make a great teacher. You're smart, experienced, and articulate. Students would love you."

"Nice to hear, but I prefer the field."

She made a conciliatory nod. "I understand that, but it's as if with every case you're trying to make up for the creep who killed Megan."

From someone else, that would have been cheap psychology, but he could not contradict her assessment. And there were times when he went to the shooting range with his service weapon and imagined the driver on the paper targets. "Maybe deep down that's what I'm doing, but it gives me satisfaction. And I work with some terrific professionals. Plus this case is intriguing." He took a sip of his pinot noir. Time to change the subject. "So, are you still seeing Ted Rizzo?"

"Yes, I'm still seeing him."

Some years ago, they had hired Rizzo to bump out their kitchen and later to put skylights in their bedroom. He was very handsome and charming and impressed them with his sense of design and professionalism. But it was clear in their dealings that he was attracted to Olivia, constantly addressing her when he explained how they would go about their work. Nodding and smiling too much when she spoke—giving off all the cues that his interest in her went beyond business. Over the weeks, Rizzo personally showed up during the construction to double-check on progress, especially when Kirk wasn't home. Visits that didn't seem necessary, given the expert craftsmen who did the actual reconstruction. Even back then Kirk sensed something predatory in Ted Rizzo.

"Did you know there's a lawsuit against his company?" A local newspaper reported how Heritage Contracting, Rizzo's company, was being sued for taking payments on a job then abandoning that job. "Essentially, he's being sued for fraud."

"Yes, I heard, but it's a civil suit, not a criminal one. I don't know much about it, but he explained that the job will eventually be completed once the materials arrive from China or wherever. And frankly, I don't want to talk about him, so let's change the subject."

But Kirk did want to talk about him, and beating around the proverbial bush was not his way. "Do you love him?"

"Do we have to talk about this?"

"That or I can describe the victim's autopsy."

She made a dismissive sound. "No, I don't love him. Yes, he's good company." She took a sip of wine.

"So am I."

She smiled. "Sometimes."

"Do you love me?"

She gave him a long stare as she measured her words. "Yes, I love you."

"So why did we separate?"

"Because you were dysfunctional and couldn't be reached."

"I was dysfunctional because I was supposed to protect her and failed. And it didn't help that you outright blamed me."

"I blamed you for not showing up in time to accompany her to the bike path."

"Jesus, I was stuck in traffic and told her to wait. But she was fourteen years old and decided to leave without me." They had been over this dozens of times. "Look, let's not fight, okay?"

"Okay, but we were grieving separately, and I needed you for emotional support because I was dying inside."

"I know, but I had to come to terms not only with the death of my daughter but the fact that I could have prevented that. And that left me so paralyzed that I couldn't be there for you. I had nothing left inside but guilt and despair. And I cannot tell you how sorry I am about that. I just wasn't myself."

"But you refused to go into counseling."

Olivia's eyes filled up as did his. "Only because I was emotionally numb, frozen, suffering clinical depression, withdrawal—call it what you want. The point is back then I couldn't address that with a shrink or some support team of other parents of dead kids. And the reason was that I saw my guilt as a life sentence and saw no possible relief. But I'm better now and working helps."

"So how are you better?"

"We'll never get the guy who did that, but I've come to terms with Megan's death. I've also stopped blaming myself and I hope you have."

Olivia studied his face for a long moment. "I have."

Kirk nodded and almost broke down with relief. "I needed that." He took a deep centering breath, a sip of wine, and he continued. "In a sense I have a new identity with myself. And I can tell you that being back in the field has made me more centered, more focused. Especially this case. Plus, I'm open for us seeking counseling. So I think we should give it another try."

She smiled in spite of herself. "You don't give up, do you?"

"Not on you."

She wiped her eyes and took a sip of her wine. "Kirk, I think it's best we continue to live apart."

"For now." She did not take the bait but something in her response caused a flicker of hope in him.

"So, tell me about your new partner."

"Her name is Mandy Wing. She's thirty-three years old and very bright. She has an engaging personality and a sunny earnestness. I like her."

"Is she attractive?"

"I imagine her wife would think so."

"Her wife? Interesting."

"And the mother of a two-year old son by artificial."

"Good for her." Then she added, "And a good cop?"

"She will be."

She smiled at the implication. "Are you dating?"

"No."

"Why don't you?"

"I prefer you."

She tucked her hair behind her ear, a gesture he loved. "Kirk, let's not go around in circles."

After a few moments Kirk said, "Thanksgiving is a few weeks away. And with vacation days, that would mean a week off for both of us. I was thinking maybe the two of us could go to the White Mountains and find a cozy inn. You know, great food, drinks by a fire, snowshoeing or cross-country skiing like old times. Separate beds, of course."

Olivia puffed out her cheeks and let out an audible sigh.

"Do I hear a discouraging word coming?"

"I don't think it's a good idea."

"Why?"

But just then the waitstaffers arrived with their meals. And they ate quietly, as if at separate tables.

CHAPTER 17

MORGAN

Nineteen years ago, October 19

My father was a big Bruins fan back then and would go to the Boston Garden a few times a year with his buddies and then stop at one of the sports bars on Canal Street to celebrate, especially when the home team won. He was not much of a drinker, maybe two or three beers a night, but he loved the ritual.

It was a week before Halloween when the Bruins were playing their archrivals, the Philadelphia Flyers. It promised to be a big game, so the trains would be filled with fans, including those who didn't have tickets but headed for the bars to watch. That meant an early dinner for the family, so we ordered takeout from a local Indian restaurant. My father left shortly after that, and after helping my mom clean up, Lulu and I headed to our rooms to do homework.

Sometime in the middle of the night I woke up with an upset stomach, which I blamed on the shrimp curry. I was about to go to the bathroom when I heard someone cross the landing. I opened the door a crack to see my father enter Lulu's bedroom and quietly close the door behind him.

For a moment, I thought that he had had too many beers and made a mistake in the dark. In a second or two I expected him to emerge, whispering apologies. But he didn't, and I heard muffled voices—his and Lulu's—but not like an exchange over a mistake. Then all was silent for a long time until I heard him groaning and heard Lulu make muffled gasps. They were having sex! Sometime later, I heard him tiptoe into the master bedroom and close the door.

At first, I was stunned with horrid disbelief, until it crossed my mind to go in there and scream at them or to wake Mom and tell her. But either way would have turned the night into hellish chaos. And I had no idea how my mother would react, if she'd explode and throw them both out of the house or call the police or even have a heart attack. Not to mention what it would do to Richie who wouldn't understand and would become hysterical. Instead, I crawled back into bed and pulled the covers over my head, wishing I could fall into oblivion. Wishing I had been stuck in a disgusting nightmare. But I lay there insanely rattled and shaking, my mind in a frantic scramble:

Was this something that just happened because he was drunk?

Or had he gone in there on other nights?

Were they carrying on an affair under our roof?

And what was wrong with him that he'd do such a shameless thing with a girl less than half his age?

And why did she let him?

I had once adored my dad and was so proud to be his daughter because he seemed to be the perfect father—smart, funny, and so handsome. His presence would fill a room the moment he entered. Even my girlfriends were envious, especially Krista who said he was the hottest dad of all the kids she knew. So, how could he do this to me? To Richie? And to Mom who had loved him and was such a faithful and devoted wife and mother?

Suddenly my world had taken on a brutal new shape.

I didn't sleep all night, twisting and turning in bed, sweating, my heart banging in my rib cage. Flashing through my mind were replays of my father's interaction with Lulu over the weeks—saying something witty at dinner then winking at her, holding her in prolonged eye contact, how he would playfully touch her arm to get her attention or try to make her laugh, the way he complimented her new outfit we had bought for her at the mall, on his Amex card. And her demure innocent little foreign-exchange-student responses. All along I had thought that he was just trying to make her feel welcome in our house. Instead, it was because he was fucking her.

And how do I face them now?

It would take every ounce of will not to crack.

The next morning, I texted my mother that I didn't feel well and was going to sleep in and not to wake me—some kind of indigestion from that Indian food. I couldn't bear the sight of my father or Lulu, not knowing what I'd do if I saw them. My skin crawled at the thought of laying eyes on him. As for Lulu, I wanted her out of the house, out of our lives. But the thought of explaining why to my mother meant having to tell the hideous truth—that my father was a disgusting, heartless pig of a man who had sex with that fucking Gypsy whore.

CHAPTER 18

After questioning more Cambridge neighbors, the next morning Kirk was satisfied that Sylvie Thornton had no known enemies. However, some hinted that Harry Thornton did not share the same popularity. Since they had not confirmed his alibi, he was still a person of interest, and high on Mandy's suspect list.

Sylvie's tennis friend, MaryAnn Liczek, was frank in her dislike of him. "In all the years, I could never warm up to him," she began. "We had the typical neighborhood cookouts and garden parties. He came a few times but struck me as aloof and ill at ease, as if he wished he were someplace else."

"How would you characterize his interaction with Sylvie?" Mandy asked.

"Not particularly warm. At first, I thought it was just his conservative manner, you know, no demonstration of affection like some husbands. And at times he'd be short with her, fact-check her, or roll his eyes when she said something he questioned. I'm not saying that spouses should be monolithic in their behavior, but he was sometimes disrespectful of her."

"Sexist?" Mandy threw out.

"Frankly, yes. But what turned me off was how he betrayed Sylvie at the worst possible time. Their child was dying of cancer, and he took up with another woman, Amy something, his new wife."

Kirk played ignorant. "How do you know that?"

"Vickie Cantor across the street spotted him at a restaurant in New Hampshire being cozy with another woman—the woman he later married."

Mandy shot a look at Kirk to say Thornton had hit Number One on her perp chart.

"Then Sylvie told me herself. She found exchanges on his cellphone that he was having an affair with this Amy. Whatever, he apparently played the sympathy card, using their sick child as an excuse to seek comfort with her. Such malarkey. He was carrying on a full-blown affair while their son was dying and Sylvie was drowning in grief."

"Did you ever sense that Sylvie felt threatened by Harry?" Mandy asked.

"Aside from his adultery, not in the sense you mean." Then she recalled something. "Well, actually I do remember her saying that he pushed her once during an argument. But not that he beat her or anything."

Just as Kirk concluded that there was nothing else MaryAnn Liczek could tell them, Mandy cleared her throat. "Ms. Liczek, did Sylvie ever mention an incident of extortion?"

"Extortion?"

Kirk cut her off. "That has nothing to do with anything," he said and flashed Mandy a hard look. He stood up and pulled out his card. "If there's anything else that might shed light on the investigation, please call anytime."

"Of course."

They left, and as they approached their cars, Mandy asked, "What did I say?"

"MaryAnn Liczek is a lawyer who has ties to the AG's office, which has ties to State and other municipalities such as the Belmont PD, which handled the extortion stuff. I don't want to compromise this case with other agencies mucking things up. This is strictly ours alone to solve.

"Secondly, if word gets back to Thornton that we're looking into the extortion thing as a possible motive, he scrambles to fabricate some sweet-smelling explanation and lawyers-up, and we find ourselves up against a brick wall. In short, we lose the element of surprise."

"So you think I'm a fuckup."

"Mandy, we've worked together for what, forty-eight hours? It's just that you need to modify your modus operandi."

She nodded. After a moment she said, "Okay, sorry."

"Accepted. But just think before you charge." He could see her ears turn red with embarrassment.

Kirk watched her drive away, leaving him feeling lousy. Two days on the job and he'd made her feel inadequate.

He turned onto Brattle Street and took a right heading toward Watertown. The Prentiss School was a cluster of red brick buildings and looked like a small college campus.

It was one thirty, and the lot was full of cars. On his cellphone he had looked up the head of the science department. He parked and headed into the main office and identified himself to the receptionist. "I'd like to speak with Letitia Khouri, please."

"Doctor Khouri is on a lunch break right now, if you care to wait. She should be free in twenty minutes or so." He nodded to a small bank of chairs around a coffee table.

"I'm here on a murder investigation that cares not to wait."

"Oh, oh! Right, sorry." He picked up the phone and called.

In a matter of seconds, a woman dressed in a lab coat stepped into the reception area. Kirk showed her his credentials and asked to speak with her in private. She led him down the hall to her office, a small space walled with stuffed bookcases.

He first apologized for interrupting her lunch, and she said that was not a problem. "Doctor Khouri, you may have heard that Sylvie Thornton was found dead two days ago."

Khouri shook her head in rueful disbelief. "Yes, and we're all heartbroken."

"What can you tell me about the kind of person she was?"

"She was just great. Devoted to her students, took them on field trips to biology labs at MIT and Harvard. Brought them to the Museum of Science. She was faculty advisor to several student clubs, went to all the sporting events. And they loved her, and three years ago she got her second Excellence in Teaching Award."

"As you may have read, her death is being investigated as a homicide. Can you think of anyone who might have wanted to hurt her?"

"No, and that is positively shocking. Everyone was very fond of her."

"No signs of animosity from colleagues or staffers, issues with begrudged students—anything like that?"

She shook her head. "No, nothing like that."

"How well did you know her former husband, Harry?"

"Not very well. He did accompany her on school events, a play and maybe a few baseball and soccer games. But that was infrequent."

"Did she ever let on that things might not have been right with them?"

"Well, he wasn't terribly personable, and always struck me as distracted—you know, like he was not comfortable in social situations."

It was the same kind of response that Kirk had heard from everybody they had questioned: that Sylvie was universally loved, and that Harry was not Mister Popular. They talked a little longer until it was clear Khouri had nothing else to help the investigation. Before Kirk left, he gave her his card to call if she thought of anything.

In the car on the way back to the station, he called Mandy. "I think we should take a closer look at Harry."

"I was hoping you'd say that. By the way," Mandy said, "Annette Volpe just heard from Sylvie Thornton's primary. She had never been given a script of atropine. That came from the outside."

"Then get her to check Harry Thornton's primary—what meds *he's* on."

CHAPTER 19

MORGAN

Nineteen years ago, October 20

THERE WAS NO way I could spend another night in that house.

Luckily it was Friday, so I texted Sylvie to invite me, Riley, and Krista for a Saturday sleepover. I was desperate and needed to be with them. She got back to me a few minutes later saying that it was all set, but she wanted to know why. I said only that I needed to talk.

I spent the day trying to be invisible, avoiding my parents and that bitch, staying in my room, pretending to still be recovering from that stomach bug. Richie spent the day with friends, and Lulu went to the town library to do homework. My mom went to a yoga class at my father's gym, not just to shape up but to avoid being reminded that she was fat and frumpy. As for how my father spent the day, I didn't care. I just wanted not to see him, not knowing what I'd do if I did. Later, I texted my mother that I was going to Sylvie's for dinner and a sleepover, and she approved.

To avoid contact, I bicycled over to Sylvie's house where we ordered pizzas and retreated to her room. It was then I told them what had happened.

"I don't believe it," Sylvie said. And Riley and Krista agreed that it was wicked insane that he had done that with Vadima in the room adjacent to mine and across the hall from where my mother lay asleep.

"I'm so fucking scared, I don't know what to do," I said, tearing up. They hugged me. Nothing would be normal ever again. One word—and my family would be destroyed. "But it's like having an evil demon in the house."

"Oh my god, this so sucks," Riley said. "I told you I never trusted her, like she's sneaky, got this phony innocent mask, but underneath watch out! The way she stares at you, kind of like she's boring a hole in your face. Friggin' creepy, like she's giving you the Evil Eye or something. Plus, she's a fucking little slut the way she comes on to Gee Gee."

"Did you say anything to her?" Sylvie asked.

"No, because I'd have clawed her face off if I did."

"What about your dad?"

"I couldn't even look at him I'm so fucking sick."

"What about telling your mom?"

"God, no. It would kill her. I mean, he picks on her a lot, but I think she loves him. Fuck! I don't know what's real anymore. I mean, why would he do this to her, and in the next room? It's so fucking sick." My tears had dried up, leaving me wanting to smash things.

"But she has to know; it's the only way," Riley said.

"If I tell her, she might get a divorce or something. Plus, that would kill Richie. It would kill all of us. I could lose my family." I started tearing again in spite of myself.

Krista and Riley hugged me for a long moment until I gained control.

"What if you tell her to go back home?" Sylvie said.

"I do that, and my parents will want to know why. She's got three fucking months left."

"Maybe talk to your dad," Sylvie said. "Tell him you know what he did, and if he doesn't want you to tell your mom, get him to get her to leave—say there's an emergency back home and she's got to go back early."

I thought about that. "Except no one would believe that. Besides, they'd have to contact the organization and would find out there's no emergency."

"Force her to lie."

I had come over for consolation and some ideas of what to do, but there were no options. I was trapped in this insane nightmare. I'd have to cut myself off from all of them, pretend everything was normal—go through the house doing laundry, having breakfasts and dinners, helping clean up, going to school, sitting through classes. How could I do all that and not crack? "I can't believe this," I muttered. "I hate him for doing this. And I want to kill that bitch."

* * *

I struggled to get through the next day when I returned home. It was Sunday and a beautiful fall day. After breakfast alone, Lulu took her sketchbook and headed off. My mother had gone to yoga class at the club. I avoided my father who was out back cleaning the garage. So I slipped out of the house and left a note that I was meeting Sylvie in the center.

I took my bike to Horn Pond where I found her scratching away on my favorite bench, drawing swans and cygnets against the blue water. I knew she'd be there, appropriating my own favorite hideaway the way she had my tattoo and now my father. I felt malignant resentment seeing her there.

She greeted me with a cheery smile. "How ya doing?" she said, showing how American she'd become.

I settled next to her on the bench, my face feeling like hardened concrete. "Listen to me, Vadima," I said in a low scraping voice, vowing that I'd never again address her as Lulu. "I know what you and my father did the other night. I saw him sneak into your room and heard you fucking."

"What?" Her face froze in horror.

"You heard me. He came back from the hockey game and sneaked into your room. And I saw him. And he was in bed with you for half an hour."

She held my gaze for a long instant and then looked away. When she turned her head to me again, she said, "Yes, and I'm sorry, but I could not help it. He came into the room, and I didn't know who it was at first, and I was scared," she said. "He was drunk and confused, I think. But then he laid down on the bed and started kissing me. I was horrified and didn't know what to do."

"Bullshit! You could have pushed him off and told him to leave."

Her eyes flooded. "I did, I tried, but he pulled off the blankets and got on top of me and started touching me."

I fought against the images forming in my head.

"Then it was too late because he told me not to make noise, not to wake everybody."

"So you let him. You let him, but you could have resisted, pushed him off, told him it was wrong, told him you'd scream if he didn't stop."

"I couldn't. He's very strong, and on top of me, and he told me not to fight. Men do these things, Morgan. They do. I could not stop him. I'm sorry, very sorry."

"So, you're saying he raped you—my father raped you?" I heard my own voice hitch at the thought. God! This was getting worse by the minute.

She started crying. "I could not stop him. Please believe me."

I didn't know what to think or what to say, but I couldn't let myself side with her.

"If I did, he might want to send me home. I was scared, very scared."

For a moment it passed through my mind that maybe the sounds I had heard were not gasps of pleasure but fear, desperation. *But no!* And at the moment I did not care what happened. "No matter what, I want you out of my house. I want you gone—do you understand? I want you out of my family, out of our lives."

"What, to send me back?"

"Yes. Say there's an emergency at home, someone is sick and dying. Say you're fucking homesick—anything."

"No, please."

I pressed my face close to hers. "If you don't, I'll tell my mother and she'll make sure you're out, you understand? She'll call the student exchange office and report you, and they'll ship you home on the next plane."

"Please no."

"Please no, nothing! You're destroying my family. You get it? You've poisoned us."

"But your father was drunk, and I could not stop him." I heard her voice crack. "It was not my fault."

She was insisting that he had raped her, and I did all I could not to claw at her blubbering little face. "I don't fucking care anymore. The damage is done, and I want you out of my house. I want you to leave the country."

She began to cry, but I told myself they were crocodile tears. Then I added, "And for the next few nights you sleep in the treehouse, you understand?"

She nodded.

I got up to leave. "Make up something and pack your fucking bags."

Suddenly her face hardened to a look I had not seen before. "If you banish me, you will be sorry."

"Is that a threat?"

She did not respond, just stared at me with those night-black eyes.

I started to walk away but looked back. "And by the way, don't think that Gee Gee likes you because he's in love with Justine and thinks you're a fucking weirdo."

CHAPTER 20

For a long time, Kirk stared at his monitor as numerous apps seemed eager to jump into service.

This was juvenile and pathetic, he told himself. But an impish compulsion made him key in the name into the search field. He scanned for any information on Theodore A. Rizzo, but all that came up were a few complaints about his company's tendency to overcharge for construction projects and a few parking tickets.

But two addresses were listed for Rizzo—the home in Wellesley and a condo in Gloucester.

Since Annette Volpe and Mandy were working their leads, Kirk had a free hour that morning to locate Unit A in an upscale condo complex consisting of adjacent town houses perched proudly on a granite outcropping high above Good Harbor with a view to die for. According to Zillow, Rizzo had purchased the place two years ago for $2.2 million.

Rizzo's black Mercedes SL 550 was not in the driveway, nor in the garage.

Kirk rang the bell. When nobody answered, he banged on the knocker until the door in the adjacent unit opened and a woman in her sixties stepped out. She scowled at him until Kirk crossed over to her and flashed his badge and identified himself. "I'm looking for Mr. Rizzo."

"He's out of town and won't be back for a while." Her eyes narrowed expectantly at him. "You a cop?"

"Yes, Cambridge Police."

"You going to arrest him?"

"No. I just need to speak with him about a business complaint." Which, of course, was a lie. In fact, Kirk was not sure why he was here, and so unlike him not to have a mission.

Her expression fell. "I was kind of hoping he was finally getting what's coming to him."

Kirk's heart jogged. "Pardon me?"

"I shouldn't be saying this about a neighbor, but he's not a good person."

"He's not?"

She made a regretful expression. "No. Frankly, he disgusts me . . . what he did to his poor wife."

According to records, Rizzo had been married to a Nora Montana, but no domestic charges had been made. Kirk felt a rat uncurl in his gut. "What did he do to his wife?"

"What he did to his wife was cheat on her big-time. Poor Nora, such a nice lady. And very pretty."

The woman clearly could not wait to lance her blister of contempt, so Kirk played dumb. "He cheated on her?"

"Yes. The way he carried on when she wasn't around."

"How did he carry on? What are you saying?"

"He's a whore hound. There, I said it."

"A *whore hound*?" Kirk hadn't heard that term in years. "You mean he has prostitutes come here?"

"I don't know what they are, but he has women coming and going here, and all hours, day and night. I don't know who they are or what his secret is. Yeah, he's good looking, but he's a prick, pardon my French. Nora would go off to visit her father in New Jersey for a few days, and he'd go to town in here."

Kirk continued to play dumb. "Go to town?"

"You know, the cat's gone and the mice come out to play. He'd bring in women he picked up somewhere."

Kirk felt the rat take a bite. She was giving him something on Rizzo, and it made Olivia a potential victim. Like she might be one of his throwaways. "Okay, so he cheated on his wife, but do you know if he ever abused her?"

"Not physically, as far as I know. Look, I already said too much. But there should be laws against his kind of adultery is all." She shook her head but seemed satisfied that she got all that out.

"Right. Do you have any idea where I could find him?"

"Yeah, Wellesley someplace." She went inside and returned with a slip of paper with the address that had been etched in Kirk's brain.

"So, this Wellesley address is where I could find him?"

"If he's not on some tropical island with one of his women."

"I don't follow."

"He finds a woman who tickles his fancy and takes her to some exotic locale then brings her home and drops her for good. The guy is a first-rate prick, the way he picks them up, wines, dines, and beds them, then he moves on to the next one. And the way he cheated on Nora." She made a hissing sound. "What he had put her through, she should have divorced him years ago."

"You said he didn't abuse her physically, but are you sure he never did?"

She shrugged. "She never said he'd hit her or anything, but he's dangerous if you fall for his charm. And he turns it on like that if he wants something from you."

"May I have your name, please?"

"What do you want my name for?"

"Just in case the Vice Squad does a follow-up on his womanizing." He said that trying to keep his expression serious. There was no Vice Squad, and womanizing was no crime.

"Rona Zuckerman, but don't tell him I said anything. I don't want him coming after me."

Kirk thanked her and gave her his card. And in fifteen minutes, he was back on 128 South when he made a call to Mandy.

"Do me a favor and see if you can find an address for a Nora Montana."

"Who's she?"

"The ex of the guy my wife is dating."

There was a pause. "Kirk, what the hell are you doing?"

"I'm checking to see if he's going to be a problem for her."

"What kind of a problem?"

"That's what I'm trying to find out."

"Kirk, this is nuts, and could take you places you shouldn't be going. She's got a right to live her separation the way she wants."

"True, but if he's dangerous, I want to know. And I want her to know. So please do me a favor and get me an address."

"Yeah, okay. But this is a distraction that you don't need." She then clicked off.

He knew in his heart of hearts that she was right and only thinking of him.

Several minutes later, Mandy called back. Nora Montana lived in a condo in Wellesley and was a CPA at an office in that town. And she had a number.

CHAPTER 21

MORGAN

Nineteen years ago, October 23

VADIMA HAD SLEPT in the treehouse that Sunday night, telling my parents that she wanted to sleep under the stars, like she did back home. She claimed that she and her brother would sleep outside more times than inside, using tents or the inside of a covered wagon. I guess that was the Roma custom. Also, there was supposed to be a meteor shower that night. They said that was fine and gave her the kerosene lantern, a sleeping bag, and extra blankets. At the least, she was out of the house for the night.

I was back in school that Monday, as was Vadima. The only two classes we shared were math and English. We entered separately and sat apart because I could not stand the thought of occupying the same breathing space with her, as if she had carried a plague as Riley had said.

Mr. D'Amato's English class was the only one I looked forward to because we were doing readings from *Macbeth* at the front of the room. These were always fun because some of the kids really hammed up the roles. Last week I had played Lady Macbeth in the "Out, damned spot!" sleepwalking scene with candle in hand, overacting the delivery with exaggerated torment, which the kids enjoyed, even applauding when I was done.

Today's reading was from Act 4, Scene 1, where Justine would play the Second Witch, Trisha Renaldo would read Hecate, and Gee Gee Gallagher would play Macbeth. The scene was the one in the cave where the three witches are cooking up a ghastly brew—eye of newt, toe of frog, dragon's scale, wolf teeth, and other awful stuff. Macbeth had come for a prophecy of his future, hoping the three weird sisters would confirm that he would someday be king.

Toward the end of the scene, Justine and the other two witches recited in unison,

"'Double, double toil and trouble; / Fire burn and cauldron bubble.'" That was followed by Justine with, "'Cool it with a baboon's blood, / Then the charm is firm and good.'"

Then Trisha entered the little circle of witches, and in a sharp voice of Hecate said, "'O well done! I commend your pains; / And every one shall share i' the gains; / And now about the cauldron sing, / Live elves and fairies in a ring, / Enchanting all that you put in.'"

Justine nodded and recited, "'By the pricking of my thumbs, / Something wicked this way comes.'"

Then she stopped without finishing the next two lines before Gee Gee was to knock and enter. Trisha cleared her throat to cue Justine to finish. But she made strange gasping sounds, and her eyes cue-balled in their sockets as she clutched her chest and fell to the floor.

My first thought was that she was clowning around before Gee Gee entered. But suddenly people began screaming as Justine lay there twitching and trying to breathe. Gee Gee was instantly on his knees.

"Get help," he screamed.

"Oh my God!" Trisha cried, and suddenly people were scrambling for help.

Mr. D'Amato cried out for someone to call security while Gee Gee began giving Justine CPR.

I stood frozen in place trying to make sense of what was happening, stunned to see Justine unconscious on the floor with Gee Gee moving from CPR to mouth-to-mouth resuscitation, and Mr. D'Amato yelling for Justine to open her eyes, to wake up.

"Oh God, she's not breathing," cried Trisha.

"Please, no," Gee Gee cried.

He continued to press her diaphragm and blow air into her lungs, but she was not responding, and people were crying and muttering prayers.

Gee Gee cried out, "Oh God! No!" His fingers against Justine's carotid artery. "No pulse. I can't feel her pulse."

The attempts to revive her continued for several minutes until three EMTs showed up with equipment and a stretcher.

Behind them some teachers appeared to clear us out of the room, but like others, I was stunned. Before I was corralled into the hall, I looked back to see the EMTs slamming Justine's chest with defibrillator paddles.

From the hall I watched them paddle her over and over again until one of them shook his head. Justine was dead.

And behind them staring blankly at the scene stood Vadima Lupescu.

CHAPTER 22

THE ADDRESS HE got from court records was a flossy condo complex in Wellesley overlooking a large pond. It was where Nora Montana, formerly Nora Montana Rizzo, now lived, having settled a prenup agreement that left Rizzo in the big Wellesley place. She had agreed to meet at the bar in a restaurant just off of Route 95.

Kirk arrived early and secured a booth where he sipped a beer while waiting for the hostess to escort the woman who showed up sharply at seven.

She looked to be in her forties, attractive and smartly dressed in black slacks, a lavender colored sweater, and black leather jacket. Despite her cordial smile, he could see her estimating him. Meeting the divorced wife of a man who was seeing his own wife was clearly bizarre.

As he explained to her on the phone, he was not here as a police detective but as the estranged husband, concerned about his wife. When the waiter came over, she ordered a glass of pinot noir. They also agreed on some light appetizers since she had already eaten dinner.

"This must be a first."

"Probably."

"So why are we doing this?"

"I'm concerned about some things I've heard about your ex-husband."

"What, that he's a sociopathic serial adulterer?"

"Something like that."

"Then you've been talking to Rona Zuckerman."

"Right."

She made a dry chuckle. "Well, she's seen and heard it all point-blank. That's his little love nest by the sea. He'd bring women up there when I was away or when he claimed he was working remotely and have his little orgies."

The thought of Rizzo in bed with Olivia made his stomach leak acid. "I want to know if he's dangerous."

"Dangerous? Only if you're in business with him . . . or in bed. In either case, he's a fraud and a cheat. You know he's a contractor and he'll do a great job putting an addition on your house."

Kirk said nothing about having hired him in the past and nodded her on since she was on a roll.

"But you got to read the fine print, like not telling you there's a twenty-dollar disposal fee for each cubic foot they excavate for your cellar. Nor the fact that he then sells that same dirt—your dirt—for thirty dollars to another customer who needs fill. The same with leftover materials—lumber, bricks, stone, whatever. Or he'll charge you in full then abandon the job claiming materials never got delivered, or some bullshit."

"One nail, no jail."

"Exactly, and the courts can't touch him, nor will they." She leaned forward. "The same with his sex life—he's a fraud and a cheat. And he'll use you. Is he personally dangerous? Only if you expect a real relationship."

"I'm listening."

"Ted Rizzo uses his good looks, his charm, and money to get a woman in bed then move on to another because he's got some kind of pathological libido that he can't satisfy. And, believe me, I learned the hard way."

Her pupils dilated like a cat's.

"When we started dating, he announced that he was 'polyamorous,' which is a fancy term for screwing a lot of women. He claimed that the main reason marriages failed was infidelity. So he made it clear from the get-go that he was into consensual non-monogamous relationships that meant he had more than one partner at a time. And his justification was that he was looking for Ms. Right. So when he proposed to me, I figured I was it, and that his gunslinger days were over."

Something shifted in her expression.

"Then a year or so later, his intimacy with me began to cool. He wasn't dysfunctional, I can assure you that. In fact, I'd wish he were. I began to wonder if it was me, that he no longer found me attractive. I still looked the same and weighed the same as on our wedding day. Then it occurred to me that he was probably getting his satisfaction in another bed."

She took a sip of wine and shook her head in dismay.

"How did you know he was still gun-slinging?"

"Because I did the bills, I discovered hotel and dinner charges that he couldn't explain. I pressed, and he griped that I was spying on him, but I had hard evidence, so he fessed up that he had been having an affair. But the reality was that he was having affairs—plural. Different venues, different cities. He was back to his polyamory because he was fucking his brains out with a lot of different women."

"And you questioned him on it?"

"Yeah, and he villainized me for snooping, claiming I was paranoid and imagining things, swearing he'd been faithful and doing his explainer thing that he was at conferences with colleagues and that those bills were all about business, wining and dining clients—all to the point that I began to question my own suspicions. He was *gaslighting* me is what he was doing."

"But you said you had hard evidence."

"Yes, and when he was out of town the next time, I had a hidden security camera installed outside and in our bedroom at the condo. Over the next month, I counted four different women, and they were engaged in kinky sexual activities I won't go into, but it was evidence I presented to my lawyer. And that resulted in a nice out-of-court settlement."

The thought that Olivia was being lined up for next filled Kirk with heat.

"I should add that he'd hide all evidence that he was married—photos, my clothes, toiletries, you name it. And unless his women explored the place, they'd never know he shared it with a wife."

Her eyes pooled with tears, and she had fingered the toothpick from the appetizer tray until it snapped. "Sorry," she said. "I'm emotional not because I miss him, but because of the incredible humiliation of being married to a fucking lie. If your wife is seeing him, I suggest you convince her to move on."

"I'm hoping she'll do that on her own."

"In time she will."

CHAPTER 23

KIRK LEFT NORA MONTANA, not knowing what exactly he had.

Rizzo was a reckless serial Lothario, but apparently not physically abusive. He was also a business cheat, although never convicted in courts. But would a womanizer, a pathological liar, and an inveterate crook pose a threat to Olivia? Or was Kirk being overly protective in his concern?

Nora had said that Rizzo had gaslighted her, tried to make her believe she was delusional about his affairs. But the term reminded him of the disturbing movie source—Charles Boyer tricking his wife, Ingrid Bergman, into believing she was insane in order to steal her wealth—and possibly her life.

And what should he do with what he knew?

If he told Olivia that Rizzo was a sick sociopath who might be using her for sexual conquest, she'd probably be furious that Kirk was being intrusive, that she didn't need his protection, that she could handle herself. That he should mind his own business. Also, with a Ph.D. in clinical psychology, she was too aware and too strong to let Ted Rizzo manipulate her. That, on her own, she'd realize that he was pathologically disordered.

"In time she will."

Kirk latched onto Nora's promise and headed down 95 North to the Mass Pike, which would take him to the Cambridge P.D. via the Allston exit.

The setting sun enameled red the Charles River as he headed east toward Boston along Storrow Drive. Sweet memories passed through his mind like taunting flashcards. Olivia and he pushing Megan in a carriage along the Esplanade. Swan boat rides in the Boston Garden. Picnicking along the tranquil lagoons with Megan, age three, quacking at the ducks. She and Olivia poised at a clutch of red tulips in outrageous blossom, each in floppy hats and flowing white dresses like figures in a painting by John Singer Sargent. Making sweet love while a crescent moon smiled down on them through the skylight.

And the wonderment that this was as good as life gets.

Then as he cut onto the Longfellow Bridge at Mass General Hospital, a nasty flash of Megan dying in there sent through him a wave of horror that he could not reach her in time. Nor spare Olivia from annihilating grief.

He flushed all that away and called Mandy to assemble the team in his office. Minutes later he made his way into the Sixth Street headquarters and up to his office.

Assembled were Mandy, Annette Volpe, Greg Lainas, and two others investigators on the Thornton case.

Mandy handed him a mug of coffee as he positioned himself at the corkboard with photos of Sylvie; her ex-husband, Harry Thornton; their son Aaron; Erin Cox Delmonico; Paul Delmonico; as well as maps and crime scene photos and grim autopsy images.

"So what do we have?" he said to the group.

Greg Lainas began. "We're still going through security footage from intersections on Brattle, Mount Auburn, Huron, Mem. Drive, and all other routes that would lead to the Thornton address. The problem is the window from six to ten was a high traffic time because it was a nice day and people were getting out. We've also got the construction people, Ubers, Lyfts, and locals moving in and out. But no one stopping at or entering the Thornton place. We also don't know what kind of vehicle we're looking for—or pedestrian."

Kirk thanked him and his associates and told them to keep digging. All they needed was a single lead, a single individual who didn't belong on that street in that window, and that might be their perp.

Next was CSI investigator Annette Volpe. "We went through the foyer, kitchen, and the whole downstairs, but no prints other than Sylvie's and some latents of her ex and her son Aaron, who checks out since he was at his dorm at Dartmouth that day. My guess is the perp was wearing gloves. And because it was cold that morning, it didn't raise suspicion on the part of the victim. Or he wiped the place clean."

"What about Harry Thornton?" Kirk said.

Mandy stood. "Sorry to be the bearer of shitty news, but Harry Thornton's alibi checks out."

Kirk felt a slight slump as he listened.

"One of his neighbors spotted him going down his driveway in his PJs for the morning paper about the time Sylvie was killed. Also his Visa records show he bought groceries at the Winchester Stop 'n Shop around nine thirty, half an hour before the landscaper showed up."

"So he's off the list," Kirk said.

"Yeah, I can't say I'm not disappointed," she added. "I didn't like the bastard from the get-go."

"Right, but we're looking for the killer, not the least popular," Kirk said.

"Yeah, but the thing is, the longer it takes, the colder the trail."

She was right, and Thornton would have made the case easy. "As we all know, every investigation's a game of beat the clock. Statistically the best leads are found within the first forty-eight hours when memories are still fresh and clues haven't dried up, and evidence is still not totally corrupted, and witnesses haven't disappeared, and suspects haven't taken off to places unknown."

"But outside Harry Thornton, we have no other leads," Lainas said.

Kirk did not need to be reminded. All the people of interest had solid alibis. But it seemed certain that Sylvie knew her killer. So, it meant going deeper into her circle of family and friends.

"Sylvie Thornton's funeral is tomorrow at Saint Bonaventure's in Arlington," Kirk began. "The one consolation is we got the green light to do a surveillance from across the street. It's a long shot, but as you know killers sometimes show up at their victims' funerals. Either because they were friends and were expected to show—or they attended to satisfy some sadistic impulse or for a sick thrill."

Kirk had known of cases where killers had appeared at wakes and funerals and even signed the memorial guest books. Perhaps in a final act of cruel revenge, they would shake hands and hug family members with weepy condolences. Or they might attend to divert attention from themselves, putting on acts of mourning, comforting the children of their victims, handing out business cards to survivors to call if they needed anything. In some past cases, killers also served as pallbearers.

And on rare occasions, a killer face-to-face with the grieving family, especially children or grandchildren, would become so consumed by guilt that they would confess.

Kirk did not know what to expect, but they would have unmarked cars and a van with cameras and blackened windows.

Sometime before seven, he arrived at home. Daisy greeted him at the back door with a small pile of Q-tips on the floor. He didn't know what ancient feline ritual she was fulfilling, but she was a retriever. They had discovered some years ago that she loved to have Megan toss Q-tips across the floor or down the staircase for her to bat and, remarkably, to bring back. Their daughter would spend a good part of an hour holding retriever games with the cat. They also discovered that Daisy would bring them gifts from the basket of toys Olivia had bought her—stuffed mice, fish, furry tails, and other things including an old red slipper of Olivia's. In the middle of the night, she would go down to her basket, and when they'd wake up the next morning, they'd find a stuffed mouse or furry tail on their bed brought up while they slept. They had surmised that she was reenacting some ancient female instinct to bring kills back to her litter, like Serengeti cheetahs returning to her cubs with a gazelle carcass.

Kirk changed her water and poured some kibble into her dish. He then went upstairs where he showered. When he stepped into the bedroom, he spotted something lying on his pillow and heard Daisy let out a soft yowl of longing. He clicked on the light. She was sitting at the foot of the bed where she usually slept. And lying on his pillow was Olivia's old red slipper.

Kirk felt his throat thicken. "Yeah, me too," he said and turned off the light.

CHAPTER 24

MORGAN

Nineteen years ago, October 25

THE OBITUARY SAID that Justine Renaldo was an aspiring violinist, full of energy and high enthusiasm. She was an excellent student and a popular young woman who loved life and had so much to live for. "She was a giving spirit who was always there to help with anything. She will be missed terribly," said Mrs. Wellington, the Headmaster at St. Bonaventure's Academy.

According to the Medical Examiner's autopsy report, no drugs or alcohol had been found in Justine's system. Her family physician said she had no history of heart problems, nor had any family members in memory died of sudden death or under the age of fifty. Doctors added that there were no overlooked heart defects, abnormalities, or arrhythmia in her medical record; and when young adults did die from heart attacks, as rare as they were, they often occurred during physical activities such as school athletics. Also, such deaths more often occurred in males. As one doctor said, Justine's death was a big medical mystery.

"Big medical mystery, my ass," Grayson "Gee Gee" Gallagher said, as we sat in the student cafeteria at St. B's. "That bitch Vadima put a friggin' curse on her is all."

Choked up with tears, Riley nodded. "I told you she was weird. My parents always said they were dangerous, those Roma people. They started the Black Death in ancient times and spread it around the world. I think she's evil."

Gee Gee was in a daze. "She cursed her. She killed my girl."

We sat there in grim silence. And none of us contradicted him.

We had gathered at Dot's Donuts after school, huddled around coffees and Cokes. I could still see the expression on Vadima's face as she glared at the scene of the EMTs trying to bring Justine back. Like she knew. Like it was what she had expected. Like she had done it.

I didn't know where she was at the moment; neither did anyone else since she did not go to school that day. But two days ago, the wake for Justine was held at a funeral home in Arlington. Surrounded by a mountain of flowers, she had lain in an open casket dressed in white with a single rose in her hands, folded in prayer. She looked like Sleeping Beauty waiting for a kiss from her prince.

The sight of her had everybody weeping helplessly, including Vadima. I had not wanted her to attend, but I would have had to explain to my parents. So she came with them and did her part, keeping to herself in a corner. Sniffling and wiping her nose and eyes with tissues. Looking like the grieving best best friend and classmate.

That night she slept in the treehouse even though it rained.

Thankfully, she claimed she was sick the next day and stayed in bed. During lunch, everybody in the cafeteria was subdued, still trying to process Justine's death. Every so often, Gee Gee would put his head down on his arms and quietly sob. Riley rubbed his back as we all cried with him. "I loved her. She was my best friend," he muttered. "What am I going to do?"

Krista suggested that he talk to Father de Souza. More than just a priest, he was a thoughtful and kind man and had always made himself available for students going through tough times whether with studies, social life, or family problems. I had gone to him once in the past because my parents fought so much. I'd even considered telling Father de Souza about my father and Vadima, but I stopped short because it was too painful and too humiliating. Nor could I imagine myself going through the scene.

"Father, forgive me for I have sinned."

"What is your sin that you are confessing to, my child?"

He always said "my child" even if you were eighty years old. *"I hate my father."*

"You hate your father? Why is that?"

"I caught him sneaking into Vadima Lupescu's room where I heard them having sex."

"Is that so?"

"Yes, and it was horrible. If my mother finds out it could mean the end of our family."

"I see. Then it might be best not to tell her."

And then what: *"Say ten Hail Marys for being a tattletale"*?

No. I knew I had no recourse but to burn inside until she was back in Slovakia and forever out of my life.

CHAPTER 25

SINCE OLIVIA HAD moved out, several mailings for her still came to the house, most of them alumnae materials, Christmas catalogues, and junk. The only important item was a renewal reminder from the Registry of Motor Vehicles. So he bagged all that to drop off at her place before heading to headquarters.

As he approached Olivia's condo complex, a flare went off in Kirk's gut. Ted Rizzo's sleek black Mercedes was parked in front. He pulled out of sight behind some parked cars, expecting to see Olivia step out of the building. But after several moments, Rizzo got out of his car, and in a flush of despair Kirk watched Rizzo let Olivia out of the passenger seat, take her arm, and walk her up the path to the front door—thinking that in those little innocent rituals Ted Rizzo had replaced him.

It was Olivia's day off, and he didn't know if they had just returned from a brunch or, worse, that she had spent the night at his place.

Suddenly he wished he were not here watching this. He wished he were not seeing Olivia with another man, giving him a hug and kiss, before she disappeared inside. He wished he had never driven here. He wished her dating was just some unpleasant abstraction. But seeing them embrace filled him with annihilating hurt.

Ted Rizzo.

It had been years since he'd last laid eyes on him, the then-friendly, neighborhood contractor who had bumped out their kitchen and put in a skylight in their bedroom. He'd been dressed in jeans, a sincere company shirt, and seasoned work boots. Now he wore a navy blazer, gray slacks, and pricey silky scarf, maybe having spent a brunch with Olivia at some chichi eatery after an overnight. No longer the friendly Mister Contractor, he was a guy with whom Olivia might be happier.

For a deliberative moment, Kirk watched the Mercedes turn back to the highway. Free-floating jealousy clouded his brain as he braced himself against the steering wheel. Then, in a mindless reflex, he put the car in gear and did a U-turn after the Mercedes.

He knew it was perversely self-vexing, and that he should head to headquarters. But he was transfixed on that sleek black roadster, wondering how his life had come to this—having lost his only child to a hit-and-run driver, possibly his wife in an urge to move on—and now tailing a guy who might help lead to the loss of his wife forever.

In the near future, he could end up a childless, wife-less, pathetic middle-aged man whose days were spent chasing killers. Olivia had been the only thing that separated him from the mean streets, the only thing that kept him from a mind of winter. And possibly his own death.

So, why the hell am I doing this?

Some wounded male-ego compulsion? Or was it some cop premonition of discovering something dark about Rizzo?

Nora Montana's words echoed and reechoed in his head: *He's a fraud and a cheat.*

Kirk followed him for ten miles back into Boston to a Starbucks on Cambridge Street where Rizzo pulled over to pick up an attractive woman in a red coat who had been waiting for him. Kirk did a fast stop at a hydrant two cars behind the Mercedes, keeping out of sight. The woman in red slipped into the Mercedes, which took off to a traffic circle, thick with cars.

Kirk held back as he followed the Mercedes over the Longfellow Bridge into Cambridge and up Broadway to the front lot of the Marriott Hotel. He pulled into the far side and watched Rizzo pull into the drop-off area at the front entrance, get out, look around, then open the passenger door for the woman in red. She exited, and he took her arm and headed through the main doors.

He didn't know if that woman was a prostitute or another paramour. But all Kirk could hear was Nora Montana: "He's a sociopathic serial adulterer." And Mona Zuckerman: "He's a whore-hound."

And Olivia was just another notch on his gun.

Kirk waited for maybe ten minutes then headed to headquarters to consult with his captain about the Thornton funeral tomorrow and to make some calls. He then left to speak with the presiding priest at Saint Bonaventure's but, against his better judgment, detoured back to the Marriott. An hour had passed, and Rizzo's Mercedes was still parked in the entrance circle.

CHAPTER 26

MORGAN

Nineteen years ago, October 25

IT WAS AROUND four o'clock when I left Dot's Donuts and headed home alone, still hating my father and my life for what he had done to us all.

It was not yet Halloween when the clocks got turned back, so it was still light when I got home. The only one in the house was my mother making dinner. Thankfully, my father wouldn't be home from the club until six. I didn't know where Richie and Vadima were at first, but I found them in the treehouse where she was giving Richie drawing lessons. When they saw me, Vadima climbed down with Richie following her reluctantly when I signaled him.

Vadima could read my expression and sense my smoldering inside.

"We were just drawing," Richie said with a whine in his voice.

"That's fine but go inside. Mom wants you."

He looked at the kitchen windows through which we could see my mother prepping the dinner. "No, she doesn't."

"Richie, I said go inside." He could hear the gravel in my voice.

He scrunched up his face. "No fair," he muttered and went into the house with his pad in hand.

When he passed into the back door, I looked at her. "When are you going back?"

"What?"

"I told you to pack your bags and leave."

"Your father says I can stay until the term is over."

"Is that right?" I said, scrambling for a response. "Well, I'm going to talk to him and make sure you're out of here."

That was an empty threat because talking to him would get nowhere because he could deny everything. And we both knew I wouldn't tell my mother and risk her throwing him and Vadima out of the house—not with having to explain to Richie that Dad couldn't live here anymore. The bitch had me.

I didn't know what she was thinking at the time because her face was unreadable. I didn't know if she was terrified or satisfied that I could do nothing without destroying the family, and would have to wait things out for the next two freaking months.

She glared at me in anticipation, but I had nothing in tow.

But before I turned and went into the house, I flashed her a toxic grin. "Congratulations—you got rid of your competition."

She gave me a baffled look. "What? I don't understand."

"You killed Justine."

"*What*? No! I did not kill her. How can you say that?"

"That night at Sylvie's party when you did your palm reading. You freaked out because you saw something in the lines in her hand, like you were looking into the future. And isn't that what palm reading is all about? Predicting what's to come?"

"You keep asking me this, but what I saw was Gee Gee is in love with her and that they would be married someday. That's all."

"And not married to you."

"Yes, yes. She was his girlfriend." She began to cry. "But how did I kill her? This is a terrible thing to say to me."

"Bullshit. You did some Gypsy black magic and when you looked at her hand you saw that it was going to come true."

"No, this is not true. I cannot change the future."

"Did you do it up here?" I said and snapped my head at the treehouse.

"Do what?"

I don't know if I actually believed it at the time, but my best best friends were convinced, especially Riley. "Cast a spell on her. Put a curse on her."

"No. this is crazy. I cannot do these things."

"Maybe you can and don't even know it. Like your magic happens when you wish really hard, like 'I hope Justine Zajac dies.'"

"No. This is impossible."

"Is it? Maybe you don't even know you have those powers. And when you looked into her hand and knew they were someday going to get married, you just wished it was you instead. And you wished that she would die."

She shook her head again, her face scrunched up in disbelief at what I was saying. "How could I do these things? How can I predict or make people die?"

"Because you're a witch."

CHAPTER 27

KIRK WALKED DOWN his driveway the next morning to retrieve the newspaper when Olivia pulled up in her car and rolled down her window. Her face was puffed with anger.

"You stalked Ted Rizzo. How dare you!"

Kirk was taken aback by her intensity. "What?"

She got out of the car and slammed the door. "Last night. You followed him from my place all the way into Cambridge, like he was one of your damn suspects. He saw you in your car."

Shit. He had taken his own instead of an unmarked vehicle. And Rizzo had no doubt checked with her for confirmation.

"Kirk, we're separated, dammit. You have no right to stalk or spy on me or anyone I see."

"I've never stalked or spied on you, Olivia."

In his years, Kirk had had his fill of sick, twisted men who'd sit outside of their ex's place, stunned with grief while a magma of rage bubbled inside as they watched the windows, waiting for bedroom lights to go on, then dim, and when they couldn't take it any longer, remove a firearm from under their seat and either break inside and shoot them both in bed and/or blow off the top of their own heads. "That's not me."

"And that's a lie because I've got it right here," she said and snapped her cellphone at him. "He texted me photos of you tailing him from my building."

What he saw was a blurry outline of him through the windshield, but it was clearly Kirk's Ford Explorer.

"This is goddam creepy. We agreed on an open separation, and you know it. So don't spy on me like I'm one of your *perps*. And that goes for people I socialize with."

Her eyes blazed at him as if discovering he had turned deviant in their separation. "I did not spy on you, and I never would. I went to your place to deliver your mail when I saw him drop you off, and that's the truth. And so is the fact that I would not violate your privacy by stalking you."

"Then why follow him all the way to Cambridge?"

"Maybe it was a bad impulse, but I was afraid he was using you."

"*Using me*? How the hell is he using me? We're social friends."

He did not want to betray Nora Montana or Rona Zuckerman by announcing that he'd heard that Rizzo had an uncontrollable yen for sexual conquests. "Ted Rizzo strikes me as the kind of guy who plays the field and probably has a lot of women. So on a hunch I followed him."

"How did you know he wasn't just going back to work?"

"Because his office is in Arlington, which was the other way."

"He could have been off shopping."

He tried not to sound catty and said, "Apparently, he was. Twenty minutes after dropping you off, he picked up some woman, drove to the nearest hotel, and went inside with her. Maybe she was someone else he was seeing or maybe a hooker. But at that hour the restaurant was closed. So draw your own conclusion."

She glared at him in dismay. "Where exactly did he pick her up?"

"Starbucks."

"Which Starbucks? Where?"

"On Cambridge Street next to Mass General."

"And what hotel did they go to?"

He did not like hearing her concern, as if wanting to know if Rizzo was cheating on her. "The Boston Marriott of Cambridge."

Her face was suddenly alight with anger. "Jesus Christ, Kirk! That was his sister, Lucy."

"His sister?"

"Yes, his sister! She was at Mass General for chemotherapy, because she's got breast cancer."

"I didn't know. I thought—" he began, hoping she'd hear his explanation, but she bore down on him, her eyes black with outrage.

"Yeah, you *thought*, and you were dead wrong," she said, as if reprimanding a child. "She lives in New Hampshire and comes down once a week for treatments and overnights at the Marriott because they leave her exhausted."

"All right, but it didn't look that way."

"I don't care how it looked—she's his sister. And she's very sick and Ted looks after her when she's in for treatments."

Kirk stood there feeling confused yet angry— confused because he had read things wrong. And angry at her cozy defense of "Ted." But there was no point in keeping this going, and after a deflating moment, he let out his breath. "Well, looks like I'm a horse's ass."

"Yeah, you are, because you jumped to a stupid conclusion."

Maybe so, but the son of a bitch was still a whore-hound dating his wife. "Well, what can I say but I'm sorry. And you can tell him."

"Tell him yourself."

He felt a sinking in his gut. The last thing he wanted to do was call Rizzo and apologize. "Okay, will do," he said.

She nodded, as the heat in her eyes cooled. "Let's just be clear that with regard to Ted or anyone else I socialize with, I don't need your protection, Kirk. I can handle myself."

"I know you can. I'm sorry. That won't happen again."

"And maybe instead of tailing me or my friends you might spend your free time meeting other women."

"I don't want to meet other women."

She made an accusatory sigh. "Kirk, we agreed on an open separation."

That was true. He had proposed that as a last-ditch effort to hold on to her, even though he had no interest in playing the field. "All right, but just how long are we going to do this trial separation thing?"

"I don't have a deadline."

"Maybe not, but I hate waiting for things to turn around."

"Then maybe you should get a plan for yourself."

"What kind of a plan?"

"Go back to the gym, go biking, go out with friends, make new ones. Do something, anything instead of sitting around the house brooding."

Her expression hardened, and at the moment he wondered what he could offer her, what plans he could come up with or changes in himself that could win her back—or if that were even possible.

Since their separation, he had stopped going to the local gym and was turning soft; he had quit doing his weekly sixty miles on the Minuteman bike path and was putting on weight. He had neighborhood friends, but almost never commiserated with them because cops did not open up to non-cops. Likewise, new friends didn't come easily for him. He had friends in the force, but if one had psychological issues from all the killings and mayhem they constantly witnessed, there were private counselors one could turn to. The same if someone had personal problems. But Kirk did not do that.

"Okay, say I find a plan, see a counselor, become more socially active, join a book club, go dating, how will we know when it's working again?" It was a ridiculous question and they both knew it.

"I don't know," she said checking her watch. "Look, I'm late for class." She opened the car door and got in.

"We also agreed to see each other on date night. That's next Thursday. Or are you going to cancel again?"

"I don't know, but just don't follow us again. I have a right to my privacy."

"I didn't follow you, nor will I. I followed him because I had a hunch he was exploiting you."

"Nobody is exploiting me, Kirk. He's just a friend."

"A male friend."

"Yes, and something I've not done since high school." She started the engine.

"Don't leave yet." He went back in the house and came out with her mail. "Time to renew your registration." Something he always did for her.

She nodded a thanks, put the car in gear, and left.

Kirk watched her move up the street, thinking that yesterday's escapade had exploded in his face. And that as a result he may have strengthened Rizzo's hand. It also occurred to him that if he lost Olivia, he faced being stuck in the same oppressive life of a homicide cop, dealing with people at the low end of the human species chain, seeing only cruelty and grief with nothing good to come home to but a black hole where the love of his life had once glowed.

CHAPTER 28

MORGAN

Nineteen years ago, October 27

ON THE DAY of the funeral, St. Bonaventure's Church was packed with kids, parents, teachers, and family friends—more people than I had ever see before including Christmas and Easter. My parents also attended and, unfortunately, brought Vadima with them. The sight of her made me want to puke. But I couldn't protest because they would have wondered why.

The Funeral Mass was conducted by Father de Souza who offered a comforting eulogy that brought people to tears. "Justine's life was taken far too soon, and we are numb with grief and greatly need to find solace."

So true, and I was happy that he didn't launch into some sappy explanation that God needed another angel in Heaven. Instead, he was more cynical:

"The Book of Matthew tells us that we know not what hour our Lord doth come. Nor do we know why a lovely young woman's life was taken from her. But God saw otherwise, and yet we are left crying out for some way to soothe the burning in our hearts."

I'm not one to cry like everyone else in the church, but I sensed that burning in our hearts in the tension within the church—mostly in us kids. We sat in tandem pews, my parents and I beside Sylvie and her parents in one, and Krista, Riley, and their family in front of us. All throughout the eulogies, our eyes kept shifting to each other's, yet all lines of awareness converged on Vadima who sat by herself in a pew at the back of the church—a look on her face saying that she knew.

It was the phrase *burning in our heart* that had moved Gee Gee Gallagher to go to Father de Souza the day before.

It was after school yesterday while we were hanging out at Dot's Donuts when Gee Gee joined us after having visited Father de Souza. We had expected that he had gone to him for spiritual solace. But he outright confessed that since Justine's death, he had gotten no guidance just talking to God in prayer and wanted real answers to real questions. So he said he had made an appointment with Father de Souza, which at Gee Gee's request was conducted in a confession booth.

"So what did you tell him?" Krista asked.

"That I wanted to know about the nature of sin," he said.

I could feel my face scrunch up in puzzlement. "The nature of sin? What did you want to know?"

"I told him that according to our catechism, there are all kinds of sins, you know, like venial sins and mortal sins and what they were. But there were some which I wanted to ask him about: the ones called *peccata clamantia*."

"That sounds like some shellfish thing on the menu at Legal Seafood," Riley said.

Krista snickered. "That's Latin for sins that cry to heaven for vengeance!"

She had taken Latin; I hadn't.

Gee Gee nodded. "Right. And that's what I asked him about. He explained that according to the Bible, there were four sins under *peccata clamantia*." He glanced at his notebook. "He said the Bible mentions only four that cry out to heaven for vengeance: murder, sodomy—you know, weird sex—oppression of poor people, and cheating workers out of fair wages.

"I wanted to know about mortal sins and what would happen if one commits one. He said that if you commit a mortal sin, your soul would not experience grace. When you died, you'd be barred from entrance to heaven."

"I could have told you that," Riley said. "Same with suicide. You kill yourself; you commit your own murder and go to hell."

We didn't know if that was true or not, but we all nodded to shut Riley up. Even though we were BBFs, she was something of a flake, latching onto every weird notion and conspiracy theory.

Gee Gee continued. "I wanted to know how one deals with the sin of murder that cries out to heaven for vengeance."

Of all our friends, Gee Gee was the most serious about religion. He had read up on arcane theological issues and could quote the Bible—verse and passage. He had also taken four years of Latin and a course in Roman Catholic Church History. Also, another on Religions of the World. Back then I had half-expected that he would enter the seminary and become a priest someday.

"You know how Father de Souza likes to hear himself talk. Well, he went on about how murder is extreme anti-social behavior, the taking of a human life for the sake of achieving personal benefits. And that's evil, a mortal sin—and the greatest since it violates the right to life from God."

"Not exactly a newsflash," I had said.

"No, but he did say according to the church it was lawful to kill when fighting in a just war. You know, how people are considered innocent as long as they haven't hurt or killed others. But when an evil is so great that it may result in the destruction of human lives, then homicide is permitted. Like in war."

We looked at Gee Gee blankly until I said, "So what are you saying?"

"I'm saying that according to him, when certain crimes cry out to heaven for vengeance, some good comes out of evil."

"Grayson Gallagher, what are you thinking?" He shook his head, got up, and walked away.

CHAPTER 29

THEY COULD NOT get permission to install closed circuit TV cameras inside the church where Sylvie Cox Thornton's funeral took place the next morning, but video photographers were poised across the street in an unmarked van as well as a black-windowed police SUV, posed as one of the funeral escorts. With clearance from his captain, Kirk wanted to record everybody who attended the funeral service.

Meanwhile, Kirk sat in a pew in the middle of St. Bonaventure's Church amidst friends, neighbors and former colleagues of Sylvie Thornton from the Prentiss School including Dr. Khouri and others he had seen on his visit there. Mandy sat in a pew across the aisle two pews farther back.

Erin and Paul Delmonico arrived early and filled one of the front pews with their children and nephews.

About ten minutes before the service was to begin, Harry Thornton and his wife walked down the aisle with his son Aaron, and that was when the murmurs began.

In front of Kirk sat two couples who lived across the street from Sylvie, the two wives sitting shoulder-to-shoulder, and beside them MaryAnn Liczek. As Harry Thornton and his wife settled a few pews in front of them, Kirk heard one woman lean over to the other and mutter, "I can't believe the gall of him bringing her."

"He has no shame . . . cheated on her for years, as Devon was dying," said the other woman.

"Married her six months after they divorced," replied the first.

"Poor Aaron. Such a sweet boy. What he must be going through."

"Poor Sylvie. She left her job and settled for a pittance. Talk about cheapskates."

Kirk had little doubt that were a poll to have been taken of mourners at the church, Harry Thornton would have been top pick for Person of Interest in the killing of his former wife.

According to the Order of Service program handed out, three people were named to offer eulogy reflections. The first was Sylvie's sister, Erin Cox Delmonico, who barely got through her words of praise and remembrance. "She was the most doting mother, who would look on her children and whisper, "'My cup runneth over.'"

Next was her son Aaron, who recalled Sylvie's passion for her family and friends, "an uncompromising strength of love" that had fortified him through some tough times as a kid, especially the death of his brother. She also had a great passion for literature and art and was active in community fundraising programs for the homeless.

The next eulogy was delivered by a man who introduced himself as Brother Grayson Gallagher, a Justinian monk who had gone to school with Sylvie. He wore a white robe with a black cowl and looked authentically ascetic with closely cropped hair, a pale sunken face, and wire-rimmed glasses that gave him an owlish demeanor. He gave touching praise of Sylvie's Christian values, saying she had lived a virtuous life of compassion and charity.

"I had known Sylvie from kindergarten through twelfth grade at St. B's where she and her friends named me Gee Gee. Over the years we were like brother and sister. As a young girl, she was a true tomboy who wouldn't hesitate to join in a pickup baseball game with us boys in the neighborhood, and yet, at the flick of a switch, she could be frilly and feminine when she wanted to be. She was a permanent resident on the honor-roll and a track star. She was popular with both girls and boys and honored for her organization of student entertainment at senior centers. And until we lost her, she was still serving others in her community out of pure compassion.

"In fact, Sylvie showed a near-saintly compassion as a community leader who helped launch Neighborhood Servings for the homeless—those suffering from addictions, and battered women. Although she struggled through hardships in her own life, Sylvie was a woman of faith, which sustained her even through the unimaginable loss of her son Devon.

"Sylvie Cox Thornton was truly a handmaiden of the Lord, embodying the same compassion and kindness as does our Savior Jesus Christ."

He went on with lavish words of comfort for her son Aaron, her sister Erin, and her family, friends, and neighbors.

And Kirk made a mental note to set up an interview with Brother Grayson Gallagher since he had known her well and may have information to help the investigation.

The final eulogy was from a woman who introduced herself as Krista Barber Saliba. She began by saying that she and Sylvie were best friends throughout middle and high school and had gone to the same college together, staying close for years after until Krista moved away. "From grade school on, Sylvie was very loyal to friends and very honest and always thinking of others."

Saliba was halfway through her eulogy when a man stood up and screamed, "You killed her. You killed my sister."

The outburst sent an electric buzz across the pews.

"What?" someone cried.

"You killed her. You killed my sister."

The place was suddenly in an uproar as people rose to shout down the man. Kirk shot to his feet to see who had made that outburst. Three pews ahead of him was a man pointing to the woman at the podium.

People rose to see who was making such claims.

"That's not true," Kristen Saliba cried through the PA system.

The priest moved to the podium and took the microphone. "Please, sir, calm down, sit down . . . please, let's all calm down and sit down and . . . please, let us move on."

The place was suddenly chaotic.

From two pews behind the man, Mandy pushed her way down the aisle, her gun pressed at her side. She grabbed the guy by the elbow, flashing her badge, and yanked him free of the pew and hustled him up the aisle at gunpoint. Kirk dashed after them.

"She killed my sister."

PART II

CHAPTER 30

"Am I under arrest?"

His name was Milosh Lupescu, thirty-four years old and an immigrant from Slovakia, which explained his accent. For the last seven years, he had been living in Portland, Maine, where he worked for a construction company. He was not armed, nor did he resist being apprehended and brought to the Cambridge station. He wore skinny jeans, a black sport coat, white shirt, no tie, and black sneakers. He was sweating and his right leg bounced in place as he sat across the table from Kirk and Mandy in the interrogation room. He was about six feet tall, athletically fit, with large meaty hands.

"That remains to be seen," Kirk said. According to records, he had no prior arrests. "Mr. Lupescu, we brought you in because of your outburst, accusing Mrs. Saliba of killing your sister. You want to explain that to us?"

"They all did. They bullied her into killing herself."

"Who was your sister, and when did this happen?"

"Vadima Lupescu. She was exchange student and came here on scholarship to study. She stayed with the Bolt family in Lexington. She hoped to go to university someday. Nobody in our family ever went to university. We were all so proud of her. When she died, my parents died in their hearts. And they blamed each other for sending her to America, for not sending her to school near home, in Kiev or Bratislava."

He spoke as if he didn't have enough time to get it all out. "Okay, let's slow down. When did this all happen?"

"Nineteen years ago."

"Nineteen years ago? So what does this have to do with the death of Sylvie Thornton?"

"She was one of them."

"One of what?"

"One of the people who humiliated her, who threatened her, saying she was a filthy Gypsy witch and better off dead." After a gasping sob, he added, "She was so depressed and humiliated . . . and they pushed her to set fire on herself."

From his jacket pocket he pulled out a small pad. "This is her sketchbook. She was an artist. Look what she drew. Look!"

One page was a pastel drawing of a female engulfed in flames at the stake. It was signed *Vadima*. The rendering was disturbing. "Your sister did this?"

"Yes."

"And this is her, your sister . . . Vadima?"

"Yes, and because they convinced her she was a witch and made curses on people." His voice cracked, and tears filled his eyes, and his leg was bouncing as if electrically powered. "And they praised that woman like she was a saint, kind and good. Bullshit! She was one of them." And he slammed his hand on the table.

"Okay. Calm down," Kirk said. He glanced at Mandy who was transfixed by the man. "You said she set herself on fire?" Old television images of Buddhist monks self-immolating passed through Kirk's mind. "Can you tell us the circumstances of that?"

"When we were kids, we always slept outside when the weather was good. It was how we got to know the stars and night animals. But they pushed her so hard that one night she got drunk or took medication and did this to herself." He nodded at the drawing.

"And where was this?"

"In the treehouse in Morgan Bolt's backyard in Lexington, Massachusetts."

"Whenever there's a fire resulting in a fatality, there's an investigation and a report is filed. Do you recall what the investigation concluded?"

"They say accident, but that's a lie. They bullied her to do that to herself."

"Who bullied her?"

"Morgan and Sylvie and Krista and Riley and the rest of them. They convinced her she should die."

"So why did they bully her?"

"Because she was different. Because she was vulnerable. And bullies go after people who are vulnerable and needy."

"How was she vulnerable?"

"I knew my sister better than anybody. We were twins, and we had a special bond. Vadima was very kind and nice to others. She wanted friends. She wanted to fit in with the others. She wanted their approval. But those fucking girls—they persecuted her. Spread rumor of evil about her."

Now he was openly crying. "Mr. Lupescu, what connection do you see between your sister's death and the death of Sylvie Thornton?"

He shook his head and wiped his face. "I don't know. I don't know."

"But you showed up today at her Funeral Mass. Why is that?"

"Because I read in the newspapers."

"But what was your intention?"

He did not respond for a spell. "To let the world know what they did."

"By yelling in the middle of her Funeral Mass?"

He shrugged.

Kirk nodded to Mandy to take over.

"Mr. Lupescu, where were you on the morning of November six, four days ago?"

"What?" His face suddenly stiffened. "I was at work, Portland, Maine."

"And where was that?"

"ABC Construction Company."

"Can anyone verify that?"

"Yes, my wife, my boss, friends at work." And he gave them contact information. Then he looked up at Kirk, his eyes red and wet. "Are you going to put me in jail?"

"No, but let me tell you that if there's any complaint that you harassed, stalked, or threatened any of these women you named or any family members or get within a hundred feet of them, we will arrest you. And first we will check your alibi with your wife and colleagues. And if you had anything to do with the death of Sylvie Thornton, we will get you."

Astonishment filled Milosh Lupescu's face. He had been brought in for disturbing the peace in a church, and now he was told that he was a person of interest in the death of Sylvie Thornton. "I did not do anything to this woman."

Kirk nodded, still skeptical. Before Lupescu was released, Kirk asked if he could make photocopies of the few sketches in Vadima's notebook that he had brought. He agreed, and while Mandy walked Lupescu out of the office, a department technician,

Sergeant Kevin Fugita, texted Kirk that the website he had been trying to reach was up and running.

Kirk moved to his computer. He opened his cellphone to the shot of Sylvie Thornton's tattoo—a four-leaf clover, unexceptional but for the fact that three leaves were blank and one—first leaf on the top left—was filled in red.

The site shared with local police departments was a sophisticated FBI database for tattoo recognition on the same order of technology as that for facial identification. After photographing and scanning the Thornton tattoo, Kirk ran the image through the national database, TATT-C, which included millions of images from imprisoned criminal offenders as well as tattoos from unidentified crime victims. One original intention was to identify members of drug gangs, cartels, and human trafficking rings, hate groups, et cetera.

The search turned up several hundred clover-leaf hits, but only one that involved a fiery death—a five-leafed clover belonging to Vadima Lupescu.

CHAPTER 31

"HE'S BEEN OBSESSED with her death for nineteen years."

Sergeant Detective Jemma Jones, now retired from the Lexington, Massachusetts PD, was a tall Black woman in her sixties and dressed in a navy-blue pants suit and red print scarf. She also appeared to be wearing a wig. She had been the lead investigator on the Lupescu case.

Kirk met her at The Harvest in Harvard Square at three o'clock that same afternoon when the restaurant was between shifts and half empty. They sat at a large corner table where they could have privacy and ordered soft drinks and two appetizer plates.

"How did you end up with this?"

"I was on night shift, and the call came in around one thirty. By the time I got there, the treehouse was engulfed in flames and firefighters were scrambling with hoses. The driveway was blocked with cars. Uniforms were trying to keep residents and neighbors back. Someone cried there was a girl up there."

She shook her head—probably against a strip of images replaying in her head.

"When did you meet the brother?"

"Milosh flew here to claim Vadima's remains a few days later. He was convinced she was driven to suicide. She had written home how kids picked on her at school, including Morgan Bolt, the daughter of the host family, and Morgan's friends. They had ostracized her, called her names, referred to her as *Va-demon*, said she was a witch. He claimed all that depressed her to the point of wanting to die."

"Why didn't she contact authorities in the exchange program or return home?"

Jones nodded. "You would think, but he said she was too proud given all that it took to get her into the program. He also said that she probably didn't think anyone would believe her—not given the well-vetted host family and top Catholic school in the area."

"Must have been a tough call to make to the parents."

"Horrible and made worse by having to go through a translator because they didn't speak English. I had to keep repeating that Vadima was dead because they were in such shock."

Kirk remembered the shock and denial of his own reaction when a colleague called that Megan had been hit by a car and was in the ICU at Mass General.

"Milosh said that before her death, his parents were happy and full of pride that Vadima was smart enough to win a scholarship. But after she died, they fell apart, blaming each other for sending her here, all because her father wanted her to see the world. To have what they didn't have, an option to be something other than a pig farmer."

Jones went on to say that Vadima had been the hope for her family who dreamed that she would eventually go to an American college and make something of herself, perhaps becoming a medical doctor and even returning to provide care to their village.

"Remember they were Romany people, pariahs who were barred from going to local universities or even med schools in Slovakia or surrounding countries. From what I understand, Romanies were taught to hide their ethnicity because it brought out discrimination, old hatred of Gypsies, rumors of evil that sometimes provoked violence. They were their Blacks living under Jim Crow."

Jones added that the mother died two years after Vadima's death, and the father, who was in his seventies, sold the farm and moved in with relatives.

"Did the school know about the bullying?"

"Some kids and a couple of teachers claimed that she was harassed because she was foreign. You know, racial prejudice."

"But the coroner's report says she was white."

"White, but Romanies are of Indian descent, which meant she was dark-skinned. Whatever, kids heard that she was a Gypsy and jumped to all sorts of stereotypes—that they had supernatural powers, cast voodoo curses, possessed the Evil Eye. Because she read palms, they accused her of witchcraft."

"Read palms, like storefront fortune tellers?"

"More likely student cafeteria or pizza parties," Jones said. "The point is that she was singled out as an outsider because she had an accent, wore scarves, and slept outdoors. In a word, she was dark and foreign. And out of ignorance, the other kids scapegoated her."

"Did you believe she committed suicide?"

"It was a consideration, but without any evidence like a note or witnesses, we could only conclude it was an accident."

Kirk showed her a photocopy of the witch-burning drawing. "What do you make of this?"

She nodded that she had seen that before. "That maybe she was becoming convinced."

"But by fire? I can't think of a worse way to die."

"Neither can I, but according to her brother, she became convinced she was a witch," Jones said. "And if you look at European history, that was how witches were executed from the fourteenth century on. In this case, self-immolation."

Kirk shook his head. "How do you convince someone they're a witch?"

"Remember the Salem witch trials? Women were convinced that they were vulnerable to the powers of the devil, and some mothers actually confessed serving Satan by suckling his imp. In fact, all that began with the black slave Tituba who claimed to be innocent of causing the hysteria of the children in the Parris household, so she told the magistrates at her trial what they wanted to hear—that she had dealings with Satan and flew around on a broomstick and had apocalyptic visions of wolves and cats. That sparked fear and more hysteria that led to the indictment and hanging of other women. There's no limit to the power of suggestion, especially if you were vulnerable to occult beliefs, or if you're a kid."

"Yeah, but that was sixteen ninety-something."

"Then how about the Slender Man case—two girls nearly stab to death their girlfriend to satisfy some internet cartoon character."

"But weren't they determined to be mentally ill?"

"Yes, but the point is that a lot of people, especially children, have a mental framework different from the rational world. They embrace what they believe as true and not what's scientifically demonstrated. A lot of bullies dabble in Satanism and black magic, and many are young. And not just children. Think about the Flat-Earthers, people who believe the moon landing was fake, climate-deniers, or those who claimed Barack Obama was born in Kenya, or Joe Biden lost the election."

"Right." They were quiet for a spell as Kirk sipped his iced tea, thinking that now their investigation had taken on a cold case. "Maybe you can fill me in on some details. Who put in the 911?"

"A neighbor spotted the flames through his window. He called the Lexington P.D. and the fire department because he knew the kids next door often slept in the treehouse."

"Was a crime scene investigation done?"

"No, because it was determined an accident, either by the lantern overturning or sparks from a nearby fire pit the kids sat around earlier. And no report that it had been extinguished before they all went to bed."

"But in your report, you say that her death was undetermined."

"Based on circumstances after the fact."

"But it could have been an accident or suicide," Kirk said.

"Except for three things. First, at the time of the fire, Milosh claimed that she was used to sleeping outdoors with kerosene lanterns. And never once had she let one burn while sleeping.

"Two, she would have been aroused by the heat, the light, and noise. Plus, she had two means of getting down from the platform—a set of two-by-fours nailed into the trunk, and a ladder. So, there is no way she could not have escaped even if it meant just leaping down twelve feet."

"Unless she was drugged. Or the structure was soaked with an accelerant. Or both."

"There was evidence that the kids had been drinking and did some weed," Jones said. "But unfortunately, there was no way to do a tox analysis of her remains." Jones took a sip of her coffee.

"So, what's the third thing?"

Jones reached into her briefcase and produced a photocopy of a strip of letters cut out of magazines. "This came in TIPS care of Lexington PD." She handed Kirk the sheet.

VADIMA LUPESCU WAS MURDERED.

"When did this come?"

"Last week. The thirty-first."

"Halloween."

"Yes, the anniversary of her death. When I heard Sylvie Thornton was possibly murdered, I called you. She was with Vadima a few hours before she died, and one of the last to see her alive."

The words on the tip sheet looked to have been photocopied from different sources, cut and glued in line on another sheet, then photocopied so that the actual published sources could not be determined from the obverse sides. "Any prints?"

"Of course not, nor a postmark."

"It could be a hoax," Kirk said. Or the work of a meticulous mind.

"Except the timing makes me suspect that it's not. The suspicion of murder first appeared in social media, then yesterday the newspapers reported rumors that Sylvie Thornton's death was being treated as a homicide. If that, in fact, is the case, it's possible the two deaths are linked, and this person suspected Sylvie Thornton's death was to shut her up about what she may have known about the Lupescu death."

"So you're saying the sender may have been privy to what happened back then. Possibly a friend and/or classmate of Sylvie and/or Vadima."

"Yes," she said.

"Or brother of Vadima."

"Possibly, although my gut tells me that it came from someone who knows something about that night."

Kirk nodded. "You said you began to suspect foul play after you talked to the brother back then, which meant the scene had been corrupted."

"Unfortunately, yes." She took a sip of her drink to down her regret. "So what about this Thornton case?"

Kirk explained the ME's forensic conclusions about Sylvie Thornton's death. "So we have two suspicious deaths nineteen years apart. The victims hung out as kids, went to the same school and church, et cetera. And one key link is they had similar tattoos."

"Right." From her briefcase Jemma extracted the Lupescu file she had picked up from the Lexington P.D. With it were death scene photos. She slid the file to Kirk with the warning, "You can take a look, but you may wish you hadn't."

He steeled himself and opened the folder.

The top shot was a studio photograph of the girl who was young and lovely and smiling brightly for the camera. She had black hair that was braided and coiled on the sides of her head in Eastern European fashion.

The next was a close-up of her five-leaf clover tattoo. It was done in the same motif as that on the Thornton woman, but with an extra leaf at the bottom, filled in red. The style suggested the same tattooist.

Then Kirk turned the page. "Jesus!" he muttered.

According to the police report, she had slept in an outdated bag made of combustible material and didn't have time to escape before she was consumed by flames. Smoke must have been the cause of death because her body was covered in scraps of charred material that had melted into her. The outline of her legs and lower body were scorched and blackened with flaps of the nylon-cotton composition. She lay on her side with her arms curled in the pugilistic pose of fire victims. Her scalp was a charred skull, her face blunted black by the flames. The horrid images reminded him of those of Pompeii victims.

Also in the folder were shots of the remains of the treehouse structure—fallen in and charred, and the tree seared of leaves and branches, and the trunk and supporting limbs, stripped black. There were also photos of firefighters, police, and family members, their faces frozen in shock. A couple images of a younger Detective Jones bent over the girl's remains. The photos made his eyes fill up.

Jemma noticed and nodded in sympathy. "Yes, very tough. As with most fire victims, she died of smoke inhalation," she said. "It was that tattoo that got us to positively ID her since she had sent drawings of it to her brother. Given the position of her body, it appeared that she became unconscious trying to escape."

Kirk took a deep breath and handed Jemma the folder. "Does the host family still live there?"

"The husband and wife got divorced and the two kids are now adults living elsewhere. Sally Bolt, the mother, died three years ago, but Jordan Bolt is still at the Lexington house." And from her file folder she showed Kirk a photograph of the man, in shorts and tank top with the letters "Fitness You." On his forearm was a heraldic looking tattoo.

"Is it officially a cold case?"

"Yes, but I have notified the County DA to reactivate it because I want to see Vadima get her justice." She gave him a supplicating eye.

"But you're saying that anonymous tip isn't enough to reopen it."

"Unfortunately, it's not, and Lexington doesn't have a cold case unit. I checked with Middlesex County, and, hard to believe, but they have only a two-person unit in an office with nearly forty thousand active cases a year. So they're super-overwhelmed."

"Which means I'm on my own."

"Unless you come up with other leads."

From what he had heard, Detective Jones had taken a medical leave, which segued into retirement. "Right." He would have to convince his captain to allow him to look into the Lupescu case if he could make a link to the death of Sylvie Thornton. "But that tip could be a hoax, and her death could still be suicide."

"True. But I've been a cop for thirty-five years, and my gut tells me this kid was murdered. And there's no statute of limitations on murder—whether it's twenty years or fifty years."

Her eyes started to fill up. "Before I start drooling on my walker, I want to see this case reopened. And if she was wronged, I want to see justice done and to restore some faith in law and order. There are still pieces of the puzzle missing, and I hope you can find them."

"I'll do what I can."

"Good, because I hear you pay close attention to details."

And because I had a teenage daughter who died in a hit-and-run and the killer was never found.

CHAPTER 32

MORGAN BOLT CASSIDY lived in a shingled, white-trimmed multi-gabled Cape Cod styled beach home in Hyannis Port with a sprawling lawn, a circular driveway around a flagpole ringed with pink hydrangeas, and a gazebo on the back lawn that led to a sweeping view of Nantucket Sound. The place sat on several acres and must have had twelve rooms. According to Zillow, the place had sold nine years ago for six million dollars. It was probably worth twice that today.

"I don't think she's teaching English anymore," Mandy said.

"Unless it's to a Saudi prince."

"So, remind me why we're here."

"Jones thinks her cold case might be connected to the Sylvie Thornton murder. That she was killed because she knew who might have torched the Lupescu girl."

"And Morgan might remember something not in the report."

"Possibly. Her report says eight or nine kids were in the backyard that night whooping it up on booze and weed and burning a witch effigy. And except for those overnighting at the Bolts', each had an alibi that they all went home about the same time and confirmed by their parents."

"So we're revisiting those former kids who slept over at the Bolts' beginning with Morgan."

"Right."

"How come Jones has dropped the investigation?"

"She has stage-four lung cancer."

"Oh, the poor woman!"

"Yes, the poor woman."

Morgan Bolt Cassidy met them at the door. She was a large woman dressed in workout tights and was glistening with perspiration. She wiped her face with a monogrammed towel. Someplace on the other side of the house she had her own gym.

According to her profile on Facebook, she was married to Martin Cassidy, owner of a prosperous civil engineering firm in Hyannis. They had no children and traveled extensively to Europe and beyond.

She led them to the glassed-in sunroom at one end of the house with a full view of the azure sound that sparkled under the sun as if covered in diamond dust. The walls were decorated with travel photos from the Alps, Ireland's Cliffs of Mohr, Santorini, Machu Picchu, and other scenic places Kirk didn't recognize. Terra cotta sunburst hangings decorated the wall, vases full of assorted shells sat on white wicker tables, and against one were beer steins from different European cities.

"Your name was given to us because you were a close friend of Sylvie Thornton's."

"At one time we were," she said without hesitation. "I'm still in shock, and I regret that I was out of town for the funeral."

"Of course," Kirk said, taking note that she did not mention Sylvie's name or said *her funeral*. "How well did you know Sylvie?"

"Not very well of late. We grew up in the same town and went to the same schools, but after college I moved away, and we lost contact. Then I got married and moved here."

"So when was the last time you saw her?" asked Mandy.

She rocked her head as if to summon recollection. "I guess ten years ago at a class reunion at St. B.'s—Saint Bonaventure Academy."

"Did you still communicate in any way—letters, email, telephone calls . . ." Kirk trailed off for her to fill in.

"We sent Christmas cards now and then. Then there was an email about a twentieth reunion."

"That you had sent?"

"Yes, I was on the committee and assigned some of the names."

"Was there any indication in your communications that she was bothered by something, upset, or scared?"

"Not really, just the standard greetings, you know." Then she shook her head with a look of dismay. "I mean, who would do such a horrible thing to her?"

"Horrible thing?"

Her face flushed. "Well, she was murdered, wasn't she?"

"Where did you hear that?"

"Well, from rumors. I mean, you're homicide detectives, right? So isn't that what happened?"

"We have not ruled out foul play, but no official statement has been made. So where did you hear that?"

"Well, a mutual friend—Riley Malone, another classmate from St. B.'s. I guess she saw a posting from a community newspaper that the police were treating her death as foul play."

"Rumors do travel," Mandy said. "So where were you when Sylvie died?"

Her expression tensed up. "Like I said, I was out of town."

"You said you were out of town for the funeral, not when she was found dead on November six."

She paused, collecting her thoughts. "November six . . . Saturday . . . I was visiting my brother, Richard, in Portsmouth, New Hampshire. He was hosting a family event."

"May I ask what kind of family event?"

She looked offended by the probing. "The birthday party of his five-year-old son." Her delivery was flat with irritation.

"Can someone confirm that?"

"I can't believe you're asking me this—as if I'm a suspect."

"This is a possible homicide, and standard procedure is to question everybody familiar with the victim, so please don't take offense."

Cassidy hissed out her breath. "Yes, Richie can verify my being there." And she pulled up her cellphone and recited his contact information.

Mandy's face knotted in exaggerated dismay. "I'm just wondering how you couldn't spare a few hours from a kid's birthday party to attend the funeral of a girlfriend you grew up with who still wore your Best-Friends-for-Life tattoo. I mean, it's only an hour's drive down 95."

That was absolutely the wrong delivery, yet Kirk got satisfaction at the discomfort that rippled across Morgan Cassidy's face. "I frankly don't like what you're implying, Detective."

"What am I implying?"

"You're passing judgment on me, saying that I just blew off a dear old friend's funeral. I've not seen Sylvie Thornton for ten years. Plus, I had family obligations that were long planned. And, frankly, I resent the suggestion that I had anything to do with her death."

Kirk cut in, uncertain if Mandy was going to make things worse. "Look, Mrs. Cassidy, we're not suggesting you disrespected a past friend or had anything to do with her death. Again, it's protocol to ask the whereabouts of everybody who may have known the deceased in a suspicious-death investigation. Can you think of anyone who had issues with Sylvie, who could have done this?"

"No, but you might contact Riley Malone who I think was closer to her." She checked her phone again and recited an address. "Except for that email, I haven't communicated with her in years."

"How many years?"

Cassidy shrugged. "Three or four."

According to the report, Riley Malone was one of the kids in the Bolt backyard the night Vadima Lupescu died. "Does she still go by Riley Malone or a married name?"

"Still Riley Malone. I don't think she ever got married."

Morgan made a motion with her body that said she wanted to end the questioning when Kirk pulled out his cellphone. "I'd like to ask you a few questions about Vadima Lupescu." He held up the girl's photograph to her face and studied her reaction. She made a barely noticeable flinch of recognition. "Remember her?"

"Yes, I remember her. She was a foreign exchange student who stayed with us. Why do you ask?"

"Do you remember what happened to her?"

"Of course, and it was horrible tragedy. She died in a fire. But what does that have to do with anything?"

"We're not sure, but evidence has come to light suggesting that Vadima may be part of the picture."

"How do you figure that?"

"That her death was neither an accident nor a suicide but foul play, and that Sylvie Thornton's death might be connected."

"That was twenty years ago!"

"Nineteen. Can you think of any possible connection between the two?"

"Like what?"

"Like maybe she was murdered, and Sylvie knew who did it and was silenced."

She squinted in disbelief. "That's insane. Vadima died in an accidental fire. We told her not to use a kerosene lantern, but an electric one. But she insisted. She said she liked the warmth and the smell. It's what she used back home when she camped out."

"And how do you think the fire started?"

"I don't know, I was asleep," she said, her tone indignant. "Maybe the wind, maybe she knocked it over in her sleep, maybe a raccoon. We had told her time and time again to get a battery-powered LED lamp. They're bright, they're light, and they won't start fires. But no, she wanted the kerosene lantern."

"According to the police report, there was speculation that she may have committed suicide."

"I guess that's possible too. Look, they went all over this nineteen years ago, and no one said anything about murder." She stood up, her face hot with scorn. "Sorry, but I have another appointment."

"Fine," Kirk said. They each gave her their cards and followed her to the front door, which she closed and locked behind them.

"She knows something," Mandy said as they drove away. "You mention possible murder investigation, and suddenly she has an appointment."

"That did seem to ruffle her feathers," Kirk said.

"Another thing, who told her friend Riley it was a criminal investigation? And why would this Riley email her that after not having communicated in three or four years?"

"They were probably in communication about their reunion. Neighbors of Sylvie see the tape and squad cars and ME van, and the word gets out on social media, and it gets picked up by the local media and spreads like Covid. Whatever, check her alibi with the brother, and I'll do a drop-in on this Riley Malone."

"Get the feeling she was trying to distance herself from her?"

"It crossed my mind." It also crossed his mind that Morgan Bolt Cassidy was an angry woman, and angry people are often afraid of something.

Kirk drove back to Cambridge where he dropped off Mandy to do background checks on the other kids at the Halloween gathering nineteen years ago while he headed north on Route 3 to interview the next name on the list. Riley Malone.

CHAPTER 33

MORGAN

Nineteen years ago, October 29

WHENEVER WE HAD sleepovers, they were almost always at my house because we had more rooms and a large backyard with a fire pit and, of course, the treehouse. But that night Riley Malone was insistent that we all overnight at her place. My first thought was that since Sylvie had just gotten a new Nokia cellphone for her birthday, she and Riley wanted to show some goofy shots they'd made in gym class.

The Malone house was a basic ranch on the other side of town, with only one guest room, which would be fine for me and Krista; Sylvie would sleep on a couch in Riley's room. It would be tight, but I welcomed not being under the same roof as my father or fucking Vadima Lupescu.

But it wasn't about Sylvie's new cellphone. It was Riley. She was beside herself, nearly hysterical about Gee Gee's charge that Vadima was responsible for Justine's death.

"She put a curse on her that night she did the palm readings," Riley said, her face so puffed with conviction that it looked as if it were ready to explode. "We were all there. We saw her. She looked at her hand, mumbled something weird in Gypsy talk, and then left without a word because she'd put a curse on her. And then when she died, it was like she had expected it all along."

"You mean like she's psychic or something?" Sylvie said.

"That's what I'm telling you. She's a Gypsy, and Gypsies cast spells on people they don't like and can see the future."

She was attesting to what I had half-seriously accused Vadima of to her face. But as Riley went on, I felt a chill.

"How do you know that?" Sylvie said.

"Because I checked. She's from Slovakia, but she's not a Slovakian. I looked it up. She's like pure Romany—fancy name for Gypsy. And guess what? Her name—Lupescu—means 'like a wolf.' Yeah, like in werewolf."

"You serious?" Sylvie said.

"Yes. And those people are all over Slovakia and Slovenia, Romania, and the rest of those backward places. And that's where Dracula's from. He was one of them. And they're known for putting hexes on people because they have these psychic powers and do black magic and stuff—which is why they're banned from so many countries."

"That's kind of hard to believe," Krista said, always the skeptical one—a female doubting Thomas.

But Sylvie was all eyes and ears. "Oh my God! You think she has supernatural powers?"

"Yeah, or something," Riley said. "I knew she was weird from day one. There was something sneaky and really off about her, the way she just stared into space and mumbled to herself in Gypsy, but was suddenly super sweet when you talked to her. She's wicked weird is all."

The thought jogged through me that Vadima had put a sexual spell on my father, casting him into some kind of horny trance that lured him into her room that night.

"I'm telling you, she's pure evil," continued Riley. "She put a curse on Justine. You know that little notebook she's always drawing in? Well, I checked it out one day during study period." She had made photocopies and handed them to us.

"Oh my God! Is that Justine?"

"Yes."

It was a drawing of Justine lying on her back dressed all in white with her hands on her breast holding a red rose with petals strewn on her front and around her—except she did not look asleep in bed but dead in a coffin.

"Oh my God!" I said. It was Justine at her wake.

"Yes, and she knew because she caused her to die, I'm telling you."

"I don't believe this," Sylvie said.

Riley nodded. "This scared the shit out of me." Her face turned dark as she glared at me.

"What?" I said.

"There's one more," Riley said. She held another photocopy in her hand. "Sorry," she said, and turned it to us.

The second drawing, done in pen and pastels, was of my dad lying in bed, except the female in his arms was not my mother but Vadima naked. I was too stunned to respond.

"It's not your dad's fault. She put a curse on him the way she did Justine."

Krista put her arm around me, and I felt pressure behind my eyes.

"But why?"

"To get back at me," I said. "Because I told her that she had no right to get a tattoo like ours. That she's not one of us."

"Yeah, and you know what Gypsies fear the most?" Riley said. "Rejection. Banishment. And that's why they put curses on people—people who expel them from society. I know, I looked it up. She's wicked freaking dangerous."

No one said anything for a long moment. And in my head like a closed loop of video I saw my father slipping into her room then coming out when they were through.

"Another thing," Riley said. "That tattoo she got with the five clover leaves? I looked that up too, and a five-leaf clover is wicked rare, like one in a billion. And guess what it symbolizes. It symbolizes a demon."

She turned over another photocopy. "According to the book of magic, the grimoire, the first four leaves represent hope, love, faith, and fortune. But the fifth leaf represents Satan. Satan!"

"Oh my God!" Sylvie cried.

"Yeah, and I also found out that they spread diseases in the olden times like the Black Plague and syphilis. Really. They're also raised to steal, which is why they keep getting thrown out of countries all over the world. I mean, I read a ton of stuff on them and they're evil. She's a freaking witch is all."

"So what do we do?" Krista asked.

After a long silence, someone said, "What did they used to do with witches?"

CHAPTER 34

Number 18 Shady Pines Lane turned out to be a mobile home set back from a country road by a scruffy patch of grass and a dying perennials garden fenced off with chicken wire. An old Honda Civic with Massachusetts plates and a bumper sticker that said "Jesus Saves" sat in front at a crazy angle because a pile of split logs had been dumped on the gravel driveway beside the house. The flue of a wood-burning stove ran up the side of one end of the structure releasing a curlicue of smoke.

As usual, Kirk had not called in advance. He rarely did so as to catch a person of interest off-guard. He knocked at the door but was answered by a volley of barks, behind which he heard the sound of a television, probably to give the dog company. To the right of the door hung an America flag.

After several minutes' wait, he drove down the street a few miles before turning around and heading back to the mobile home. The street was a winding wooded road of humble capes and ranches. Yet nearly every one of them was decorated with pumpkins, skeletons, and witches and signs announcing a Halloween scavenger hunt last weekend—all but number 18.

Kirk was nearly back when he spotted a woman jogging in his direction, then turning into the trailer home.

He pulled in front and rang the bell. Another volley of barks until a woman looked out the side window. Kirk held up his badge, which she studied and then opened the door.

"Yeah?"

Riley Malone was a thin woman with a hard, sallow face, magenta buzz-cut and dressed in navy blue sweats. He identified himself and explained he was here about Sylvie Thornton. She hesitated at first, then without a word let him enter.

As he stepped inside, a pickup truck went by and tooted, the driver giving Riley a wave, a large flag attached with the silhouette of a witch on a broom. "Your neighbors go all out for Halloween."

She waved back with a grimace. "Stupid holiday," she muttered and closed the door.

"I saw all the signs up the road."

"That was the other day, and they're still up," she sneered. "I run every afternoon, and I've been looking at them for weeks."

Clutter was the immediate impression of the interior. Boxes and bags were full of glassware, dishes, household goods, clothing, towels, et cetera. She removed a box from a chair and dropped it on the floor.

"Sorry about the mess. It's for the church charity shop."

Kirk sat down. On one wall was an illustration of a beatific Jesus with a glowing heart; on the opposite wall, a large wooden crucifix. Then his eye stopped at a framed illustration of Saint Michael spearing a winged Satan at his feet.

The other impression was the smell of dog—an aged black mongrel that snuffed around Kirk's feet. With a remote, Riley clicked off the TV. "This is Felix, and it's time to do our business," she said and let him out the back door then took a chair opposite him. "So what do you want to know?"

"We're investigating the death of Sylvie Thornton who I understand was a friend of yours," Kirk said. "We want to know if you could shed light on her death."

She shook her head woefully. "I was shocked when I heard, but I really don't know anything. We haven't stayed in contact for years, not since I moved up here. But I knew she had a terrible time with her son's death a few years back, and then there was her divorce. So I guess it all caught up with her."

She wore a septum-piercing piece that ended in two silver beads hanging from her nostrils like silvered snots. Kirk could never understand why people thought that was a good look. She also wore a gold crucifix.

"You may have heard that her death is now being investigated as a possible homicide."

Her face darkened. "Yeah. It was on Facebook."

Either a local reporter or neighbors had posted that rumor. Kirk and Mandy had seen the same reports that authorities had not ruled out foul play, so Malone's story was covered. Same with Morgan Cassidy.

"I understand you were close as kids and that you and other girls shared a tattoo."

Something dark crossed Malone's face. "What about it?"

Kirk showed her his cellphone shot from Sylvie Thornton's arm. "Like this?"

She made a sigh of resignation and rolled up her sleeve, revealing a greenish shamrock with a single leaf in red, identical to the one on Sylvie's right arm, but a different leaf. "Yeah, same thing."

"Who else has that?"

"Morgan Bolt and Krista Barber."

"Is that the same as Krista Barber Saliba?"

"Yeah, that's her married name. We got them back in high school. It was just a silly thing to show we were friends."

"Right. And whose idea was it to get that?"

"I don't know. Why's it so important?"

Kirk just gave her a silent glare.

After a prickly moment, she said, "It was Morgan's idea."

"Is that Morgan Bolt, now Morgan Cassidy?"

"Yes. So, what's this have to do with Sylvie's death?"

"I'm not sure, but would you say Morgan was the power figure of your group?"

"I guess. I mean, she had a car and a fake ID and a big house for parties and stuff. Her dad had a boat. She was good at getting what she wanted." She made a humpfing sound. "Good enough to marry money. Beat the crap out of me," she added, tipping her head at her surroundings.

Her resentment was palpable. Morgan Cassidy lived in an august seaside mansion within a mile of the Kennedy compound. Likewise, Sylvie Thornton was born and died in a stately family home in the most prestigious mail zone in eastern Massachusetts—Harvard Square. And here was a sad, lonely, wrung-out woman living in a trailer with Jesus and an old dog.

"When was the last time you communicated with Morgan?".

"When I heard about Sylvie and that maybe it was a homicide."

"Uh-huh. And when before that?"

"A few weeks ago. She wanted to know if I was going to the reunion."

While they talked, the woman kept wringing her fingers as if her hands were at war with each other—a nervous gesture that maybe suggested she knew things she was struggling to hold in.

She wiped the sweat from her brow onto her sleeve and got up. "I need some water. Can I get you one?"

"No thanks."

She got herself a bottle of water, twisted off the cap, and guzzled down most of the contents. Kirk pulled out his cellphone and held up the photograph of Vadima Lupescu. "Do you recognize her?"

Riley sucked in her breath with an audible wheeze with her hand to her mouth, her eyes gaping in horror.

"Are you okay?"

"I—I don't want to talk about her."

"Why not?"

She shot to her feet and dashed for the bathroom, shutting the door. Kirk followed her and could hear her make gagging sounds followed by the flush of the toilet.

He tapped at the door. "Ms. Malone, are you all right?" Silence. He tapped again, and when she still didn't answer, he rattled the door, but it was locked. He was about to call 911 when she opened the door.

Her face was red and wet. She walked past him into the middle of the room and sat down stiffly in her chair. He sat opposite her. "Can I get you anything?" She shook her head. "Are you okay to talk?"

She looked at her hands and made a slight nod.

"I was asking you about Vadima Lupescu. I'm wondering if you could shed some light on what happened the night in Morgan's backyard—the night she died."

Her eyes still closed, her mouth trembling. He waited, and she held still, but for her mouth, twitching as if she were having a private conversation inside. Then she opened her eyes, looking straight ahead, and in a barely audible voice said, "I killed her."

"What?"

"I killed her, I killed her, I killed her." She said that while striking the crucifix on her chest with her fist until he grabbed her hand.

"Okay, okay, please calm down." He got another bottle from the refrigerator and handed it to her. She took a few sips. "Tell me what happened."

Through tearful gasps she said, "I convinced them she was a witch, that she was evil."

"Whom did you convince?"

"My friends, the kids at the school."

"Like who?"

"Morgan, Krista, Sylvie, Gee Gee, Timmy D., Justine, and the others. Because she was a Gypsy, a Roma, and that she cast spells and made curses, and things."

"What do you mean *cast spells*?"

"I saw her. She did palm readings and tarot cards and made creepy chants. I didn't believe it at first, but then weird things began to happen. Things she predicted."

"Like what?"

"At first, dumb things, like which school was going to win the next game. Who was going to score with scratch tickets. Who'd make varsity. Then more serious stuff. One night she did palms and told us who'd be the first to die. A week later, Justine had an aneurysm and dropped dead in class." Tears puddled her eyes. "And she was only seventeen."

"And you believed Vadima caused it?"

"Yeah, that she'd put a hex on her because she was jealous. She had a crush on Gee Gee Gallagher, but he liked Justine. Then she died. And I was convinced Vadima had killed her by Gypsy magic."

"And where did you learn about Gypsy magic?"

"Books. Online. It's all there about how Romas hexed people they don't like. How they speak the language of animals and worship Satan. How they carried the plague and sacrificed Christian babies."

"You really believed that back then?"

She nodded. "I was pretty religious, and in the Bible it says 'anyone who casts spells is detestable to the Lord.' And 'thou shall not suffer a witch to live.' And I believed that. I even asked Father de Souza, and he said witches were anti-Christian and worshipped Satan. And the thing is—Vadima was not religious. She went to church, but just to look good and stay in school. But I was convinced she was an imposter and dangerous to us."

"What do you mean *dangerous to us*."

"She knew that we didn't like her and didn't trust her, so she made bad things happen."

"Like what?"

"Like my mother coming down with shingles, and Krista's dog getting killed by coyotes. Like she put a curse on us. And then Morgan's father . . ." She stopped dead.

"What about Morgan's father?"

She shook her head. "Nothing."

"What about Vadima and Morgan's father?"

"Nothing. It wasn't important."

"If you know something that could shed light on either case, please let me know."

"It's not important, okay?"

She was rattled, but she wouldn't talk. Kirk made note and moved on. "So why did you say you killed Vadima?"

"I convinced everybody she had evil powers and was a danger to us and our families, so we met and had a ritual of cleansing. It was all very dumb—you know, the book, the bell, and the candles stuff. But we even convinced her that she was possessed by a demon and had to die."

"So you're saying that you, Morgan, Sylvie, Krista, and others convinced Vadima that she was a witch and had to die by setting herself on fire? Is that what you're saying?"

She made an involuntary groan and nodded, her eyes puddling again. "It was Halloween, and we had a sleepover at Morgan's. It was cool and foggy, so we all sat around the fire pit in her backyard and got stoned on weed and vodka nips. And then we decided to do an exorcism to drive the demons from her.

"We'd made a voodoo doll that looked like her, even used her hair from her brush. And the plan was to burn it on the fire, you know, in effigy."

"And Vadima knew about this?"

"Yes. She was in favor of it, because we convinced her that after that the demons were gone, and she'd be our friend again."

"And she was convinced?"

"Yeah, I mean she was there and went along with it."

"And where were Morgan's parents?"

"They were out having dinner with friends, you know, to avoid trick-or-treaters, or whatever. They had no idea. We did the incantations and all, then cast the effigy on the fire to cleanse Vadima."

"How did she react?"

"I think she was relieved, like we were all together on this, and she'd be our best friend."

These were the same kids who only a few years before believed in Santa Claus and the Tooth Fairy. "Okay. So after you burned the effigy, then what?"

"We were all still zonked out, so we just went to bed."

"What about Vadima? How did she seem after the cleansing rite?"

"Relieved, I guess. I really don't remember because we were all still stoned. She went to sleep in the treehouse. She did that a lot."

"And what happened after she went up and you all went to bed inside?"

She shook her head and fought back tears. "There was the fire."

"How did you learn about the fire?"

"All the noise and commotion. Fire trucks, police, people yelling."

"So between the time you went to bed and heard all the commotion you were sound asleep, right?"

"Yeah, blotto."

"So what do you think started the fire?"

She shook her head. "I think she wasn't convinced we'd cured her. I think she did it herself."

"And not an accident or the wind?"

"It was foggy but not windy."

Kirk pulled up his phone again and held up the tip from Jemma: VADIMA WAS MURDERED.

"Can you explain this?"

"What? Oh my God. Who said this?"

"We don't know. It was an anonymous tip to the Lexington Police Department. But there's reason to believe that there may be a connection between the death of Vadima Lupescu and Sylvie Thornton. So, do you know who might have sent this?"

Her face was ashen. "No." She shot to her feet. "I can't talk about this anymore. I told you all I know." She moved to the door.

Hers was the reaction more of fright than horror that the two deaths may be connected. As if she sat on something relevant. But at the moment, she looked spent.

"Okay, but we may need to question you again." He handed her his card. As he followed her, his eye fell on a four-pack of beer with a familiar looking label. "*Monk's Brew*. Is it any good?"

"I don't know. I don't drink beer."

"It says brewed and bottled at Saint Julian's Monastery, Smithfield, Mass."

"Yeah, from a friend who's a brother out there."

Then it came to him—the same label on a magnum at Sylvie Thornton's house. "What's your friend's name?"

She flashed him an anxious look. "Grayson Gallagher. We called him *Gee Gee*."

"Right. He gave one of the eulogies at Sylvie's funeral."

She nodded. "I didn't go." Then as an afterthought, "I'm sure it was great."

"It was heartfelt."

"I believe it. He was a very spiritual person even as a kid. Never missed Bible class. He had an opportunity to go to medical school but decided instead to live a life of prayer. God bless him."

"And brew beer. Can you tell me why you didn't go, because you were best best friends at one time?"

She glanced at the Fitbit on her wrist. "Look, I've got to leave." She yanked down her sleeve and opened the door.

"Right." Kirk thanked her and left; his mind's eye stuck on the long white scar on the inside of her wrist.

Ten minutes later he was heading back to Boston when his cellphone jingled. It was Mandy. "We contacted Richard Bolt who confirms that Morgan Cassidy was at his son's birthday party. So she's off the list."

"Unless he's lying."

"Yeah. Learn anything from Riley?"

"That she felt responsible for Vadima's death by spreading rumors about her being a witch. Apparently, she had a lot of bottled-up guilt over it."

"That may explain why she's kept a low profile."

"Might also explain why she doesn't celebrate Halloween."

CHAPTER 35

He picked up Mandy at the Cambridge station and headed south on Route 3 toward the Cape.

"Harry Thornton may be off the list," Mandy said, "but Morgan Cassidy did visit her brother, Richard Bolt, in Portsmouth and apparently went to the next town to pick up a few things for the nephew's birthday party. The thing is she didn't come back until afternoon."

"What time did she leave her brother's?" Kirk asked.

"He said she was gone when he woke up. Remember it was Saturday morning and people with normal jobs sleep in on weekends."

She was right. Police work was anything but nine to five with weekends off. While working a case, which was most of the time, a detective's personal life was indistinguishable from his or her professional one. You brought it home obsessively, keeping at it around the clock, examining notes, replaying interviews, spending hours online searching for clues, backgrounds, databases. It defined you, your mental state, and your life. What at times had bothered Olivia, such as calls in the middle of Megan's birthday party or while they were asleep. "So she could have left at five a.m. and driven to Sylvie's, killed her, and gotten back before noon."

"Possibly, although that's a long stretch. But here's one that might not be," Mandy said. "Riley Malone's parents were arrested twenty years ago in an anti-immigrant protest against refugees displaced from the second Gulf War in Iraq and from Somalia's civil war. Her father was also part of an online group called Citizens Aware, which maintains that Third-World immigration is rooted in anti-Christian values—namely Muslims—and ruining America. The ACLU pegs this as one of the most extreme groups, having gotten worse over the years. But even back two decades ago, there was strong racist language that may have fed Riley's anti-Roma attitudes toward Vadima Lupescu."

"Nice social values to pass on."

"Right. And according to Jemma Jones' report by her history teacher, Riley was the most hostile toward the girl. She wrote a paper claiming that Romany people started the Bubonic plague and drank the blood of Christian babies."

"The hits keep on coming."

* * *

It was a little before six that same day when Kirk and Mandy showed up at Morgan Cassidy's house for the second time. The place was lit up by lanterns, path lighting, gazebo lighting, and spot lighting that showcased trees and shrubs. Sitting in an open three-car garage were a gray Tesla sedan and a silver BMW SUV. A John Deere tractor sat in the third bay.

Morgan's husband, Tom, met them at the door. After identifying themselves, Kirk explained they needed to speak to Morgan.

"We're in the middle of dinner."

Kirk apologized while Mandy blurted out, "You have a micro, right?"

Even Kirk was taken aback by that and almost snickered. *Smooth, Mandy.* Morgan came to the door. "Sorry to interrupt, but we'd like to ask you a few more questions."

She did not look happy. "Can't you come back tomorrow?"

"Not really," Mandy said, cutting off Kirk again. "I think it's best if we talk now."

Morgan muttered discontent under her breath and led them into the same sunroom and turned on the lights. Her husband began to settle with them, but she said she could handle this, and he left.

"I really resent you're barging in like this, Detective."

"We understand, but the investigation has taken a new turn. There's a suggestion that the death of Vadima Lupescu was foul play and that it may be related to the death of Sylvie Thornton." Kirk then pulled out a photocopy of the crime tip sent to Jemma Jones.

That got results. Morgan stared at the sheet, took a deep breath, and let it out slowly. "I did not send that, if that's what you're asking."

"Fine, but do you have any idea who did?"

She made an exaggerated frown of disdain. "Of course not. It could be a damn joke."

"Yes, but if true, it could be a link to the murder of Sylvie Thornton."

"Based on what?"

"That Sylvie was killed because she knew what may really have happened that night. So, please tell us what happened the night Vadima Lupescu died."

"What makes you think anything happened?"

"We talked to Riley Malone."

"And?"

"And we'd like you to fill us in."

"Just as it appeared in the report. There was a fire in the treehouse and she died in it."

"And maybe you can tell us what led up to that?" said Mandy.

Morgan paused for a moment as her eyes narrowed shrewdly on Mandy. "I know about you, Detective Wing," and she pronounced that like a swear. "How you were put on leave because your partner nearly lost his life when you abandoned him during a riot."

Mandy let out a long audible breath. Kirk glared at her to let it go. "Good to see you've done your homework. Now where exactly does that get you, Mrs. Cassidy?"

"I don't like you showing up in the middle of the dinner hour and questioning me about some accident that happened twenty years ago. And frankly I don't like your holier than thou attitude, Detective."

Kirk cut in. "Mrs. Cassidy, this may be a double murder investigation, and I'm asking you to please answer our questions."

She closed her eyes for a spell to center herself. "All right, what do you want to know?"

Over the next several minutes she described pretty much what Riley Malone had iterated, with interludes of prompting. "So after the effigy burning what did you do?"

"Everyone else went home, and the rest of us went to bed, and Vadima to her sleep pad in the treehouse."

"And when did you learn about the fire?"

"When my father woke me."

"And what did you see?"

"The whole treehouse was engulfed in flames, and police and firefighters were everywhere trying to put it out."

"Right," Kirk said. Yet he suspected she knew things that she didn't want to share. "I understand you kids burned a voodoo doll. Maybe you can tell us about that."

"Is that what Riley Malone told you?"

"Yes, and she said she was convinced that Vadima cast spells on people and that she seemed to predict stuff."

"So we believed."

"Such as what?"

"I'm sure Riley named some."

Kirk nodded but to draw her out said, "Just to corroborate."

"Oh, dumb obvious things like who would make the honor roll, who would score the most baskets or win the next game."

"There were also reports that some of the kids believed that Vadima might have been responsible for the death of Justine Zajac."

She rolled her eyes. "Yeah, but look, we were dumb gullible kids, and she did some tarot card stuff and muttered something about seeing something bad in the future. But that was just a terrible coincidence. Kids who seem totally healthy sometimes just die without clear medical cause. We had one last year at my school. It's tragic and a mystery."

"Of course. There was also a rumor that Vadima put a hex on your father."

Her eyes suddenly hooded. "What are you talking about? What hex?"

"That she somehow lured him into having sex with her."

"Where—who told you such crap? Did Riley tell you that? Huh? Yeah, who else, the little jerk."

"Riley did not tell us that," Mandy said. "As you may recall, Vadima Lupescu was a talented artist. You must remember how she was always sketching in pen and ink in a small bound notebook, right?"

Morgan's expression flattened.

"I remember."

"Well, I don't know if you knew this, but a few of her sketches, which she dated, were of you and your father in compromising poses suggesting illicit intimacy. Illicit because she was still fifteen at the time. Her birthday was six days later."

Morgan's face looked like a wax mask of herself. "It *was* Riley, wasn't it? Riley Malone told you this."

"Riley Malone only said you kids believed that Vadima predicted things, but she did not say what she claimed to have foreseen regarding your father." Mandy produced a photocopy of one of the sketches. "This is what's telling."

"Where did you get this?"

"From Milosh Lupescu, Vadima's brother. She had sent home some of these, and he had thought the male in the picture was some kind of romantic fantasy. But the likeness to online photos of your father is unmistakable, including his tattoo. So please answer the questions: Did you know that your father was having sex with Vadima Lupescu?"

Morgan made a gasp of resignation as she glared at the image of the half-nude Vadima in a bed and in the arms of a naked male with the facial likeness of Jordan Bolt and a tattoo on his forearm. "Yes," she said in a near whisper, and appeared to deflate in her chair, as if relieved that it was out.

"I know this is difficult for your," Mandy said, "so, we appreciate your being frank. How did you learn that he was having sex with her?"

"I saw him go into her room one night and heard them make sexual sounds." Her face was full of disgust.

"Do you think their sex was consensual?"

"No. I think he threatened to send her back home if she resisted."

"Or told."

"Yes."

"So you're saying you didn't believe that Vadima was a witch who cast a spell on him, right?"

"That was Riley's harebrained idea. She was a superstition freak, believed every cockamamie theory."

"But back then you believed that, right. I mean, the voodoo ritual, burning the effigy?"

"We were kids. If she said Lulu escaped from Area 51, we would have believed she was a Martian. I mean, teenagers sometimes have an irrational view of things, especially kids at a conservative Catholic school. Believing in witches is just a sidestep to believing in saints."

"Did your mother know?"

"She later found out."

"How was that?"

Morgan made a sigh that came out as a whimper. "When she found a box of condoms on his boat—a thirty-six count, more than half of them missing."

"How did your mother know he was not having sex with other women?"

"Because she checked with other boaters and the harbor master. On days he claimed to take Vadima and other kids fishing, she found out that he ended up dropping anchor in a secluded cove off Peddocks Island. And there were no other kids."

Mandy was on a roll, and Kirk nodded her on. With Thornton off her list, she now had her claws out for Jordan Bolt. "Is that why your parents separated?"

"What do you think? She threw him out of the house."

"When was that?"

"A few months after the fire. She later filed for divorce."

"Did you know what he was doing?"

"Not until I saw him sneak into her bedroom that night. Then it hit me—really hard." She took another deep breath. "And I hated them both for it. At first, I blamed her for seducing him, thinking she was a little tramp. But later I realized he was taking advantage of her, threatening to report her to immigration if she didn't comply."

"Did you approach him about what you knew?"

"Yes. We had a terrible fight, and he claimed that he was drunk and didn't know what he was doing."

"When was the last time you spoke to your father?" Kirk asked.

"Four years ago."

"So you're not close to him."

"That's a fair deduction."

"What brought you together then?"

"My brother got sick."

"I just wanted confirmation." Kirk checked his notes. "It's our understanding that there were seven of you in the house that night—you, Sylvie, Riley, Krista, your parents, and your brother, Richie, with Vadima sleeping in the treehouse, correct?"

Morgan nodded.

"Anyone else?"

"No."

"Mrs. Cassidy, I don't know how to ask this without asking it," Kirk continued, "but do you believe your father had anything to do with Vadima's death?"

She glared at him point-blank. "I really don't know."

"But you wouldn't dismiss the possibility."

She thought for a protracted moment, closing her eyes. When she opened them again, her eyes had shrunk to ball bearings. "No, I wouldn't."

"Why do you say that?"

"Because he had every reason to. She was underage. You can figure out the rest."

"Right." Proof would have sent him to prison. Even the accusation of pedophilia could have ruined him for good.

"What about your mother?"

"She had damn good reasons, but no, because my mother was not capable of that. Besides, she suffered vertigo. The last thing she'd do would be to climb a ladder, even if she wanted to get rid of Vadima."

He recalled from the photos that the ladder showed no signs of fire damage, so the fire was started from inside the treehouse, which might eliminate Sally Bolt if she, in fact, had suffered vertigo. "Clarify what you mean that she may have had reasons."

"It's pretty obvious, isn't it? I mean adultery with a teenage girl. She was the ultimate competition. She was young, attractive, and sexy, and my mother was middle-age and overweight. And my father never let her forget it."

"Do you communicate with your father?"

"I haven't seen him, but we exchange texts now and then."

"Would you know where we could find him at this hour?"

"He may be at his club. The website said they were installing a new security system today." She checked her watch. It was after seven. "But most likely at home."

Kirk nodded. They had the time and the address.

She walked them to the front door and opened it. Before they stepped outside, something shot by Kirk's feet from the outside.

"That's Elmo," Morgan said, looking back at a long-haired black cat. "Another reason I've not seen my father—he hates cats."

Morgan closed the door behind them. As they walked to the car, Mandy said, "I think she just threw her father under a bus."

"I think you're right."

CHAPTER 36

"THE SON OF A BITCH is a damn pedophile."

"And Morgan knew, which explains her contempt. And humiliation. That's also something that Jemma Jones didn't know about."

"So we've got a suspicious death nearly twenty years ago that may be connected to the Sylvie Thornton murder."

"That's Jemma's theory."

"Except she couldn't put it together."

Kirk nodded. "Only because she was dealing with an old puzzle. But Morgan may have handed us a missing piece."

"And a big one. He had the motive, the means, and the opportunity for killing the Lupescu girl. And for Sylvie, definitely the motive since she may have known he torched the girl."

"Except sometimes the pieces don't quite snap into place, and you're tempted to force them, which produces greater problems." Like my marriage, he thought.

Mandy grunted an affirmative.

"The other problem," Kirk added, "is that the overall picture keeps changing."

It was half an hour later, when they turned off Route 6 to 3 North to Boston. It was past seven thirty, and a cold rain fell. It would take them oven an hour to reach Lexington. They were both exhausted and each running on another French roast grande. He took a sip. "By the time we get there, I'll need a straitjacket."

Mandy chuckled. "Really, and won't he be happy to see us."

"Off guard, and the better to catch him."

"Unless she calls ahead."

"Doubtful. She just sicced us on him."

It was nearly nine o'clock when they pulled up in front of 37 Liberty Tree Lane. Lights were on in several rooms.

They hustled up to the front door portico in the driving rain with Kirk yearning for his warm dry bed. He rang the bell and heard some scurrying and muffled voices from the second floor. A light went off in an upstairs bedroom. A few moments later the inner door opened on a man in a t-shirt and jeans. His long graying hair was ruffled.

Kirk and Mandy held up their badges. "Mr. Bolt, we'd like to talk to you about a murder investigation."

Shock lit up his face. "What? Yeah, okay," he said, and shot a look up the stairs behind him before opening the glass door.

"Jordy, is everything okay?" A female voice from upstairs. Then a flash of a young woman in panties and a t-shirt from a darkened bedroom. Maybe in her twenties, maybe younger. And according to their records, Jordan Bolt was sixty-two.

He looked as flustered as he did rumpled. He swept back his hair, revealing a bright red hickey on his neck. "Can't this wait until tomorrow?"

"Not really."

"But it's the middle of the night."

"Right, and there's a freezing rain coming down, so let's get on with it," Mandy said and brushed by him into the living room, shaking off the rain.

Kirk followed her with a grin as Bolt called upstairs that everything was fine. They all took seats as Kirk turned on his recorder.

"What's this all about?"

Bolt's feet were stuffed into loafers without socks and his mouth looked raw from sexual activity. On his right arm was a blue tattoo of a shield with red lightning bolts shooting out of the center—the same image on the male figure's arm in the Lupescu girl's drawing.

Kirk explained that the death of Sylvie Thornton was being investigated as a homicide.

"Good God, who'd want to kill her?"

"What we're hoping to find out," Mandy snapped, shooting him a withering look.

"When was the last time you saw her?" Kirk said.

"Jesus, I don't know," he said, clearly uneasy. He scratched his head. "Years ago. She was a friend of my daughter's back in high school."

"And not since?"

"I don't think so. No."

Mandy looked at her notes. "You're owner of Fitness You, right?"

"Yeah."

"A standard question," she continued. "Can you tell us where you were on the morning of November six?"

"The sixth? I was here."

"And not at your health club?"

"Saturday's my day off."

"Okay, so any way to confirm that?"

"Well . . ."

From upstairs, a female voice: "Jordy, what's going on?"

Bolt moved to the bottom of the stairs as did Mandy. "It's nothing." And he flashed his hand for her to disappear into the bedroom. She did, the door snapping closed.

"By the way," Mandy said returning to the living room, "how old is she?"

"I don't like that question."

"You'd like it less if she's under eighteen," Mandy said. "So maybe you should have her bring down her driver's license."

"Jesus!" Bolt muttered and headed up the stairs, and Kirk gave Mandy a wink of approval.

"Likes them young," she said.

"Some things don't change." Kirk was pulsing with contempt for Bolt—a guy who had sexually abused a fifteen-year-old exchange student under the same roof as his wife and kids. Unfortunately, it would be nearly impossible to convict him of the violation of a child almost twenty years ago without a formal complaint, hard evidence, a written confession, and, sadly, with the victim dead. But Kirk would love to take him down. Not to mention Mandy who looked poised to shoot him.

The woman came down. She was now in jeans and a Fitness You sweatshirt. She wore her hair in pigtails, and her young face was frayed pink—from Bolt's beard, no doubt. Her expression was sullen, and she barely made eye contact as she handed Kirk her license. Her name was Siena Martinez, age eighteen, and just two months legal.

He handed it back to her, and without a word she crept back up.

"Look, can't we do this another time? I told you I've not seen Sylvie in years."

"No, we can't," Kirk said. "We have reason to believe that Sylvie Thornton's death may be related to the death of Vadima Lupescu."

"Vadima? What? That was twenty years ago."

"Nineteen, and there's evidence she was murdered."

"What? There was a full investigation, and the police determined she died by accident."

"Recent evidence puts that determination in doubt," Kirk said.

"What evidence?"

"That's not anything to share. So maybe you can tell us what you recall from that Halloween night." Kirk checked his notes. "What we know is that she returned to your house after school around three that afternoon. Take it from there."

Bolt made a dramatic sigh of exasperation. "Yeah, yeah, yeah, it's all on record that I didn't get home until sometime before six. Sally showed up a little after that, and because it was a Friday night, yeah Halloween, we ordered pizzas for the kids."

"Meaning who?"

"Sally, Richie, and Morgan, and a few others including her girlfriends who slept over that night, and me."

"And what did you and your wife do?"

"We went out with friends to a restaurant. Got home around ten and went to bed."

"And where were Morgan, Vadima, and her friends when you got back?"

"They were in the backyard sitting around the fire pit."

"Do you recall who was there?"

"I don't know, a bunch of kids, a dozen or more."

"I know it's been years, but who exactly do you recall was there?"

"Jesus!" he muttered to himself. Then he named Morgan and her best girlfriends, plus Grayson Gallagher, Tyler, Timmy D., and others. Kirk jotted down the names.

"Do you know what time Vadima went up to the treehouse?"

"No. I tucked in around ten with my wife and fell asleep."

"How about your wife?"

"I assumed she fell asleep too."

"Do either of you take any kind of sleep aids, medications, sedatives, whatever?"

"Not really. I mean, sometimes Sally would take a melatonin if she needed it."

"Right. So do you remember anyone leaving the house while you were in bed?"

"No. I didn't wake up until I heard first-responders banging on the doors."

He went on to describe the chaos once the police and fire fighters arrived.

"How do you suppose the treehouse caught fire?"

"We've been all through this." He made another audible sigh. "Our guess was that she fell asleep and had forgotten to turn off the lantern, and the wind knocked it over, or maybe she bumped it while sleeping."

"Did you see any signs of stress in her? Or did she seem worried about anything?"

"Not really. She was a private person." Then, pulsing to go back upstairs, he said, "Look, we had to live with this terrible event for nearly twenty years. She was a bright and charming young woman. In spite of that detective—Jones and her conspiracy theories—that girl died in a terrible accident. Simple as that."

"And maybe not," Kirk said. "Putting your skepticism aside, do you think any of your daughter's friends might have been capable of murdering her?"

"No, I don't."

"What about Morgan?"

"God, no. Look, all this was settled years ago. I mean, why are you asking all these questions?"

"Because it's been reported that you regularly had sex with Vadima and that she didn't resist because she was afraid of being deported."

He made exaggerated frowns and his head cocked to the side as if Kirk had spoken in a foreign tongue. "What? That's bullshit. Absolute bullshit. Who the hell said that?"

"That's not important," Mandy said and from her folder pulled out a photocopy of one of Vadima's sketches of her with Bolt sitting naked in each other's arms in bed.

"How do you explain this?"

He looked at the drawing as if for the first time but said nothing, although the artery in his neck throbbed like a frog.

"Given the likeness," Mandy said, "including the tattoo, who would you say the figures represent?"

"Cut the shit," Bolt said. "Where did you get this?"

"It came from the sketchbook of Vadima Lupescu who, you may recall, chronicled her experience in drawings instead of a camera."

"Yeah, so what?"

"So, who would you say the figures are?"

"This is fucking entrapment."

"That didn't answer the question—who are the figures?" Mandy said, her eyes sparking like Tasers.

"Me and her."

"So how would you interpret this?" Mandy said.

"I don't know. Maybe she had some kind of fantasy about me." He stabbed the image. "But this didn't happen. Okay? Just fucking bullshit."

"So, your answer is to blame the victim."

He glared at Mandy. "I don't give a sweet shit. That never happened."

"What did happen is that Vadima was murdered, and that you may have had a motive."

"Fucking bullshit. I did not have sex with her, and I did not kill her. She died by accident. I mean, this case was closed nineteen years ago."

"Your daughter claims she saw you sneak into Vadima's bedroom one night," Kirk said.

"What? That's fucking outrageous."

"So is sexual abuse of a minor. Vadima Lupescu was fifteen years old," Mandy shot back.

Good, Mandy!

"I don't care what Morgan claims. She saw nothing. And you have no warrant to be here. Now get out of my house."

He was right, and Kirk nodded for them to leave. They had gotten some of what they had come for. Bolt had displayed all the basic clues that he was lying—his voice skating an octave, loud denials, the body language, the fluttery eye movement, the repeated words, the sudden swearing. The nastier the language, the more likely they're lying.

As they moved to the door, Bolt said just as they stepped outside, "If you want someone with a motive, maybe you should pay a visit to Riley Malone, because she had a serious thing against Vadima Lupescu."

"Such as?"

"Such as extreme prejudice against foreigners. Her own parents belonged to some anti-immigrant groups that rubbed off on her. Did you know she was suspended from school for beating up a refugee girl from Somalia? She also told my daughter that Romany people ate Christian babies. I don't know if she had anything to do with her death, but if you're looking for someone with a motive, maybe you should drop in on her."

* * *

"There's no statute of limitations on rape of a child in Massachusetts," Mandy said.

"True, but we have no victim to make the charge, just some sketches of her in bed with Bolt—something a savvy lawyer could claim was the girl's fantasy, not documentation of what happened."

"We have his own daughter's confirmation."

"Right, and she clearly loathes him," Kirk said. "But would she be willing to testify in court?"

"We could drop the suggestion to the press."

"To what end?"

"To ruin the bastard."

Kirk snickered at her dogged determination to bring Bolt down. "The problem is he lawyers up and brings charges against us for defamation of character based on circumstantial evidence with the hope that his own daughter would testify against him, which probably wouldn't happen. And, I remind you, no live victim but rumors that are nineteen years old. Not much there."

"Fuck!" she said. They drove on in uneasy silence. "So what do we do and what do we have?"

"What we do is solve a murder or two and not pedophilia," Kirk said. "What we have are three people in the Bolt family who each had motives to kill Vadima Lupescu—Jordan, Sally, and Morgan—all because Dad may have taken sexual advantage of an underage exchange student. He was lying about sex with the girl, but I'm not sure he killed her. We'd need more about that Halloween night.

"We also have Riley who apparently had loony racist motives. The mother is dead, and reports claim she was sound asleep when the fire broke out and suffered vertigo, which could have kept her off the ladder."

"The other thing is that if Sylvie was killed to shut her up on Vadima, someone may be gunning for the others who were there that night."

"Right," Mandy said. "So what's our next move?"

"Check out the other female in the sleepover, the woman who gave a eulogy for Sylvie Thornton—this Krista Barber Saliba. I'll do that in the morning. Meanwhile, you check on Bolt's alibi and anything you can find on Riley Malone."

"Want to grab a beer and pizza?"

"Would love to, but I have a date."

Mandy grinned brightly. "A date? With who?"

"My wife."

CHAPTER 37

MORGAN

Nineteen years ago, November 1

WE WERE ALL pretty rattled by the fire death of Lulu. My mother took it particularly hard, crying and blaming herself and my father for letting Lulu use a kerosene lantern. He shot back that she insisted on it like what she used back home without problems. But my mom wasn't satisfied with that and carried on, also about the few empty nips of vodka later found on the lawn by the police—ones I had missed before we went to bed.

They didn't know about the effigy burning. All they knew was that we were toasting marshmallows in the fire pit and singing "Kumbaya."

Mom was more broken up than my father since she was fond of Vadima who was like a second daughter, helping around the house, bringing her flowers and drawings of her and us kids. I felt as if she wished Lulu really was her daughter.

Riley was in a state of shock, muttering prayers, whipping through her rosary beads. I think she was more rattled because she believed Lulu really was a witch and died the way witches did in olden times—as if the fire was divine intervention. "You know, an act of God!" she had claimed. "Like he did in Sodom and Gomorrah." I just said, "Yeah." Such a dipshit.

Krista just cried in horrid disbelief. She liked Lulu who had helped her with math homework too. I mean, Lulu was a whiz at math. In return, Krista, who had nice clothes, helped Lulu with her outfits and gave her a stack of fashion mags and high-end clothing catalogues.

Richie was just plain numb with fright, rattled by all the firefighters and cops buzzing around with hoses and lights. Plus the sight of the treehouse in flames and then collapsing in a burst of sparks made him cry even more, since Dad had built that for him and because he had loved going up there, especially with Lulu who would read to him and give him drawing lessons. Every so often, he'd start weeping into my mother's bathrobe.

The night passed in a crazy blur. I remember my father slamming open the bedroom doors to get us out of the house in case the sparks from the treehouse spread.

He carried Richie terrified and crying down the stairs. The other girls threw on sweats and shoes and with my mom poured into the backyard where firefighters and police had gathered with my father who sprayed our house with a garden hose.

The scene was wild. Flames shot into the tree, engulfing the treehouse, which eventually collapsed to the ground in a burst of sparks with water blasting from the fire trucks in the driveway.

The police and fire marshal pulled us aside and questioned all of us, together and then separately. According to the fire marshal, the lamp was an old-fashioned model, a "dead-flame type," which was dangerous if tipped over since the fuel could combust. Instead of snuffing out the wick like safer models, when the lantern turned over, fuel spilled out and spread the flame to a nearby pile of magazines and notebooks and then along the floor and upward on the railings to the roof. They guessed that in her condition with all the alcohol and weed, Vadima forgot to turn off the flame and passed out.

We all pretty much had the same story—that nobody knew how the fire started. But later, we were questioned again by a Detective Jemma Jones. I didn't know Lexington had any Black cops, let alone a woman. She was nice, but she seemed suspicious that the fire had spread so fast and that Lulu never woke up in time to escape. They had found the damn nip bottles. We fessed up to those, but no one said anything about the voodoo doll thing.

I don't know what time it was, but the police told the other girls to call their parents to pick them up. Richie, my parents, and I eventually went back to bed, but none of us could sleep. The police and fire people stayed for the rest of the night.

Richie slept with my parents because he was so spooked. I headed for my own room. For several minutes I watched from my window as the police and fire inspectors walked around the charred remains. Before the medical examiner people showed up, the police set up a blocking screen as they removed what was left of Lulu.

CHAPTER 38

It was date night.

Kirk did a fast change of clothes in the men's room of a gas station and headed to pick up Olivia for a concert at Symphony Hall. Tonight, the BSO was performing Mahler whose music she loved. He was halfway to her condo when he got a text saying that something unexpected had come up and that she had to cancel. "Sorry, but maybe tomorrow night?"

He pulled over and called her. "What's going on? I've got tickets for the BSO."

"Oh no, I'm really sorry, Kirk, but something's come up. Are you free tomorrow night?"

"Yeah, but the BSO isn't."

"God, I really didn't know. Maybe we can go for dinner tomorrow. I mean, you're flexible, right?"

That almost sounded like a cut—like you haven't got a social life. "So what's on for tonight that you can roll me?"

But she disregarded the question. "Look, it's late and I'm on my way out. Sorry, but call me tomorrow and we'll get dinner someplace. I promise. Again, I'm sorry, Kirk. I really am, but please don't take offense." She clicked off, leaving him staring at the red call-ended circle on his screen.

Don't take offense. "Right!" he said and drove to her place.

As he pulled up to the curb, he spotted Rizzo's Mercedes in the driveway, and a hot wire flared in his gut.

Christ, I'm losing her.

He texted her. I'M OUTSIDE. WE NEED TO TALK.

A minute later Olivia came out of the building, in her overcoat draped over her Sarah Campbell dress—the one that always reminded him of Sinatra's "The Way You Look Tonight."

Kirk got out of the car and met her. "What the hell's going on? This was our night."

"I'm going to a fundraiser for Youth Villages."

He glanced at the Mercedes. "With Rizzo."

She didn't like that. "With *Ted*."

He could not gauge his emotions, torn between hurt and anger, and feeling the press of tears. "Look, either we have a total separation or we get back together, because I hate this fucking in-between thing. Really, it's killing me."

"I'm sorry. Really," she said. "Maybe we should just not do date night."

He gut flared again. That was all he had left. He took a deep breath. "Olivia, do you love me?"

"Kirk, it's not a matter of loving you or not."

"Just please answer me: Do you love me?"

"Yes, I love you, but I need time to work things out by myself."

"But you're not doing it by yourself. You're dating Ted Rizzo. That's not working things out by yourself."

"Kirk, please lower your voice," she snapped. "Seeing others was part of our agreement."

"Do you know that a slew of complaints have been brought against him and his company?"

"What are you talking about?"

"Construction fraud. They'd start a job, take the money, then never finish it. The old 'One nail, no jail' scheme. Prosecutors never touch them because the fine print says that if they run out of materials or supplies there's some insurance adjustment and they won't be taken to court. So it becomes a civil case, and homeowners don't have the money to press charges. The point is your boyfriend's a fucking crook." In spite of himself, he was about to declare what a predatory Lothario he was, but Rizzo suddenly emerged from the building, dressed in a suit and tie, glowing to hit the gala.

"Hey, Livie, is everything okay?"

Livie? You smug, presumptuous bastard.

"Everything's fine, Ted. Please leave us a moment so we can talk, okay?"

But Rizzo kept approaching, his face a mask of innocent concern. "I could hear your voices from inside, and they didn't sound friendly." He turned his face to Kirk's. "Is everything cool, bro?"

With every scintilla of control that Kirk could muster, he said in a flat voice, "Ted, this is between us so please do as *Livie* says and go inside, *bro*."

"Well, I'm not sure I like what I'm hearing." He walked up to Olivia. And with his hand on her shoulder he muttered, "Are you feeling harassed?"

She turned toward him point-blank. "No, I'm not feeling harassed." She was barely able to disguise her indignation. "I can deal with this, Ted, so please go back inside."

Rizzo glanced over her at Kirk, no doubt sensing that Kirk was near volcanic. "Are you sure?" he said, turning to her with feigned concern.

She flashed Rizzo a steely glare. "Yes! I said I can handle this." And she put her hand against his chest urging him back. "This is between me and Kirk, okay? So go back inside."

But he still held firm, studying them. After a prickly stare-down, Kirk said, "Ted, if you don't get the fuck inside, I will make you."

Olivia flashed around. "Kirk, no!" she shouted to prevent him from lurching at Rizzo.

Rizzo narrowed his eyes at him. "Are you threatening me, Kirk?"

"Yes, I fucking am, *Ted*."

After a moment of consideration, Rizzo's expression softened. "Look, bro, let's not scrap, okay. I'm sorry for what happened, and I understand the difficulty of what you're going through, what you're both going through. Believe me, I've been through a divorce myself, so I know your pain."

Kirk stabbed his finger at Rizzo. "You don't have a fucking idea about me or my pain, you smarmy piece of shit."

Olivia shouted, "Jesus Christ, Kirk, stop it!" Then she snapped her face to Rizzo. "Goddamn it, go inside *now*."

But Rizzo stood his ground and with open hands of conciliation he moved toward Kirk.

"Look, Kirk, Olivia's my friend, and I'm supporting her as best I can in this difficult time."

Again, Kirk lurched forward. "And Olivia is my wife. My wife, you got that. And we're still married, and you're seeing my wife!"

Kirk could hear Olivia shouting and feel her pushing him, and he knew he was a membrane away from grabbing Rizzo and pummeling that greasy self-satisfied smirk.

"Look, she made it clear that you were going through a trial separation, and that you both had agreed to see other people."

"Yes, a trial separation and not a fucking divorce, you got that? We're still married, so find yourself a real date, not someone else's wife." So that he wouldn't sic Rizzo on Nora Montana, his ex-wife, and Rona Zuckerman, Kirk stopped short of calling him out for his serial philandering.

"Look, Kirk," Rizzo said in that cheesy ingratiating tone, "we go back a few years, the three of us. So when I heard that you two had separated, I gave Livie a call to see if there was anything I could do."

Now the son of a bitch is trying to gaslight me! "Yeah, see a spot of blood and jump right on it."

Before Rizzo could respond, Olivia slapped Kirk's chest. "Goddamn it. Stop it now." Then to Ted, "Both of you. You're making a goddamn scene."

"I was just trying to make amends," Rizzo muttered.

But Olivia disregarded him, and in a low grating voice to Kirk: "Please, Kirk, for me, please leave!"

He froze, his eyes flooding as he gazed at her, her expression damning him. And she was right—he had caused a scene, lost his cool, and made a pathetic ass of himself. "Sorry, baby," he said.

"I'll see you next week," she whispered. "I promise."

I promise. He nodded, feeling the press of tears behind his eyes. "I love you," he whispered and headed for his car.

As he did, he heard Rizzo say, "I don't care if he's a damn cop. Get a restraining order on him. He's dangerous."

"You haven't got a fucking clue," Kirk muttered and started his car to take him to the pistol range.

CHAPTER 39

KIRK SPENT A fitful night replaying that scene over and over in his head, in stunning disbelief that Olivia had sent him off with his tail between his legs and Rizzo feeling triumphant.

He had gone to the pistol range where he got a box of bullets out of his system, letting the cathartic succession of exploding jolts work its therapy. Then he went home to bed feeling purged, like puking after a bad meal.

But by daybreak, his only options were to gnaw on the barrel of his gun, call in sick and not get out of bed, or throw himself back into the case to get hard around the egg of pain in his chest. He opted for Door Number 3. Their case was breaking, and he wanted to see it play out, no matter what.

Given the traffic, it took him an hour and a half to reach York, Maine, and the address for Krista Barber Saliba. By the time he got there, he had regained his ballast.

The home was a handsome single-family structure with high pitched ceilings and set back from a manicured lawn with a clutch of birches and maples, all enviably neat and cozy.

According to Sergeant Kevin Fujita, Krista Saliba's alibi checked out on video confirmation of her at her son's wrestling match at the Fryeburg Academy on the Saturday morning Sylvie Thornton was murdered.

She met him at the door wearing jeans and a navy blue WPI sweatshirt. After identifying himself, he explained that he was at the Funeral Mass for Sylvie Thornton when her eulogy was interrupted by Milosh Lupescu.

She led him into her living room where he asked her if she had any idea who would have killed Sylvie. "No, and I'm shocked anyone would do that. She was such a giving person."

He explained that they were investigating the cold case of Vadima Lupescu as it may have been related to the murder of Sylvie Thornton. "So we're hoping you remember what happened that Halloween night."

She looked genuinely startled. "How's there a connection? I thought it was an accident."

"We're working on the theory that Vadima was murdered, and that Sylvie may have known who was responsible."

She reiterated the same story Morgan Cassidy had about the kids sitting around a fire pit and burning an effigy to expel demons from Vadima.

"After that foolishness, we all went to bed. I slept in the guest room with Riley, Sylvie was in Morgan's room, Richie in his own room, and Mr. and Mrs. Bolt were in the main bedroom. I was sound asleep when Morgan woke me to say there was a fire in the backyard. Her parents were rousing everybody else."

"Who else was in the group at the effigy burning?"

"Timmy Delacroix, Leyla Lapore, Carla Lally, and Grayson Gallagher—we called him Gee Gee."

"Grayson Gallagher," Kirk said, flipping through his notes. "Wasn't he the boyfriend of the girl who died in class—Justine Zajac?"

"Yes. And that was just awful. She collapsed in class and never woke up. A heart aneurysm. It was so freaky because she had no symptoms. One minute she was reciting her lines, the next minute she was dead."

"And how did that affect Grayson?"

"As you can imagine, he was shocked, horrified like the rest of us. They were sweethearts with plans to go to college together and get married. He was devastated. He dropped out of college and had some counseling. They were very close. I don't think he fully recovered."

"And now he's a Justinian monk."

"Yes. And I think that way of life is a consequence of her passing."

In short, he had dropped out of life. Kirk nodded, scratched some notes. "Can you give us contact info for the other people who were there?"

"Timmy Delacroix sadly died in Afghanistan, Leyla I think lives in England, and Carla last I heard moved to Texas."

That meant the only other local person was the monk. "And no one else in the house?"

"No, only Richie, but he got sent inside when the alcohol and weed came out. I think he was ten at the time."

"Do you know where he's living now?"

"No. Morgan would, of course."

He nodded, knowing it was Portsmouth, New Hampshire. "Do you remember how the fire in the fire pit was started?"

Krista rummaged through her memory. "I think charcoal lighter, you know, the squirt-can stuff."

She went on, reiterating what Kirk had heard from the others.

"Can you think of anyone who may have wanted to harm or kill Vadima?"

Krista hesitated for a spell. "Not really. Some kids didn't know what to make of her because she was foreign and did palm readings and stuff."

"At the time did you believe she cast spells, put hexes on people?"

"No. I didn't believe in that stuff. In fact, I was already having doubts about what church was all about. But I attended because my parents decided that if I were to be raised with religion, Catholicism was the best option. I'm not religious, but I don't regret it. I still like the rituals. But I didn't believe in magic, white or black."

Kirk nodded. "There are rumors that Morgan's father, Jordan Bolt, may have had a sexual relationship with Vadima. Is that something you had heard?"

"Who told you that?"

"Morgan. She'd discovered her father sneaking into Vadima's room one night. Is this something you knew about?"

She hesitated for a moment. "Yes, she told us."

"Who's *us*?"

"Me, Riley, and Sylvie."

"The clover-leaf friends. Your tattoo."

"Yes, well, that was a teenage affectation. I had that removed years ago."

"I see. How did Morgan react to that discovery of her father and Vadima?"

"She was devastated, to say the least. She went into a funk and pulled into herself. She stopped eating and doing her schoolwork, became truant, missing school days and church. Her grades fell and her teachers were concerned. It was awful. We pleaded with her to tell her mother, to see the priest, to talk with the guidance counselor—anyone. But she refused."

"As far as you know, did she tell her mother?"

"Not as far as I know. But she said that her mother found evidence that it was an ongoing thing. That he would take Vadima out in his boat and they'd have sex somewhere in the harbor. I really don't know."

"Any idea what kind of evidence?"

"Morgan did say her mother followed them to the marina on a couple of occasions."

"Did Vadima ever let on to you or the others?"

"No, because Mr. Bolt threatened to have her sent back to Slovakia if she told."

The more he heard about Jordon Bolt, the more he wanted to see him behind bars for life, if for nothing else but being a disgusting, child-molesting pig. "Do you know if Morgan ever confronted Vadima about her and her father?"

"Oh, yeah. She told her that she wanted her out of their house, that she wanted her to make up something about an emergency back home, and to go back to Slovakia."

"Did she say what Vadima's reaction was?"

"No, but I guess she was crushed. I mean, she claimed that Mr. Bolt forced sex on her."

"That he raped her?"

"Yes, but Morgan didn't accept that, even if it was true. Whatever, that confrontation took its toll on Vadima. She avoided us at school, ate alone. Then one day, I noticed that the backs of her hands were all scabby. She had stuck herself with pins, like she was punishing herself. I look back now with pity for her and guilt that I didn't reach out to her." Her expression turned rueful. "Two days later was Halloween and the fire."

"So you're suggesting it's possible that Morgan and her father had reasons to want to get rid of Vadima."

"I think her father did just to hide his abuse, but I don't believe he killed her. He didn't strike me as violent."

"What about Morgan?"

"Morgan was very clever, but she was not given to violence. In fact, in all the years I knew her growing up, I don't recall her ever erupting in anger. Instead, she'd do a quiet burn inside."

"Okay, what about Grayson Gallagher? Do you think he could have killed Vadima?"

"He could have. I mean, at the time he was convinced that she had caused the death of his girlfriend."

"So you're saying he may have believed Vadima practiced black magic."

"Well, he believed in white magic."

That term again. "White magic?"

"Christianity."

Interesting view. "Okay, back to Sylvie. Do you have any idea who'd want to kill her?"

Krista's expression changed. "No."

"Or why?"

"No." She checked her watch. "I really have to pick up my son."

She got up, suddenly seeming upset. He followed her to the front door. "Are you all right?"

"This is all very disturbing."

"Of course." Kirk handed her his card, telling her to contact him day or night if she thought of anything to help the investigation.

She nodded, looking as if she herself were under a threat.

CHAPTER 40

MORGAN

Nineteen years ago, November 1

I ACTUALLY HAD dozed off, and when I woke up the next morning, the screen was gone. My guess was that the remains of Lulu had also been removed.

Detective Jones had returned with more questions, although a lot were the same from the night before. I guess she was testing to see if our answers all agreed.

Richie again was scared and answered with nods and grunts. He said he was asleep the whole night and heard nothing and saw nothing until the police and firefighters came. Throughout the questioning my father held his hand, giving him squeezes to answer the questions since he was like totally numb.

Because of all that, we didn't go to school that day. I can only imagine all the buzz at St. B's. I wish I could have been there.

Outside, people in uniforms picked through the charred remains, putting things in baggies. I overheard the fire marshal explain to the detective that lab work would have to be done to determine if the residue was kerosene and not some other accelerant, which would tell them that the fire most likely started by accident. They would also try to determine the point of origin for the flame, such as the lamp. He asked my parents when the quart can of kerosene in the garage had been purchased and how much might have been used in the lamp by Lulu.

All throughout the questioning, my dad looked very jumpy. My mom was teary-eyed, especially when Detective Jones said she had managed to contact Lulu's brother who spoke a little English—her parents did not. She had told him the news about his sister's death. I guess he took it pretty hard. Her remains would be kept at the local funeral home, and a service at Saint Bonaventure's Church would be held when he could fly here. The parents wouldn't come, but they'd have a real burial at home when her remains went back with the brother.

Then the fire marshal questioned us, wanting to know what exactly was inside the treehouse besides Lulu. I hadn't been up there in a long while, but my father said she had a foam mattress pad, a sleeping bag, probably a few items of clothes, and an extra blanket. He asked what the sleeping bag was made of, and my parents didn't know. I think he wanted to know if it was something that wouldn't burn easily.

He also asked why my father had let her buy a kerosene lamp instead of a battery-powered one. That sounded like an accusation that made my father snap back.

"Because it was like what she used back home. We tried to talk her into a battery lamp, but she refused. She said she never left it burning at home, so we were convinced it was safe."

The fire marshal didn't like that answer. "Well, it was a tragic choice, especially given that it was used in an all-wooden treehouse and not some open-air campground."

"Look, I hear what you're saying, but it is what it is."

The fire marshal looked at my father blankly and nodded. "Whatever, she had a collection of flammable material, mostly paper stuff." In his hand were plastic sample bags containing a few pieces of charred remains.

My mom said that Lulu was a talented artist and may have had some sketch pads up there. She also loved to read so she had some paperbacks Mom had given to her and probably schoolbooks. The fire marshal said those must have contributed to the spread and intensity of the combustion. But she must have had a lot more like newspapers and magazines.

"There wasn't much left of them, but we found this."

He held up a plastic evidence bag containing the partially scorched cover of a catalogue from Victoria's Secret. I don't know where she had gotten that, but it wasn't from me or Mom, and definitely not Richie.

My father just shrugged. "She must have gotten it from the mall."

My mother glared at him with a look that said *Bullshit!*—that he had given that to her—his hot little Barbie Doll.

CHAPTER 41

"So this Ted Rizzo guy takes customers' money and runs, and just inside the law. And in the meantime, he's putting notches on his gun."

"Right." *And Olivia's the latest.*

"See why I married a woman?"

Kirk laughed. "Me too."

"The thing is that maybe you're becoming a little obsessed with this guy."

Mandy was right, but Kirk did not respond.

"I know this sounds like New Age bullshit, but happiness with one's life has to come from within. Some real passion that is all your own and not dependent upon others."

"But my real passion is Olivia."

"I understand, but for the time being you should seek out new things and new people." Then she added, "I speak from experience because it happened to me."

"What did?"

"We had a baby."

"I'm not planning on getting pregnant."

"No, but can I offer a suggestion?"

"No, but you're going to anyway."

"My cousin. She's recently divorced, and, as we guys would say, a real looker."

"And she's straight?"

"Very. I think you'd hit it off with each other."

"Okay. So what do you have in mind?"

"Something casual for the four of us, maybe a decent pizza place in town."

"I'll think about it."

"No you won't."

Kirk glared at her over his sunglasses. "I said I'll think about it."

"Right. Give me the word, and I'll make the rez."

After leaving Krista Saliba, Kirk and Mandy reconnoitered on the road from where he called Riley Malone to say he and his partner wanted to ask more questions critical to the investigation. She claimed she was on her way out, but he threatened sending a local squad car to bring her in. She conceded.

When they arrived, Riley Malone was loading a suitcase into the trunk of her car. She slammed closed the trunk and led them inside. All the clutter was gone.

"Are you going someplace?"

The question surprised Riley. "Eventually. My cousin's in Vermont."

"Glad we caught you," Kirk said. "We have some more questions about Vadima Lupescu."

Her face tensed up again. "I told all I knew to the police nineteen years ago and told you the other day. I don't know anything else. Nothing."

"Fine, but we spoke with Morgan Cassidy who said that she'd witnessed her father entering the bedroom of Vadima Lupescu one night. Is that something you knew about?"

Riley's left eye began twitching. "Yes."

"But in the original police report of her death, there was nothing about Mr. Bolt having sexually abused Vadima."

"Because I was scared and confused. We all were."

"Scared and confused over what?"

"The police and all the questioning. But I also thought she hexed him to have sex with her. I told you we were kids and had crazy thoughts, okay? So I didn't say anything because I didn't know what had happened between them."

Mandy leaned toward her. "I can appreciate that. But according to Morgan, her father had extorted her into having sex, threatening to send her back to Slovakia. Looking back, does that seem credible to you?"

"Yeah, I guess. I remember him being taken by her, you know, giving her hugs and telling her how he liked her outfit or the way she did her hair, especially when she wore it in pigtails."

"Pigtails?"

"Because they made her look younger." Then she added, "He said they looked like handles, you know, likes reins for a horse."

Pigtails! Kirk had a flash of Bolt and his current baby-faced girlfriend Siena Martinez.

Mandy nodded, as if confirming Bolt's pedophilic tastes. "Right. So, how about with the rest of you girls?"

Kirk knew where Mandy was going with this.

"Yeah, sometimes. Back then Sylvie had a great figure, and a couple of times he told her that she looked 'hot'—his word."

"Too bad there wasn't a MeToo Movement back then," Mandy said.

Kirk cut in. "Do you think Mrs. Bolt suspected he had something going on with her?"

Riley made a half-shrug. "I don't know."

Despite their oaths to keep the public safe, there were times when Kirk understood a cop's urge to plant evidence on some creep you knew was guilty of nasty crimes—all to ensure a verdict in court. Yes, it was police corruption—like Mandy's grandfather. But the more he learned about Jordan Bolt, the more he understood the urge.

Riley checked her watch, looking anxious for this to be over. So Kirk moved in. "Ms. Malone, can you think of anyone who wanted to harm Sylvie Thornton?"

The first time Kirk had questioned her, she had not known that Sylvie Thornton's death was being investigated as a possible homicide, and that no connection had been offered between her death and that of the Lupescu girl. Riley Malone had settled on suicide. So the question forged an ominous link. And her expression rippled with what looked like fear.

"What? I thought Sylvie, you know, took her own life."

"Well, things have developed, and we've got reason to believe that Sylvie Thornton was murdered because she knew something about the death of Vadima Lupescu—that it may have been the result of foul play."

"No, I can't think of anyone who'd want to harm her. She was a wonderful person." Riley kept wringing her fingers as if they were fiery with hives.

"Then can you think of anything that Sylvie knew about Vadima that would have led someone to kill her?"

"No."

Suddenly her expression shifted from fear to a polished innocence—an expression Kirk knew from countless interviews, when persons of interest convinced themselves that they didn't have a clue because they hadn't witnessed anything suspicious. But

Kirk hitched his eyebrow and bore down on her until she cocked her head on a second thought.

"Well, I mean some people were upset when Justine died, you know, thinking that she'd put a curse on her. But no one would have gone so far to, you know, set the treehouse on fire."

"What about Justine's boyfriend, Grayson Gallagher?"

"God no. He was devastated, plus he was just too religious to do something like that. I mean, he's a monk for God's sake, a holy man."

So were a few hundred pedophile priests. "Right. Then can you think of anything about the night that Vadima died that would have led someone to murder Sylvie?"

"I don't know what you mean?"

"Do you think Sylvie knew who might have killed Vadima?"

Riley's mouth began twitching again. "I don't know."

"As you can tell, we're trying to determine who might have had a motive to kill her and silence Sylvie."

"But after so many years?"

"Right, and that's the million-dollar question. Nonetheless, let's keep the deaths separate. Do you think if she had known about Jordan Bolt's sexual tryst with Vadima that Mrs. Bolt could have killed her?"

Riley made a smirking humpf. "I think she would have killed him first. I mean Sally Bolt was a strong woman with a lot of pride, but he pushed her, constantly needling and shaming her about her weight—calling her names, Miss Piggy and Butterball, saying how she let herself go, and how being fat was bad for his business. I hated being there when he did that."

"But she did eventually divorce him."

"Yeah, and it would have been sooner, but she wanted to wait for Richie's sake."

"So you don't think she had enough reason to have killed Vadima."

"No."

"What about you?" Kirk said.

"Huh?"

Kirk looked at his notes. "We understand that you and your family harbored contempt for immigrants and that you were suspended for beating up a refugee Somali girl because you claimed they cannibalized Christian babies?"

She gaped at him. "For God's sake, I was an impressionable kid full of weird ideas. I didn't know any better and I did some things I regret. But I didn't kill Vadima."

Mandy glared at her. "Riley, there are reports that your parents were members of some right-wing anti-immigration groups that lobbied local officials to reject all foreigners, especially from Eastern Europe and the Middle East."

"Yeah, and I was influenced by them, but that doesn't mean I killed her, okay?" She stood up. "Look, I told you all I know. I really have to go."

"Fine," Kirk said.

She moved to the door and opened it for them, her mouth twitching for them to leave.

Kirk handed her his card.

"If you think of anything at all, don't hesitate to call."

She nodded and snap-closed the door behind them.

CHAPTER 42

"WHY DOES MY gut say she's hiding something?" Mandy said as they headed toward the car.

"Probably because she is."

"You think she killed Vadima?"

"She may have believed the girl was a witch, but I don't see her killing her or Sylvie Thornton." The woman weighed no more than a hundred pounds and was an anxious wreck. Kirk could not imagine her planning and executing such an elaborate murder. When they settled in the car, Kirk said, "I think she's scared."

"Of being a suspect?"

"No, of being next. As soon as it sunk in that Sylvie may have been killed for what she knew, it was like the flick of a switch. She couldn't wait for us to go. Probably why she's heading for Vermont."

"But what about her beating up the Somali girl?"

"Like she said, we all did stupid things as kids." Kirk pulled the car down the road toward the highway.

After a few minutes, Mandy said, "I once beat up a boy because he called me a lesbo freak in class."

Kirk gave her a glance. "Would you say that helped your decision to become a cop—getting back at bigots and bullies?"

"Getting back at men who commit violence against women because they're women."

He heard a hitch in her voice. A moment of silence passed as he sensed there was more. "I'm listening."

She took in a centering breath. "First of all, I'm not a dyed-in-the-wool man-hating lesbian," she said. "But a woman is killed by a man every three days. It's so fucking common, there's a goddamn term for it: *femicide*. Killed because of her gender. Twenty-six hundred women were murdered by men last year. One in four teenage girls have been sexually violated."

"Right, and it's appalling."

"And the consequences are devastating. *Devastating!* Women are either killed by men or left with physical and mental scars, which can lead to suicide."

"So, you view police work for yourself as a fight for human rights, especially women's."

"Yeah, and maybe at the time I was too idealistic, but I wanted to make a difference, especially for women."

Kirk was impressed with her determination in what was traditionally a man's arena, especially being a woman married to another woman. "I have to say, I respect that."

"It was also personal. My mother was raped as a girl."

"Oh no."

"At summer camp. A twenty-four-year-old counselor lured her into the woods and fed her a cocktail of wine and ketamine—what forensics found in his water bottle. She passed out, and he stripped her down, forced himself into her, put her clothes back on her when he was done, and then took off. When she finally came to, she had blood running down her legs."

Kirk let out a soft groan. "How did they get him?"

"Witnesses saw him disappear with her. When she didn't return, a search party found her still unconscious. All she remembered was going into the woods with him, supposedly to show her an owl's nest. Prints confirmed it was that bastard."

"So they got him on premeditated."

"Yeah. First degree felony because she was under age—fifteen years old. Fifteen! A girl!" The word stuck in her throat, and Kirk could see her mind drift back to that moment.

"He got seven years in Concord; and she got life in trauma, pain, guilt, depression, and self-abuse."

"I'm so sorry."

"So am I. And it only got worse," Mandy continued. "She became pregnant, and because her parents were religious, they refused her getting an abortion and arranged to send the baby to a Catholic orphanage where they had adoptive parents lined up. But because it was a preemie with medical issues, the couple couldn't claim the baby until the hospital could release her from the neonatal ICU, which took months. In the meantime, my mother's father had made her sign the relinquishment document under duress. Her sister, who was older, got her a lawyer and managed to get a judge to reverse custody to her. So she got her baby back."

"That's good news. So what happened to the baby?"

"She became a cop." She turned her face out the side window and wiped her eyes.

Kirk let a few moments pass in a hushed silence. "And how did you learn all this?"

"My grandmother—even though my mother made her swear never to tell."

"Did you ever learn who your father was?"

"Eventually, but I never met him. After two years in prison, he hanged himself."

"One bit of justice."

"Only from the outside," Mandy said, fighting tears. "Besides being a traumatic mess, that only added to her guilt—you know, because I was born, he killed himself. Whatever, she dropped out of school, suffered depression and PTS, had continuing nightmares, saw a lot of shrinks. Then her father died of a stroke, which only made things worse. Long sad story short, she turned to alcohol and opioids just to cope, and was in and out of rehab, all while trying to raise me on days off. My grandmother did most of that."

"That must have been horrible for you."

"Yeah, pretty bad. By the time I learned what rape was, I was filled with rage at what had happened to her and sadness because she was too fucked up to be a mother."

Kirk reached over, took Mandy's hand, and gave a squeeze. "I'm so sorry."

Tears coursed freely from her eyes. "The thing is, that son of a bitch robbed her of a happy, healthy life, of plans of going to college, of wanting to be a nurse. But she'd suffered such pain, such guilt, such self-doubt and hatred that she couldn't go through a day feeling normal—without booze and pills.

"She didn't even enjoy motherhood, and I never knew the kind of mother she would have been if that hadn't happened to her. So my fucking biological father had robbed her of her soul and me of my mother."

After a long, sad silence, Kirk asked, "When did she die?"

"When I turned thirteen. She OD'd and became just one more opioid stat."

"Jesus," he whispered.

They drove in heavy silence for a mile or so when she made a wry chuckle. "So that's how I became a cop. I couldn't go back and wipe out her suffering, nor make her a better life, so I joined the academy. To bring justice to men who do that to women."

She made a dismissive shake of her head as if shaking off the subject. "So, what about you?"

Kirk thought a moment. "Well, I was an English major and wanted to be a teacher. Maybe high school, maybe go all the way. But my roommate was a CJ major and that sounded more interesting. You know, courses in criminal psychology."

"So what made you become a cop?"

"I'm still trying to remember."

Two years ago, while still recovering from the death of Megan, Kirk had asked for a medical leave after a case. He and his partner, Artie Stamos, were called to a home in Cambridge where an Army vet had barricaded himself in the home of strangers after having shot a woman, her mother, and her twelve-year-old daughter. He had even killed the family dog. Later he claimed that he was following orders from God. After a shoot-out with police, the killer surrendered but had left Artie Stamos wounded in the thigh.

Kirk vividly remembered entering the house to face nightmarish horrors—floor puddled with blood and walls splashed with brain matter of the victims, including the young girl who was still alive but hemorrhaging from her abdomen and mouth where a bullet had torn through her cheeks. Kirk would never be able to unsee that girl dying against the body of her mother whose chest had been blown open.

No matter how mentally sick he was, the killer was the incarnation of evil and criminally liable and, to Kirk's mind, did not deserve to exist. And Kirk would have been willing to make that happen. But the courts sentenced the killer to three counts of first-degree murder, so he would spend the rest of his miserable life in prison.

However, Kirk would for months suffer near-suicidal trauma, exacerbated by the death of Megan and the breakdown of his marriage. He had reached dangerous burnout and was at the risk of suicide or homicide. He had no immediate support group since he was not religious. Olivia and he had drifted apart, and his only friends were other police officers who also suffered cumulative trauma and shared the same grim view of humanity. So he'd spent months in professional therapy until it was either return to the force or die of PTSD-induced depression. What got him back was a forced renewal of the need of his service to society, encouraged by the constant entreaties of his captain.

"But you must get some satisfaction from the job."

"Yeah, catching bad guys."

"And what do you not like about the job?"

"Ending up like them."

"You mean a criminal?"

"No, less human."

"'A mind of winter.'"

Kirk nodded. "In a phrase."

They rode for a few more miles, each lost in thought. Mandy finally broke the spell. "I know how ridiculous this may sound, but you know what you need?"

"What do I need?"

"What you need is a date."

What I need is my wife. "Maybe."

"Really, just get back into doing normal social things. And I have just the person in mind."

"Your cousin."

"Right."

Kirk's phone chimed. It was Sergeant Kevin Fujita.

When he got off the phone, he looked over to Mandy. "This will pick up your spirit. Three years ago, Jordan Bolt was caught in a sting operation. He responded to an ad placed on Craigslist proposing a sexual encounter with a fifteen-year-old girl for money. When he showed up at the rendezvous, he was arrested. He could have been slapped with a felony and put away for years, but unfortunately high-priced lawyers got him off on a misdemeanor."

"How come?"

"Technicality. By law police can't specify the girl's age in a sting ad."

"But it's on his record, right?"

"Right, and some justice there. But he's off our list of possible perps."

"What the fuck are we missing here?"

They were quiet for a while. After a few minutes, Kirk said, "Call Kevin and find the street address for Richard Bolt."

CHAPTER 43

ACCORDING TO THE Jones report, Richard Bolt slept through the fire and all the commotion. Detective Jemma Jones herself had questioned him and noted that he was scared and burst into tears when he saw the charred remains of the treehouse. He was barely able to respond to her questions, saying he heard and saw nothing.

"And you're wondering if a ten-year-old set fire to the treehouse?" Mandy said.

"Yes."

The possibility was difficult to get his mind around, not just because of his age but because all indications were that Richard Bolt had liked the girl, that he had spent time in the treehouse with her as she would tell him stories about living on a farm with lots of animals. She also gave him drawing lessons.

"Because he was crazy about his father and may have known about him and Vadima and worried that he'd get in trouble if the mother found out."

"That's the difficult part," Kirk said. "Would a ten-year-old pick up on his father's sexual interest in another female? At that age, a kid isn't even sexually aware of himself."

"Maybe he believed all the talk about her being a witch and he wanted to save the family. Plus, it was Halloween."

And a night crazy with mischief. "Maybe."

They found Richard Bolt later that same day at the Portsmouth Public Library where he was head librarian.

The woman at the circulation desk directed them to his office on the second floor. Bolt did not overreact when they identified themselves, maybe because two other staffers were in the room, or maybe because he had expected them.

Kirk suggested they go outside to talk privately, and Bolt slipped on a hoodie.

"What's this all about?" he asked as the three of them headed down the stairs.

"The death of Sylvie Thornton."

"Oh."

Just "*Oh.*" Kirk filed it away. Possibly another clue that he had expected their visit.

Now thirty years old, Richard Bolt was a stocky man dressed in chinos and a white shirt and tie. He was tall like his father but outsized and balding. He also had a stubby ponytail that stuck out of the back of his head like a small geyser.

He led them out a rear door to a grassy area with scattered picnic tables for patrons to relax with lunch and reading material. Because it was sunny and a comfortably mild fall day, a few people sat at tables with light outerwear. Bolt led them to an empty some distance from the others.

"Mind if I smoke?" he asked.

"No, go right ahead," Mandy said. And Kirk nodded.

"I've been trying to cut down."

"Have you tried the patch?" Mandy said. "It got me off the habit."

"I'm wearing one, at the behest of my wife. We have a young son, so I don't smoke at home. But I've cut down, so it's helping." He lit up and took a few puffs. "I was shocked and saddened when I heard about Sylvie."

He looked away for a moment. "I knew her when she hung out with my sister, Morgan, when we were young. She was a nice girl and was always friendly and taught me some card tricks that I'm passing on to my son."

"I'm sure you have nice memories of her," Mandy said. "So this may be shocking to hear, but we have evidence that suggests she was murdered."

He nodded. "That's horrible."

"Your reaction suggests that you've heard."

"Yes, I did, from my sister. She came up last week for my son's birthday."

"Then you probably heard that we're working on the possibility that Sylvie's death may be related to the death of Vadima Lupescu."

He blew a plume of smoke to the side. "Yes, although I can't imagine what the connection might be."

From her jacket Mandy brought out the photocopy of the tip note to the Lexington PD—that Vadima Lupescu was murdered. "Any idea who sent this?"

He glanced at it for a moment then looked away and shook his head. "No idea."

"Right," Kirk said. "So can you think of anyone who would have wanted to harm Sylvie?"

"No, but like I said, I haven't seen her in years."

"It's a routine question," Kirk said, "but can you tell us where you were on the morning of November six?"

Bolt pulled his cellphone out of his jacket pocket and punched a few keys to check his calendar. "That was a Saturday. I was here. We have children's hour at ten."

They would confirm that inside. "Right," Kirk said. "Let's go back to that Halloween night nineteen years ago. Tell us what you remember—anything at all."

Bolt took a drag on his cigarette and let out a weary sigh. "I was ten years old at the time, and it should be in the report that I remembered nothing. My father had taken me around the neighborhood trick-or-treating with a few other kids, and we were back shortly after dark. My sister and a bunch of her friends sat out back, then around nine o'clock, Morgan sent me to bed."

"And where were your parents?"

"They went out with friends to a restaurant."

"After going to bed, what do you remember?"

"Nothing. I fell right to sleep until my parents woke me." He took another deep drag from his cigarette and dropped it on the ground and stepped on it. "I'm sure it's all in the police report from back then. Hopefully, it still exists."

"It does. And it says that you had a nightmare about witches."

His face scrunched up as if dimly recalling that. "I guess I did. I mean it *was* Halloween after all."

"Right. But you may also have been present outside when Morgan and her friends held a little ritual at the fire pit."

"What little ritual?"

"According to some of the women who were present back then, they conducted some kind of effigy-burning exorcism of Vadima because they believed she was a witch. I'm wondering if you may have witnessed that."

"I know nothing about that."

"What about the fact that those kids believed that Vadima was a witch?"

He punched another cigarette out of the pack. "I remember nothing about that either. Keep in mind, I was ten at the time and Morgan was sixteen and shared nothing of her personal life with me. Teenagers don't do that. We had our own friends and did our own things."

That may be true, but something told Kirk that Bolt was saying what he wanted them to believe. "Is it possible you eavesdropped on them before going to bed?"

He lit the new cigarette and inhaled deeply. "It didn't happen. I went straight to bed. As I said, I wasn't interested in sixteen-year-old girl gossip."

Mandy cleared her throat. "Mr. Bolt, can you think of anyone who would have wanted Vadima dead?"

He coughed on his smoke. "No. She was a kind and gentle girl everyone seemed to like."

Kirk kept reminding himself of what Jemma Jones said: That Richard Bolt adored his father. "Not everyone."

"Well, so you believe," he said with an undertone of discomfort.

Mandy cleared her throat. "Do you think your father had anything to do with Vadima's death?"

Bolt snapped his head around to face her. "What?"

"Let me reword that," Mandy said. "Do you think your father set fire to the treehouse with Vadima in it?"

"God Almighty, no. And how can you even think that?"

"Because according to Morgan, your father had sex with Vadima Lupescu—that she had seen him sneak into Vadima's room one night and take sexual advantage of her."

"That's outrageous. Simply outrageous." He stamped out his cigarette under his foot and stood up to leave.

"Why are you leaving?" Mandy asked.

"Because this interrogation is over."

Before he stepped away, Kirk handed him a card. "If you think of anything helpful."

He snapped the card out of his hand, turned on his heel, and headed into the library.

They watched him pass through the door they had exited. "Well, that worked out nicely," Kirk said with a grin.

Mandy removed an evidence baggie from her jacket pocket and with a pair of tweezers retrieved Richard Bolt's cigarette butts.

"As we English majors would say, 'All's well that ends well.'"

CHAPTER 44

MORGAN

Nineteen years ago, November 3

I COULD HARDLY forget the day that the whole school turned out for Vadima's Funeral Mass. Just the Mass. There would be no long, slow caravan to the cemetery across town because her remains would be sent back to Slovakia once members of her family arrived to claim them. Arrangements for their arrival were still being made. I mean, her family lived on a pig farm in the middle of Nowhere, Slovakia. I'd heard that the only member of her family who could make it here was her brother—Milosh.

Also there were Detective Jemma Jones, the fire marshal, and a few first responders, two police officers in uniforms, and one of the EMTs I'd recognized.

Richie didn't go because Mom thought he was too young to be exposed to death, especially one so unpleasant. So, that morning he stayed home with a babysitter.

My mom and father sat with me in the front pew because we were like family, my mother had said. Behind us sat Sylvie, Riley, and Krista with their families. Milosh sat in the front pew across the aisle with another priest and some people I didn't recognize.

Milosh cried throughout the whole service, occasionally glancing our way and shaking his head, maybe disbelief, maybe disapproval. At the time I didn't care. And he spoke little English, so it made no difference what he was communicating.

Father de Souza conducted the service, of course. He did his usual good somber job, personalizing the sermon, holding forth on how Vadima was an intelligent and friendly girl who felt blessed to be studying in America. How she was compassionate and a talented young artist who sometimes sketched a few of us during Mass, catching one or two of the congregation dozing off. That produced some welcome chuckles. "But I suppose that was better than dozing off herself."

He went on for a while, saying what the cop had said the other night—that it was such a tragedy to lose a beautiful and talented young woman. If she weren't gorgeous and talented, would he have said, "Such a tragedy to lose a homely and ungifted young woman?" And what if it were me: a large, plain, mediocre young woman?

The thought flashed through my mind that maybe Father de Souza may have been turned on by her too.

After the service, I saw the brother talking intensely to the detective and another police officer through an interpreter. He looked very upset, more angry than mournful. He also kept looking our way. He was introduced to us, but he began sobbing in my mother's arms and eventually walked off with Detective Jones and a man from the funeral home to identify Vadima's remains, what there was of them.

After the service, we all reconnoitered in front of the church. Of course, the whole gang grouped together—Sylvie, Riley, Krista, Gee Gee, Timmy D., and the rest—all hugging and crying. We were all pretty numb with disbelief.

I hugged Gee Gee and whispered, "How are you doing?"

He nodded. "Getting tired of going to funerals."

"Of course." How could he not be reminded of Justine? How could this not make him miss her all the more?

Riley, always a nervous wreck, was convinced that Lulu's death was nothing less than divine intervention—that God himself had brought on retribution for her practicing sorcery. "Reverend de Souza says the Holy Bible forbids sorcery and the casting of spells. And that's what she did, right?"

She addressed that to Gee Gee who didn't respond, just looked away, like his mind was someplace else.

"I mean, he said that Satan uses witchcraft to distract people from worshipping God and that those who practice black magic are idolaters and they will be sent to the fiery lake."

Krista scoffed. "Come on, Rile. That doesn't mean God zapped her the other night."

Riley was incensed. "You don't believe me? You saw what happened at the party at Riley's house. She looked at Justine's hand and suddenly freaked out and left. She saw that she was going to die, because she made that happen. She cursed her and we were right there. She was doing divination—reading the future—and the Bible says diviners and witches should be killed. Right, Gee Gee? Doesn't it say that? What you quoted the other day?"

He was the biggest Bible student among us, quoting heavy-duty passages all the time. "*Exodus* twenty-two—'Thou shall not suffer a witch to live,'" he said in a voice devoid of inflection. And he fingered the gold crucifix Justine had given him for his birthday.

"See?" Riley said.

"She died by accident," Krista insisted. "She was drunk and doped up and probably forgot to turn off the lamp and maybe kicked it over in her sleep."

"Or maybe she did it herself," I suggested. "Maybe she realized she *was* a witch and did bad things and decided she deserved to die." I turned to Gee Gee. "Don't you think that's possible?"

He shrugged. "It's possible. One way or the other, she's still burning." Then he walked away, leaving us wondering at his statement.

My parents broke away from some teachers and neighbors and came over to us. My mother's eyes were swollen red with tears she kept wiping on Kleenex. She gave me a hug even though I could not cry.

"All I can think of is her family getting that call." Apparently, the police detective made that call the other day. "A beautiful, lovely girl . . . and now she's dead."

My mom sobbed because she was genuinely horrified by the girl's death, even more so than for Justine who officially had died because of some weird medical anomaly. Not only had Vadima been a guest in our house, she had been like a temporary daughter. Mom also went on about how she had died—"So cruel, so hideous," she had said, sobbing.

While we stood there, my father turned to me. "Is everything okay?"

I gave him a frigid look. "What?"

"I mean, you don't seem very upset."

He always claimed I was a "cool one."

"I am upset," I snapped—but it wasn't about Vadima.

I could barely look at him. So when the crowd of mourners drifted away to their cars, I took the opportunity to tell my parents that I was going to the center with the other kids and that I'd walk home. Because of the babysitter for Richie, they had to leave.

I drifted away, but my father followed me. "Hey, Morgan, are you all right?" He made an effort to give me a hug, but I yanked away.

"I'm fine."

He kept pace with me, and I could feel him tense up. "Hey, what's the problem?" he said. "Is everything all right—I mean besides all this?"

I kept walking until we were out of earshot of everybody else, stopped dead, and turned full-face to him. "I watched you in church crying big crocodile tears and making a show as if you lost your own kid instead of your sexmate."

"What?"

"And then outside you're grabbing everyone's hand and making big showy hugs, thanking them for their condolences, gladhanding and chuckling it up with your clients from the club, as if you were at a party. And you know why? Because you're relieved she's dead."

"What the hell are you talking about?"

I wanted to stop myself but couldn't. I reached into my jacket pocket and pulled out Vadima's sketch of them naked and in bed and flapped it in his face.

"What the hell's this?"

"She drew you having sex the night you went into her room and didn't come out for a fucking half hour. Yeah, *fucking* half hour. I heard you. And now she's dead, and you're off the hook."

"Off the hook of what?"

"Of being a pedophile. And I know she would have told people. And you would have been arrested, and sent to jail, and the club and your reputation would have gone down the toilet. And you know what else? Mom would have divorced you like that."

He was stunned speechless, his mouth moving as if trying to find the right words to conjure up. He nodded at the drawing. "This is just a fantasy of hers. I mean . . ."

"Bull! I saw you go in there. I heard you groaning. And you know what else? You would've ruined us—me, Richie, and Mom."

I turned to stomp away and saw my mother in the shadows of the awning under Dot's Donuts. She had heard everything.

CHAPTER 45

MANDY ARRANGED IT so that she'd sit next to her cousin Carol Dean while Mandy's wife, Susan, sat next to Kirk so that Carol and he would face each other in the booth.

She also picked the restaurant, Santarpio's Pizzeria in East Boston. As Mandy had promised, Carol was attractive and a lively conversationalist. Perhaps too lively. She was a senior administrator in the HR department of Boston University and was not shy or circumspect. She was forty-two years old, four years divorced, and the mother of a six-year-old boy. And Mandy was right: he could smell the Magie Noire—what Sylvie Thornton had worn to her death.

This was the first first-date Kirk had had since December 6 twenty-three years ago when he had taken Olivia to Blue Hills to ski. They had been with each other exclusively ever since. And he was not comfortable.

They had ordered beers first and would hold on the pizza until they had a few minutes to study the menu.

"You must have a picture of her," Carol declared, having asked about Olivia for the last several minutes as if she were doing a biography.

Kirk did not want to talk about Olivia, but some prideful impulse made him flash a favorite shot of her on his cellphone, one of the hundreds he had of her in digital albums going back years. He held up the photo of her in the white linen dress she wore last summer at a restaurant near where they vacationed in Martha's Vineyard. The one that reminded him of Frank Sinatra's rendition of "The Way You Look Tonight."

"Wow! She looks like a fashion model."

Kirk nodded.

"So do you."

He made a flat smile, taking a sip of his beer and wanting to go home.

This woman was pleasant enough, except she didn't catch on that he did not want to talk about Olivia or their separation. But she was relentless.

"So, she's a beautiful college professor and no doubt brainy and tenured at one of the most prestigious universities in Boston, and you're still pining for her."

He said nothing yet but felt irritated that she was attempting to striptease his psyche.

"I can understand that as she was a source of stability following the death of your child. Mandy told me. I'm so sorry, and being a mother myself, I can't imagine what that must be like."

Kirk took a sip of beer and flashed a nonplussed glance at Mandy who gave him an embarrassed eyeroll.

"So what pulled you apart? I mean, why did she leave?"

"Are you writing a journal article or something?"

"Pardon me?"

"You've not stopped asking me about what's going on between me and my wife."

Carol's glare sharpened. "I'm just wondering what Olivia sees the separation doing for her and you."

"I think it might be a more successful evening if we changed the subject."

Mandy piped in. "I agree." And Susan nodded. "Did any of you catch the latest episode of *Succession*?"

But nobody paid her attention. "To answer your question," Kirk said, "she left to give herself relief from all that had transpired." He said that with a tone of civility, hoping Carol would catch the hint and maybe talk about TV, football, or the best Medicare Advantage plans.

"Fair enough, but look, I'm trying to understand why we're here."

He looked at Mandy, thinking, What the hell did you tell her? "What do you mean?"

"Why are we on a date?"

"To get me out of the house, and maybe you also," Kirk said with an ingratiating smile.

Carol nodded. "Yeah, to get you to socialize again."

"Something like that."

With her ears bright with embarrassment, Mandy glanced at the menu. "What do you all like on your pizza?"

"Mushroom and onions," Susan said.

"Yeah, yeah, that's fine," Carol said with a flick of her hand.

She probably would have given the same dismissive answer had Susan suggested roadkill. "I like pepperoni if that's not too offensive," Kirk said.

"Fine. We can get two smalls," Mandy said, and waved over the waiter.

The waiter took the order and left.

Kirk took another tired swallow of beer. If he were home right now, he could be watching the Patriots face off with Miami.

Carol was back at it. "So you're saying that this really isn't a date but some kind of therapy for you."

"How is this pizza-and-beer therapy?"

"To help you decide if you really want to play the field or want your wife back again."

"I've already decided, and Mandy should have told you: I want my wife back, but this gets me out of the house in the meantime."

"Oh, so you're putting the rap on her."

"How am I doing that?"

"By sitting back and waiting."

"As opposed to what?"

"As opposed to changing your ways so that she feels like going back home to you?"

"Is this pizza-and-beer or *Doctor Phil*? Why do you want to know about me and my wife?"

"Because you're not being honest with yourself. You really don't want this date with me or anyone else. What you really want is to get back to being married. So the real question is what are we doing here?"

Jesus! "Having pizza and beer."

"No. Mandy said you were separated and that it may be permanent. But all I'm hearing is you not willing to give up on Olivia. I think maybe you're not ready to be back in the field. You've been separated for only three months, and you're no way near settled even on the trial separation."

"Look," Kirk said, feeling his IQ begin to drop, "this was billed as a simple casual social engagement, a way to get out of the house, not to getting back in the field as you put it."

"Then it was mis-billed. This was a getting-to-know-you between two people, one burned by divorce, the other on his way. Frankly, you're simply not there yet. In fact, I think you're just spinning your wheels in the field until she comes back to you. And I can't say I blame you. From what I hear, she's a Golden Girl. And if she's in the field, I'm sure there's a pack of guys with hearts full of hope yipping at her heels, like all those suitors after Penelope while Ulysses is gone. Yeah, I was an English major too."

Mandy and her wife, Susan, sat there stupefied as if watching some weird game show.

"So what do we do?"

"Finish the beer and tell the waiter to cancel the order since you're still holding the torch for her."

"I don't fucking believe this," Mandy said.

"No, I'm starving," Susan cried. "You two do what you want; I'm staying."

Kirk did not move, amused at the turn of events. But Carol was incensed. She leaned down toward him. "If you want a piece of advice, get some therapy, find a friend you can lean on, and get a dog. Then maybe your wife will see you've changed and come back."

Kirk nodded. "Gee, sounds like a plan."

"By the way, remember how that Ulysses poem by Tennyson ends? 'Made weak by time and fate, but strong in will / To strive, to seek, to find, and not to yield.' Good luck," she said and walked away.

Kirk took another swallow of beer. "You didn't tell me she was a frustrated marriage counselor."

"Sorry about that, but she does tend to be a tad nosy."

"Nosy doesn't come close," Susan said. "She was like pecking for blood."

"She wanted a real date, and I wasn't it. But she did strike a chord."

"She did? Like what?" Mandy asked.

"To turn over a new leaf."

"Huh?"

Kirk took out his cellphone and spent the next several minutes punching keys. By the time he was done, the pizzas arrived.

"What was that all about?"

"Tell Carol thank you," Kirk said. "I just re-upped my gym membership."

CHAPTER 46

Saint Julian's Monastery was a large fieldstone structure with a high tower capped by a belfry and sitting in the midst of open fields of grass rising to the distant Metacomet range of hills. White clouds puffed against a blue sky turning the place into a medieval postcard.

Here and there monks chatted with tourists or sat on benches under trees or pruned shrubbery. They all were dressed in white robes with black cowls.

Kirk and Mandy entered the visitors' lobby and asked to speak to Brother Grayson Gallagher. A few minutes later, the man emerged from down a long hallway. Kirk recognized him from the Funeral Mass for Sylvie Thornton. He explained that they wanted to talk to him about her death.

Gallagher nodded and led them to a small chapel with stained glass windows and plain wooden pews. On the rear wall under polychrome altar glass hung a crucifix. Kirk noticed that Brother Grayson Gallagher crossed himself with his left hand. He took to the front row and Kirk and Mandy sat in the pew behind him.

He was average height, maybe five-ten, and slender. But even in his robe he had a width of shoulders that suggested he had spent time at physical labor. From what Kirk had read, the Justinians were famous for their gardens from which they harvested products for their breads, jams, and other foodstuff that they sold to tourists.

"Outside of immediate family, you're one person who knew her best."

"But only as teenagers. Back then she was a dear friend. Once I joined the brotherhood, I pretty much receded from the social world. Yes, we exchanged holiday cards, but we saw each other infrequently."

He had a simpatico face with large soft eyes behind wire-rimmed glasses—the kind of eyes that could project solace and empathy for those who mourn, the kind that could look with reverence at the pages of scriptures as he could the flowers and vegetables in his garden—the kind of eyes that perhaps glimpsed signs of the other world. "When was the last time you saw Sylvie?"

"About three weeks ago when I passed through Boston to visit my father."

Kirk nodded, recalling the bottle of Saint Julian's beer on Sylvie's kitchen shelf, and the autopsy report of fruited muffin remains in her stomach—like the kinds of baked goods from the monastery ovens. If he had visited Sylvie Thornton three weeks ago, those muffins could have been frozen until the morning she died.

"How did she seem?"

"She seemed fine. She was happy to see me and told me about the community project she was working on. We had a lovely lunch and chatted about this and that."

"Did she seem distracted or anxious about anything?"

"Distracted, maybe, because she was busy with so many things. But anxious? Nothing I detected."

Kirk nodded and jotted notes. "If you don't mind, we're obligated in an investigation to ask everyone their whereabouts at the time of a victim's death, which was November six."

He had anticipated the question. "Of course. I was visiting my father at Bayside Nursing Home in Plymouth."

"Do you recall the approximate time you arrived and left your father?"

"It was around five o'clock the afternoon of the fifth and left around seven thirty when visiting hours were over."

"Did you return to the monastery?"

"No, I overnighted at a parish house of Saint Katherine's nearby. I think I left a little after five the next morning."

According to Saint Julian's website, the brothers rose around five to meet Morning Prayer at five thirty. So that seemed about right. Plus, an early start to avoid Sunday traffic. "And what was your means of transportation?"

He smiled at the question. "Contrary to what people may think, we do get out once in a while," he said. "The monastery actually owns a couple of vehicles, which the brothers use for business or if we're visiting a parish or giving retreats. So I drove."

Kirk nodded. "Right." If he left at five a.m., he could have made it to the Thornton woman's house in Cambridge by seven. "And did you drive directly back here?"

"Well, no, I stopped by the nursing home to check up on my father before heading back, which was just before breakfast was served."

Kirk was good at gauging people's manner, but he could not determine if Gallagher was responding normally or with calculated holy-man compliance.

"About what time was that?"

"Oh, I'd say seven or seven thirty."

If true, he would not have made it to Lexington until around nine, maybe later if he hit traffic. Too late to kill Sylvie, he thought with relief. But, of course, that would be checked.

"So, how long have you been a brother?" Mandy asked.

"Actually, more than half my life."

"I don't think I ever met a monk before."

He smiled. "I hadn't either until I came here as a boy with my parents. But years later, Saint Bonaventure brought us out here on a field trip, and it changed my life."

"How was that?"

"Well, I was walking outside and took a detour to a solitary sundial in the middle of the grass with the chapel in the distance. I looked up at the sky and felt God's presence. It wasn't like anything material was there, just a click, and I knew God was with me."

Mandy nodded in fascination. "So what made you actually join the order?"

"My mother died suddenly as I was about to enter medical school, and that proved very difficult for me. We were very close, and I needed counseling. Our priest at the time suggested I find inner peace and recommended a Catholic retreat in Connecticut. After several months, I'd decided that the spiritual life was for me. So I returned to Saint Julian's and I've been here ever since."

"And you clearly enjoy it."

"*Enjoy* in a deeper sense than the ordinary meaning. Compared to life in the real world, the life of the spirit is austere, isolating, and full of hard work. But the prayerful life is deeply satisfying. We live simple but balanced lives of liturgy, prayer, gardening, domestic basics—all that move us closer to Jesus Christ. It is what makes us happy, preserving a life that is 'ordinary, obscure and laborious' as is written in the Order's constitutions."

How unlike his own life, Kirk thought. Over twenty years under a badge and he still had to labor to preserve his humanity, to compartmentalize the dangers and horrors he faced nearly every day—what monstrous things humans do to humans—bodies blown in half by shotguns over a drug deal gone wrong, a husband killing his wife and kids then himself because he's lost his job with endless bills. So far from inner peace and Jesus.

"Can you think of anyone who would have wanted to harm Sylvie?"

"Absolutely not. In fact, I question that her death was foul play."

"Based on what?"

"I think Sylvie was so badly scarred by the death of Devon that she never recovered. I've known parents who have lost children yet who have found sustenance in their faith by turning to God and through Him gained the strength to go on. But I don't think she ever found such comfort even though she had faith. Then, sadly, she suffered a divorce, which I hear was quite contentious. Her son, Aaron, moved in with Harry, which constituted the loss of another son. So she was at her lowest."

Kirk was impressed with his detailed and fluid delivery. As if he had prepared.

Gallagher continued. "I should add that Sylvie most likely suffered clinical depression growing up, although back then the condition was neither recognized nor properly dealt with. My sense is that with such a chronic condition, the death of Devon and her divorce were just too much for Sylvie's soul to bear."

"So, you think that she was driven to suicide."

"Sadly, yes."

"But you said she seemed fine when you visited her."

"Yes, but Sylvie was always good at masking her pain. I casually mentioned how the leaves were in high color driving out and their peak should come in a couple of weeks. But I could see her face fall. Autumn reminded her of Devon's death."

"And a couple of weeks, like about November sixth."

Gallagher pursed his lips. "Yes. It was an unfortunate slip."

Gallagher's expression changed—like he was guilty for having reminded her.

They got up to leave, and Gallagher walked them down the hall and into the foyer leading outside. At a table near the reception desk was a poster with images of tourist items for sale by the brothers, including baked goods as well as bottles of Monk's Brew. Kirk nodded at the sign. "I hear the brothers make a great beer."

"Yes, we're quite proud of it."

"Are you one of the brewers?"

He smiled. "No, I work the gardens."

"I noticed that Sylvie had a magnum at her place."

"Yes, I brought her a bottle when I visited."

"And perhaps a four-pack at Riley Malone's."

Gallagher flashed a wary eye at Kirk and nodded. "Yes, except I don't think she's a beer drinker."

"So, when did you visit Riley?"

Another serene smile. "I guess I forgot to mention it was last weekend, again on my way to visit my father."

"Right. I may have to get me some."

Gallagher checked his watch. "Unfortunately, the store's closed. It's open from nine to three."

"Another time then."

"Let me know in advance, and I'll be happy to give you a tour."

Before they left, Kirk gave Brother Gallagher his card saying to call him if he thought of anything that would help the investigation. When they were outside, Mandy said, "He seems pretty settled on suicide."

"He did seem to push that," Kirk said. "He also seemed to react when I mentioned the beers."

"I noticed that."

"Get Kevin to check the visitors log at the nursing home. If he dropped by the next morning as he claimed, he'd have to have signed in." Then he added, "Also last weekend when he claimed to have visited Riley."

Mandy made the call, after which she and Kirk headed to the parking area where some brothers were spreading mulch over a garden plot, one of several lying side by side and neatly squared off by railroad ties. Wooden stakes fenced off the areas where vegetables and herbs had grown but now were being mounded for the winter months. Little signs were stuck in the ground as labels for tomatoes, peppers, beans, cucumbers, and other veggies as well as herbs in a separate plot. A few tourists wandered the gardens.

What caught Kirk's eye was a sector that was also fenced but with a large sign that said DO NOT ENTER. His guess was that this might have been for flowers because he saw dried-up blooms under stalks that had been cut down in neat piles. There were some Latinate labels, which meant nothing to him, but he before they left, he clicked off a few shots.

CHAPTER 47

MORGAN

Ninteen years ago, November 3

MY MOTHER HAD heard everything, but I think she had known all along. I also think that that had not been the first time he and Lulu had had sex. Probably for weeks and not just in the house but on his boat. He used to take us all into Boston Harbor, but after a while that got old. But he still took Vadima.

He had also taken her to the Museum of Fine Arts one day because there was a special exhibit of Cézanne. I had no interest; neither did the other girls. But she was into art, so they left together.

Looking back, I doubted they went to the museum. Probably to a no-tell motel or he screwed her on his boat. I wouldn't have put it past him. He had had an eye for young females, especially those with great bodies. And Vadima's was world-class. I also suspect they had regular sex and that my mom was aware. Wives know these things, especially when your competition is under the same roof.

I now have to admit that I had blamed him more than I had blamed her. Whatever the case, it felt good laying into him like that—like lancing a boil.

I had turned on my heel and left him frozen there in a stand-off with my mother.

I crossed the street and headed for the center where others had gathered. I had felt confused and spacey and even thought about going back to the church to pray. It was empty by now, but I talked myself out of it. I was not in the mood to ask for forgiveness, not for that blowout with my father. Not for anything. What I had craved was the company of my BBFs. My Shamrock girls. The originals.

A Starbucks sat at the corner of Mass. Ave. and the side street. There were still tables and chairs outside, even though it was November. This was our secondary hangout after Dot's.

It was noontime, and the sun was partially out, so people sat at tables with coffees and lunch including some of the kids from school. Of course, because of the funeral, classes had been canceled. That was fine, because I'd be heading for English right now and I was in no mood to get into a discussion of the theme of scapegoating in "The Lottery," a short story about stoning some woman to death. Where do writers come up with such stuff?

The plaza outside of the coffee shop was a big open space, which felt good after the confines of the church.

As I entered the area, I spotted Sylvie alone at a table. There was no coffee cup or lunch bag in front of her. Just her cellphone. She wore sunglasses because it was a bright autumn day. Also—to hide emotions. Like the person or not, funerals were sad, especially listening to Father de Souza who could pull tears out of a rock.

As I approached, Sylvie looked at me with an intense expression. My first guess was that she was still fighting back emotions. She had sat at the other end of the pew, and I had barely looked at her for all the distraction of the crowd, the service, and Anna Lawrence singing "Ave Maria."

"Hi," I said as I approached her table.

She did not respond. But even through her dark glasses, I could see her eyes lock on mine, her face rigid. "Hey, girl, what's up?"

Her face was stiff, forbidding.

"Did something happen? I mean, you're creeping me."

Without uttering a word, she clicked on her cellphone, turned it to me, and then pressed the PHOTOS button.

God no!

CHAPTER 48

THE RIDE BACK to Cambridge took nearly three hours with the traffic. It was a little after eight when Kirk pulled up his driveway. The house was dark save for a kitchen light.

When Olivia was still living here, she would leave lights on in half the rooms, giving a warm welcome home when he worked late. Because she was no longer here, he had left the garage door closed to keep out the raccoons and anyone interested in the twelve-speed Specialized Road bike Olivia had gotten him for his forty-fifth birthday. It crossed his mind to drive to the gym he had rejoined to do a half hour on the elliptical, but he really yearned for bed. Maybe the first thing in the morning.

He pressed the remote to raise the door, but after three attempts it didn't lift, which meant time for new batteries. He got out and manually raised it then pulled the car inside.

It was a cold, partly cloudy night, and through a window the full moon whitewashed the lawn.

Kirk opened the back door expecting Daisy to caress his feet as always. But no cat.

He went upstairs making kissing sounds that always got her attention, especially at feeding time. She often slept on Olivia's side of the bed, but she wasn't there, nor in the guest bedrooms, bathrooms, closets, nor in the cellar. But in the downstairs family room, he saw the draperies flutter. He pulled them open onto the window, which was raised just enough for Daisy to squeeze out. A chill went through him—he never left that window open because there was no screen. It had been torn and he had dropped it off at the hardware store to be rescreened.

Or had he forgotten to close it?

The other night he had lighted the wood-burning stove, but because the cold air in the flue was heavier than the updraft, smoke poured out of the stove and filled the room. So he had closed off the room to keep Daisy out and opened several windows to clear the air. But had he forgotten to close this one? And had he not noticed because of the draperies?

He felt a flutter of anxiety as he flicked on the back lights, grabbed a flashlight, and went outside. The clouds were now scudding across the night sky, leaving the moon a smudge of light through the gauze. The backyard was wide and dark and oddly quiet now that the night freezes had sent the cicadas back into the ground.

Daisy had never been outside in her life and for good reasons beyond sparing birdlife. The street saw commuter traffic during the mornings and evenings and had turned a lot of squirrels and rabbits into roadkill. The other reason: their backyard was alive with night creatures because of a nearby golf course, which drew coyotes, raccoons, red-tail hawks, and owls to feed on the water birds and squirrels. Besides night predators, she could be bitten by a rabid creature or sickened by consuming a poisoned rat.

With his torch, he swept the clutch of rose bushes under the kitchen windows, then the small patch of perennials behind the family room and the half-frozen birdbath near the birdfeeder, which gave her hours of entertainment from the window ledge inside. He then sprayed the upper yard of unbroken lawn but that barely made a dent in the blackness. So he climbed the six granite slabs to the upper yard. He swung the torch until the light fell onto a dark bundle.

Kirk's chest clenched. He stepped onto the rise of lawn and inched forward. He stopped. Daisy. In the torchlight her gray and white hair was matted in blood. Her neck had been savaged.

Sweet Jesus, no!

For a long moment he stood frozen. She had gotten out through the window he had forgotten to close.

With his flash he scanned the bushes that fringed the backyard, half-expecting feral eyes to be glaring at him out of the black. But nothing. Whatever had gotten to her was long gone. Thankfully, she had not been eviscerated or eaten or carried off to some den to be torn apart by coyote pups.

For a moment he had a mental flash of when he and Olivia had gotten her as a kitten from the Animal Rescue League in Boston for Megan's tenth birthday. She had loved the cat. They had loved the cat, not just because it was a bright, dappled gray beauty. But because it was a living connection to Megan. Now there was nothing left of Kirk's family.

This was going to break Olivia's heart. Because of Kirk's long days, she had wanted to take her, to spare her the boredom of ten or twelve hours of an empty house. But her condo did not allow pets. He would have to break the news to her. And face the blame.

He looked down at the sad bundle of bloodied fur. Now what?

Because of the recent freezes, he would either put her in the cellar freezer until the spring or soften a spot in the backyard with hot water to dig a hole before the deep freeze set in.

In the light, he could see her neck had been bitten badly.

He went back into the house and got two tall kitchen bags. He put on gloves, and with his stomach turning, he removed her from the grass. But because her blood had begun to freeze, he had to use a hand shovel to free her head or risk having it tear off from her body.

"I'd like to kill the thing that got to you, girl."

Gently he lay her in the plastic bag, double-wrapped it, then slipped a second bag over that and bound it with duct tape. He then brought her into the cellar and lay her in the freezer on top of packages of frozen peas and succotash. "Sorry, Daisy," he said, and closed the lid and went upstairs to bed.

But his mind kept churning about the poor cat, trying to work down that premonitional twitch in his gut that something wasn't right. Coyotes never leave dead prey. They kill at the throat and carry their catch to a secluded spot to eat it or take it to their den for their pups. Same with foxes. Raccoons, from what he had read, didn't just kill pets that strayed in their night territory and leave a carcass whole—they eviscerated their kills and ate the innards. Same with owls—pick the carcass apart until they can carry away a big chunk to finish in a tree or feed their owlets.

After several minutes of lying in the dark, Kirk got out of bed and turned on the security system app on his laptop to see what had gotten to Daisy. The screen flickered then went black. None of the cameras out front or in the back of the house were functional.

Nothing. The system had failed at 7:44 when he and Mandy were still driving back from Saint Julian's Monastery. The only explanation was some systemic failure in the spy camera software.

That, or somebody had a portable Wi-Fi jamming device that disabled his cameras. But why?

Because Daisy had free roam of the house, he could not activate the motion detectors. And no alarm had been triggered.

A chill passed through his marrow. Someone had turned off his security system to kill his cat. They'd slipped through the window, grabbed Daisy, and killed her then dumped her remains on the lawn where he would not miss it in the back lights.

Someone mean-spirited, paranoid, and out for revenge. Someone who owns his own business and knows security systems. Someone who doesn't like cats.

Jordan Fucking Bolt.

CHAPTER 49

OLIVIA PULLED INTO Kirk' driveway the next afternoon. She had texted him earlier that she would stop by, so he rushed back from the Cambridge Animal Hospital to meet her.

She got out of her car with a suitcase in hand, and for a brief moment, his heart leapt—she had decided to move back. "This is a nice surprise."

But she retreated from his approach. "I hope you don't mind, but I have to get a few things."

"Oh." And instantly his heart sank. The suitcase was empty. He led her inside. "What's going on?"

"I need a few of my clothes."

"You already got a lot of your stuff."

"Summer things."

"It's November." And snow was in the forecast for tomorrow night.

"I'm going to the Caribbean."

"You are? When?"

"I leave tomorrow morning."

"Where?"

"Saint Lucia."

"With Ted Rizzo?"

"Yes, and he's a decent guy."

"So am I."

She made a dismissive gesture, not wanting to get into another circular spat.

His mind was reeling. "So you're going with him?"

She headed for the stairs to her closet in their bedroom. "Yes. Uh-huh."

"And when are you coming back?"

"Next week."

In his head he had flashes of Olivia and Rizzo walking hand in hand down an endless white sand beach by bright blue reef water and then dining under straw cabanas and then lounging naked with mai tais in hot tubs—just like the Sandals commercials. "A little getaway with Ted in Saint Lucia."

She turned to him full-face. "Yes, and I have a right to do and go as I please, as we agreed."

"Right," he said climbing up to his office as Olivia headed to the closet.

I've lost her, he thought. It's over.

A few minutes later she called down, "Where's Daisy?"

Shit!

He climbed the stairs and entered the bedroom.

"I said where's Daisy?"

The cat would have shot out from wherever she was to greet Olivia.

She stopped what she was doing as she took in Kirk's expression. "What?"

"I have bad news."

Her hand went to her mouth. "What?"

"She got out and . . . I found her dead in the backyard."

"What? What? How did she get out?"

"I got home last night and discovered the window near the wood-burning stove was open."

"Jesus, Kirk, how could you?" Blame was all over her face.

"It wasn't me. Somebody broke in and killed her."

"What? Who broke in? What are you telling me?"

He went on to explain how he had found her with her throat torn open and how the security camera had been turned off. While he recounted the events, Olivia's expression transformed from horror to bafflement.

"What makes you think someone else did this?"

He could hear the fury at the supposition that he was fabricating blame—that he was standing there composing a bald-faced lie—that he had been careless the way he was when Megan got killed when he was supposed to accompany her biking but got delayed. He cut in before she could hurl that at him. "I had a necropsy done."

"What?"

"I wasn't completely sure if some rabid animal got to her, so I took her to the animal hospital earlier, and they said she wasn't attacked by any animal but had died from seven stabs of an ice pick."

Olivia let out an involuntary screech. "God! Who would do that?"

"I have an idea and am looking into it."

Olivia was now crying. "Where is she?"

"In my trunk. I'm going to bury her in the backyard under the gazing ball."

Tears rolled down her face. "It's one of your damn perps getting back."

It was one of the worries that they carried in the dark recesses of their minds—that an ex-con or friends of someone Kirk had put away would come for him or them in revenge. She had even said that Megan's death was payback by some criminal Kirk had arrested. "Maybe."

Without another word, Olivia finished packing and walked out of the room with her suitcase. He followed her downstairs to the front door. She turned to him, her face stiff

"I'm so sorry," he said. "But we'll get him."

She gave him a light hug. "I'll see you when I get back."

"Safe travels."

With a nod she opened the door and headed to her car.

He watched her drive away, his eyes wet and thinking that he wanted to go up to bed and fall into a bottomless sleep.

Instead, for the next hour and a half, he dug a hole in the backyard near the gazing ball. The ground was hard from the last few nights, and he had to pour gallons of boiling water over the plot to make a three-foot mud pit. The vet had put Daisy in an air- and water-tight plastic container, which he lowered into the grave, coated it with lime to keep animals out, covered it with more dirt, and surmounted with the gazing ball and stand. "Sorry, girl. We'll get that bastard," he said and headed back inside to shower. Before he stepped into the shower, Mandy called.

"Hey, Kirk, I hate to hit you with bad news, but Riley Malone's dead."

"What?"

"She was killed last night in a hit-and-run before we could get to her."

Jesus Christ! How much worse can things get?

Yesterday Malone had called Mandy to say she had something important to tell her, hinting that she knew something about the treehouse fire. But she had left no clues or names.

"Where did it happen?"

"On her road," Mandy said. "But the thing is, it would have been her last jog because her car was packed for Vermont, and the only thing left in the house was the dog."

"So, she'd do her run, go back, shower, change, and pack the dog and take off."

"Looks that way."

"Who found her?"

"A dog-walker at the side of her road. I guess it was getting dark."

"Shit."

"Yeah, and it gets worse. According to the techs, it doesn't appear to be an accident. The M.E. says she was hit from behind at a slow speed, but it looks deliberate."

"Based on what?"

"I guess her chest and legs were crushed, which couldn't have happened unless the vehicle backed up and went over her a second time. The slow speed meant no fender damage. Forensics is working on retrieving tire treads, but it doesn't look promising. Looks like the killer knew what he was doing."

"So someone knew she was leaving. Someone who knew she had a cousin in Vermont and stopped her before she disappeared. Shit!"

"Yeah. Like you said, she was scared she was next."

They should have put her under protective surveillance.

"This is a shitstorm we didn't see coming."

"But should have."

PART III

CHAPTER 50

It was a little after six by the time Kirk and Mandy showed up at the scene where Riley Malone had been killed last evening. It was a moonless night, and local police had set up Klieg lights, making glowing stripes of crime-scene tape crisscrossing the roadside. State and local squad cars barricaded the area with lights flickering, as uniforms and techs scoured the road and brush. Without the flow of cars, it looked like a set for a grim movie.

Riley's body had been found on the side of the road where she'd been thrown and then intentionally crushed by the vehicle. At the moment, her remains were in a van on the way to the Medical Examiner's office in Boston.

According to forensics, she had been dead for at least four hours, which meant she was hit just before sunset at four thirty. The streetlights had not yet gone on, which meant she was running at twilight.

"She knew too much, and the son of a bitch got her," Mandy said.

Kirk looked up at the sky, which was a cloudless black bowl studded with a million stars. When he was a kid, his father had taught him some of the major constellations, by connecting the dots. When he asked his father why people had made shapes of gods and animals, he said because it helped make sense of the randomness of life. As he stared at the Big Dipper and connected the stars of Orion, he thought how futile, how random and quick life was. What made the scramble of stars all the more fretful was the thought that someplace fifteen hundred miles to the south, Olivia could be looking at the same stars in the arms of Ted Rizzo. That too made no sense.

One of the M.E.'s assistants came over to say that Riley's body and clothing would be put under microscopic scrutiny in search of any paint chips or tire treads or anything else that might give a clue to her assailant's vehicle. Detectives from the local PD were also checking security cameras at intersections and homes along the road and would get back to them as soon as they found something.

When they were alone, Mandy said, "The way I look at it, we have two options—hang around for these people to find something or go home to bed."

"Or a third: check out Jordan Bolt's car."

* * *

They arrived at Bolt's place a little before nine. The lights were on, and the flicker of television lit up the living room windows. No red look-at-me Jeep sat in the driveway like last time, and the door on the detached garage was down. Unfortunately, they didn't have a warrant to search it.

Jordan Bolt met them at the door. "Sorry about the hour, but we'd like to ask you a few more questions."

"What's it this time?"

"I think it would be better if we did this inside."

He shot a glance behind him and hesitated before he stepped aside to let them in.

From upstairs, the sound of a door closing. Probably his nubile girlfriend who had been on the couch with him watching TV. Bowls of chips and dip sat on the coffee table.

They moved into the living room where Bolt clicked off the set and stared at the two of them.

"Do you mind if we sit down?" Mandy said.

Bolt nodded, and they sat around the coffee table where Kirk slid aside the chips and lay down his recorder and clicked it on. "Riley Malone was killed last night."

"Riley Malone? Good God, no!" It took him a moment to let that settle in. "What happened?"

"That's what we want to know," Mandy said. "Specifics aren't important, but her death is being investigated as a homicide, and we'd like to know your whereabouts late yesterday afternoon."

"Jesus Christ! I'm getting tired of this. I was at work until around six."

"Who can confirm that?"

"My assistant."

"And her name?"

"Siena Martinez."

"She's your assistant?" Mandy growled. "Assistant what?"

His face looked as if he had swallowed broken glass. And in a voice weak of air, he said, "She's working to become a personal trainer."

"I'm sure."

"Look, why the hell are you here? I did not kill anybody, period."

"There's evidence to suggest that, like Sylvie Thornton, Riley Malone was killed because she knew who set fire to the treehouse."

"So you come to me again? What the fuck!"

"Look, the only people in your house at the time were you, Mrs. Bolt, Morgan, Sylvie, Riley, Krista, and Richie."

"Ever think that somebody else slipped into the backyard—some fucking crazy?"

According to the original report, all the others in the yard that night had alibis. But that didn't eliminate the possibility that somebody other than those kids had murdered the girl. He was right, but Kirk didn't give him that.

Mandy cut in—her eyes narrowed on him like laser beams. "Mr. Bolt, the only people who would have benefited from the death of Vadima are you and your family members."

"What do you mean *benefited*?"

"We've already been through this. To protect you and your family if it ever came out that you were sexually abusing her."

His head flinched toward the stairs. "Jesus! Keep your voice down. I never fucking abused her. Who told you such shit?"

"The pen-and-ink drawings from Vadima's sketchbook," Mandy said, and handed him photocopies of a half-naked Vadima, her face down and blank with Jordan Bolt also topless with his arm around her and looking at her, grinning expectantly. "Remember these?" Mandy said. "What she did instead of selfies."

"I told you these may have been her fantasies."

"Cut the shit," Mandy said. "They're graphic illustrations of you about to rape her. What's important is how you kept Vadima Lupescu as your sex slave because she feared being sent back to Slovakia."

"We've already been through all this . . ."

"Right, and it's time to fess up because the prime witness is dead and no charges are being pressed. So stop fucking around and come clean," Kirk said.

After a wincing moment, Bolt responded. "Okay, but it was consensual. I mean . . ."

Mandy hissed. “Her shoulders are slumped, and her head is turned facedown in submission. That’s not the look of consensual.” And she flapped the pages at him—copies that were given to them by Milosh. “This was sexual extortion, and you know it.” Mandy was flaming. “And she was fucking fifteen years old!”

In a voice barely audible, he said, “I did not kill her.”

“But you had the motive, the means, and the opportunity since she was asleep in the treehouse, probably intoxicated on alcohol and marijuana,” Kirk said. “And you would have benefited the most from her death.”

“So would the others.”

“Who else are you suggesting?” Kirk said.

Bolt looked away, clearly hearing his own implication.

Morgan had said that her mother may have known but internalized things—and that if she knew, she might have seethed silently about Jordan’s having sex with Vadima instead of reporting to the police and filing for divorce. She’d not only want to shield the family from humiliation but to protect young Richie who would be crushed if his father went to jail and the family broke apart.

“Are you suggesting that your wife might have killed Vadima?” Kirk said.

“Yeah—and came back from the dead and killed Sylvie and Riley to cover up.”

“No, but she knew about you and Vadima and how you had this thing for slender young females.” Mandy made a nod toward Siena in the upstairs bedroom. “So the way I see it, she never lost her pregnancy weight with Richard, and you probably rubbed her nose in that, and to get back you took up with Vadima maybe to score with a sexy kid.”

"You have no damn right to come in here and accuse me of abusing my dead wife. That's an insult, and I resent that."

"Then how would you characterize it: a forty-year-old father of two having sex with a fifteen-year-old-migrant?"

"A damn mistake. A bad decision is all."

"Like Siena Martinez?"

He made a dismissive look. "My wife was asleep when I woke her."

"Right." She also suffered vertigo and probably would never have climbed the ladder. "So you're suggesting that someone else may have committed those murders to protect the family name?"

He did not respond but looked straight ahead at Kirk.

"If your alibi holds up, that leaves Morgan and Richard." Kirk checked his notes. "And Richie was ten years old at the time and asleep."

He glanced at Mandy, sensing she was thinking the same freakish possibility—that little Richie had set the Lupescu girl on fire and, now nearly thirty, murdered Sylvie and Riley to cover for himself and/or his parents and Morgan.

At the moment, FBI agents were checking in on him.

"Do you think that Morgan may have killed Vadima then Sylvie and Riley because they knew about you and her?"

He waited too long before saying, "I don't know. And I'm not answering any more questions without a lawyer."

"Good idea."

"By the way, where were you last night around eight o'clock?"

"Who did I kill this time?"

"My cat."

"What?"

Kirk glared at him for an answer,

"I was here all evening and all night."

"And I suppose your assistant trainer can confirm that."

Bolt didn't respond but let out a groan of defeat.

"Right," Kirk said and left with Mandy.

CHAPTER 51

An hour later, Kirk drove up the driveway into the detached garage behind his brick garrison off Garden Street in Cambridge. No matter how many times he had pulled in over the last thirteen weeks, he could not get used to how the door rose onto an empty bay where Olivia's silver Audi SUV had sat—always a comforting sign that he was home.

Nor all the holes left by her. Although she had moved into a furnished condo, gaps were everywhere—the "Crazy Cat Lady" mug he had gotten her, the empty closets, wall hangings including some handsome lithographs, the top of her dresser, the vanity table, her yoga pads and blocks, and road bike. She was a voracious reader, more than he, yet she had left most of her books because she was now reading online. What bothered him the most was the negative spaces left by photos of the three of them when Megan was still a little girl, plus those of her and Olivia. Thankfully, she had left two frames of him and Megan on Martha's Vineyard, all smiles against a sparkling slick of infinity. The only pictures she had left of them was their wedding photo.

Still, the place looked like a half-looted dig.

He stood in the kitchen that he had barely used since she had left. His coffee came from the local café. His meals were mostly takeouts. The stove had seen only one burner lit, usually for boiling eggs. The oven had gone untouched. Only the micro was his go-to appliance, mostly for restaurant leftovers. The fridge was practically bare but for coffee, milk, OJ, soy milk, and a half empty six-pack of Blue Moon. Except for the upstairs closet and a few of her effects, the place could have been a bachelor pad.

His marriage to Olivia had been a spiritual oasis between the station and the mean streets. On the day she walked out, it was as if a sandstorm had buried his little green world, leaving him bereft of child and the woman he had loved since high school—the love of his life, which had defined his life. And now it was empty, filled only by the ticking of the clock they had bought at a little gift shop on a ski weekend in Stowe, Vermont, another life ago.

He wrenched all that away and moved to the dining room table where he spread out contents of Detective Jones' files on the death of Vadima Lupescu, including transcripts of all those people questioned in the case as well as the autopsy report. Also, their own files of crime scene photos, compiled police reports from all three murders, notes, and transcripts—what in the trade was his "murder book." He would throw himself into it, because finding bad guys was all he had left from chewing on his Glock.

For the next two hours, he pored through the transcripts, feeling himself stirring with a weary rage at the dreadful inhumanity he faced every day, at his own uncertainty that what he did actually mattered, at the corkboard photos of Vadima Lupescu and Sylvie Thornton and Riley Malone. And he thought about Mandy Wing and her stoic certitude that what they did each day did make a difference—that in a small way raised the quality of civilized life.

On his laptop, Kirk made a rough spreadsheet of persons of interest and listed motives beginning with the Lupescu murder:

JORDAN BOLT

Motive: *To eliminate the victim of pedophilia whose claim could have ruined him for life—ended his marriage, killed his health club business, disgraced him publicly, alienated and humiliated his children, and sent him to prison for years.*

Alibi: *Claimed he was asleep.*

SALLY BOLT

Motive: *Eliminate a witness to his forced sex on a fifteen-year-old, an offense of pedophilia which could have ruined him for life—ended his marriage, killed his health club business, disgraced him publicly, alienated and humiliated his children, and sent him to prison for years. Same as above.*

Alibi: *Apparently suffered vertigo. Could not have climbed ladder.*

MORGAN BOLT CASSIDY

Motive: *Same as above.*

Alibi: *Claimed she was asleep.*

RICHARD BOLT

Motive: *Same as above.*

Alibi: *Too young. Asleep.*

SYLVIE COX THORNTON

Motive: *None known.*

Alibi: *Apparently asleep.*

RILEY MALONE

Motive: *Supernatural fears. Ethnic hatred.*

Alibi: *Claimed was asleep.*

KRISTA BARBER SALIBA

Motive: *Peer pressure from the others.*

Alibi: *Claimed was asleep.*

GRAYSON "GEE GEE" GALLAGHER

Motive: *Alleged curse killing girlfriend, Justine Zajac.*

Alibi: *Claimed went home to bed.*

The other kids who were at the effigy burning had been cleared in the Jemma Jones report and recent follow-up by Annette Volpe and other investigators on their team.

But as he stared at his monitor, he kept asking himself, "What the hell are we missing?" It was as if someone was always a step ahead of them.

He scanned the transcripts of the questionings of all the witnesses and people of interest.

He was amazed at the malicious racism leveled at Vadima Lupescu by some of the kids back then. One teacher had been shocked that Riley Malone had written a paper on how the Romany people were believed to have caused the Bubonic Plague. She also claimed that Grayson Gallagher shared the belief that Vadima had caused his girlfriend Justine's death, and that she secretly worshipped the devil. Because she was dark and did her hair in unusual braids, spoke in a foreign accent, she was Other. And she had gotten taken advantage of by Jordan Bolt fulfilling his sick hunger. She was vilified by ludicrous myths of Roma people, and she was murdered for whatever senseless fear. It was the same old I-Thou persecution, be it Romas, Jews, Uighurs, Chechens, Kurds, Tutsis, and Armenians, his own people, and endless other minorities.

He was also beginning to question if there was in fact a connection among the deaths. That maybe there were three unconnected murders—the Lupescu girl, Sylvie Thornton, and Riley Malone. But what scratched at his mind was that Malone was not killed by accident. She had sustained pelvic fractures, crushed leg bones, and various breaks along the spinal column. In addition, there was significant brain damage from a partially crushed skull. There were also abrasions on the arms and legs from being ground into the apron of the road. That was not an accidental death.

A winter mind.

He was suddenly startled by the ring of the back door. It was Dave Nathan who lived with his wife, Jessica, in the house behind Kirk's. Their backyards were separated by a fieldstone wall inside of which their cute pug named Ebbi would get her daily exercise. Dave was holding his laptop.

"Sorry to bother you, pal, but got a moment? I want to show you something."

"How about a beer?"

"No thanks. I just finished one."

He lay the laptop on the kitchen counter.

"I got an alert from the backyard security camera the other night, but there was no break-in or any damage to our place. But it picked up a figure cutting through our yard."

He tapped a few keys as Kirk settled beside him.

"Whoever it was disappeared, then twenty-something minutes later, he returned."

The image was dark and grainy in the dim light.

"But you can see that he appeared to leave something behind in your yard. I couldn't make it out or identify who he was. But it might mean more to you."

Kirk put on his reading glasses and stared at the screen as Dave reran the video. For several seconds, all he made out was the spread of lawn. From one darkened corner a figure with a baseball cap emerged and moved quickly toward the stone wall.

After a long stretch of no movement, the figure reappeared through the leafless trees to lay something down in the yard behind Kirk's house.

"That's my cat."

"I forgot you had a cat."

"We did before he put an ice pick in him."

"What?"

"That bastard killed my cat."

"Jesus. Any idea who that is?"

"Yes."

CHAPTER 52

MANDY CALLED KIRK to say she had some new material she wanted to review with him ASAP.

Dave was gone when Mandy showed up around nine thirty.

Kirk was exhausted and wanted to go to bed, but Mandy was urgent. Besides, he needed the distraction from an image that Rizzo had just posted on Facebook—a selfie of him with his arm around Olivia grinning victoriously. He was dressed in a Tommy Bahama flowered shirt, she in a summer beach dress that he'd not seen before. She had a smile for the camera but not as obnoxiously self-satisfied as his. He knew every expression she was capable of, and he took that look as hopeful. They were scheduled to return in four days.

Kirk and Mandy moved to the dining room table spread with files, photos, and transcripts of interviews.

"How you doing?" she asked.

"I'm doing."

She nodded, her eyes alight with anticipation. "Well, I've got some stuff on Brother Grayson Gallagher you might find interesting. Remember when I asked him why he became a monk what he'd said?"

"Something about his mother dying."

"Right, that she died an untimely death. Well, I checked, and she actually died from falling down the cellar stairs while carrying a basket of laundry. The autopsy determined that she cracked her head at the bottom and bled to death. She was found the next day by dear old Brother Gee Gee who had dropped by to check on her. The report says she was wearing a mobile medical alert device, but the batteries were dead."

"But isn't there some kind of light or beep that would say they're low?"

"Probably, but maybe she didn't notice or had bad hearing. According to records, she was sickly and on painkillers, which may have compromised her alertness and mobility."

"Her son should have noticed. Does it say where he was when she fell?"

"Tufts Medical School. And she lived in Quincy—about twenty miles. The report says he had visited her the day before."

"Then he should have checked that the batteries were low or dead." Kirk thought for a moment. "You think he may have had something to do with it?"

She shrugged. "It's circumstantial, but here's something suggestive." She glanced at her notepad. "Did you know that the patron saint of his order was Saint Julian?"

"Only because it says so on their website."

"I wasn't brought up Catholic, so I looked him up. Apparently, saints are named patrons of places, occupations—farmers, dancers, butchers—as well as people with special interests or talents—you know, dancers, fishermen, students."

"Like Saint Francis, patron saint of animals."

"Right. You know what Saint Julian is the patron saint of? Murderers."

"A patron saint of murderers? Sounds like a Protestant joke."

"Well, he was also the patron saint of innkeepers, which is why he's known as Saint Julian the Hospitaller, as in hospitality. According to legend, he was hunting when a stag showed up and told him that he'd grow up to murder his parents. So, horrified, he moved far away and married. But unbeknownst to him, his parents visited his house and his wife put them up. But thinking the sleeping couple was his wife and lover, he killed them while they slept. He was so upset by what he'd done, he started an inn for the sick and poor, and suffered penance the rest of his life. God eventually forgave him and later he was made a saint."

"So you're saying Gallagher joined the Order of Saint Julian out of guilt for killing his own mother?"

"It's possible. His mother died when he was in his first year of medical school, and a year later, he dropped out and joined the Julians," Mandy said. "The thing is he could have joined any other monastic order in the country, but he chose this one because Julian was his spiritual model. You know, he commits a mortal sin and spends the rest of his life in penance in a monastery for murderers."

Kirk smiled. "Then kills Sylvie and Riley because they knew he murdered Vadima."

Mandy suddenly looked crestfallen as Kirk's words floated in the air. "Well, you kill once and get away with it, why not again? I mean, he won't expect salvation, but he covered his tracks." After a moment's silence, she conceded. "Okay, it's a stretch."

"Maybe not."

"Huh?"

Kirk slid his cellphone to her with photos of the fenced-off garden. One of the shots was a close-up of hand-printed labels stuck in the ground where the plants had been chopped and turned. "What does that say?"

She squinted. "Belladonna."

"Right, a perennial also known as 'deadly nightshade,' 'the devil's herb,' and 'beautiful death.' The plant is deadly poisonous, totally—the roots, leaves, stalks, seeds. Eat a few berries and you're gone. It attacks the nervous system and causes muscle paralysis including the heart."

"Yikes!"

"According to legend, it's what the Romans used to get rid of political rivals. And what Shakespeare's real-life Macbeth used to wipe out the army of the Danes. The stuff is knock-dead toxic."

"So what's it doing in their garden?"

"Good question. One reason might be tradition. They built that compound after a medieval monastery in Germany, including the original gardens where they grew fruits, vegetables, herbs, and medicinal plants, including belladonna. Probably after trial and error, and a lot of sick and dead people, they had discovered that in small dosages the plant could treat headaches, arthritis, colds, irritated bowels, even dizziness. It's still the chemical basis of pharmaceuticals such as scopolamine for seasickness. That's one of the key ingredients. Another is atropine, which was found in the toxic screen of Sylvie Thornton."

"Holy shit!"

"Yeah, and according to their website, Brother Grayson is the monastery's horticulturalist."

Kirk opened a folder of crime scene photos and showed Mandy two. Sitting on a counter in Sylvie Thornton's kitchen was a magnum of beer and a package of berry muffins from Saint Julian's Monastery. "According to Davidson, she had remains of some kind of bread muffins in her stomach."

"Jesus, you're right—Locard's Principle. What the perpetrator brought to the crime scene. Those could have been belladonna berries."

"Right. And maybe he made sure she sampled the one and incapacitated her before dragging her out to the tree."

"Son of a bitch." Mandy checked her own notes. "He claims that the morning Sylvie was killed he had left Saint Katherine's parish house before six and stopped by to check on his father at Bayside before breakfast, which would be around seven."

Every nursing home had guest sign-ins. So there would be a record of when visitors came and left. Kirk called Kevin and told him to check with Bayside.

"If he lied, he could have driven straight to Cambridge, killed Sylvie and later Riley as cover-up. The real question is why kill Vadima Lupescu."

Kirk rifled through the various transcripts. "According to Riley Malone, he blamed her for his girlfriend's death—Justine Zajac. Riley claimed that he was very 'spiritual' and bought into Vadima being a witch and handmaid of Satan bullshit. And that, out of jealousy, she put a hex on Justine, causing her to drop dead in class."

"Right. He was also one of the kids at that effigy burning and could have come back a few hours later and torched the girl then ran back home."

"And maybe Sylvie suspected it was him and sent that note to Jemma."

"Yeah," Mandy said, "and she blamed herself for cranking up all the Gypsy sorcery stuff which he fell for."

"And maybe Sylvie told Riley that she suspected Gallagher and he found out or suspected and went after her."

"The son of a bitch kills Vadima and joins a monastery as cover. Like pedophiles becoming priests."

Kirk's cellphone chimed. It was Kevin who said that there was no record of Grayson Gallagher signing in or out at the nursing home early on November sixth—the day Sylvie was killed. He did add that sometimes when no one is at the reception desk, family members might visit loved ones without signing in. "Maybe," Kirk said.

"We just got a report back from the lab. In a pocket of Riley Malone's jogging pants was a partially eaten fruit and nut bar with the wrapping still on it. Monk's Kitchen, Saint Julian's Monastery, Smithfield, Mass."

A moment later two photos showed up on Kirk's phone of the blood-smeared wrappings.

"We got him."

"Why don't we send the staties out to bring him in?" Mandy said.

A state police station was only a few miles away from the monastery, and they were fifty miles east of the place. "Something about a bunch of squad cars showing up at the monastery in the middle of the night and hauling him out in handcuffs. The word gets out, and it makes for lousy optics, especially right before the holidays. No, this is ours. And we surprise the good brother, just like the stag."

CHAPTER 53

THEY MET BROTHER Grayson Gallagher in the same small chapel at the monastery.

A night clerk had let them in through the main entrance. Kirk apologized for the late hour, but said it was urgent that they see Brother Gallagher who had been asleep for four hours. They gave no reason, and although looking annoyed, the clerk left to wake Gallagher.

Meanwhile, at Kirk's request, the county sheriff had sent a team of support deputies to wait unobtrusively in vehicles outside should they need them.

"You traveled halfway across the state in the middle of the night, so this must be important," Gallagher said when he met them, again dressed in his robe. He settled in the pew across the aisle from them, sandaled feet crossed in the aisle.

He projected that same serene sense of confidence, even though he was being questioned in the middle of the night and for the second time by two homicide detectives. Kirk did not know if he was playing coy or mocking them. "We have some questions to ask in light of new evidence on the death of Sylvie Thornton."

He cocked his head. "That makes me wonder if you now consider me a suspect."

"You are a person of interest."

He nodded in contemplation. "That sounds serious."

Not knowing how exactly to respond, Mandy simply nodded.

"It is serious," Kirk said.

Gallagher continued nodding as that sank in and gathered his thoughts. "When I was a postulant, you know, a candidate hoping to become a member of our order, I was told that I was a flawed human being, full of sin and that I would need a lifetime to grow into the holiness of Jesus Christ. Like others in postulancy, I was asked to examine my intentions and commitment to the life of the spirit. I recognized my flaws and intolerance of others and was told that I would have to love our Lord Jesus Christ before I could love others."

Kirk felt his heart jog at the possibility that this was a long ecclesiastical windup to a confession. "What exactly are you saying, Brother Gallagher?" Kirk said in a voice that he had summoned so many times to inform suspects that they had no other places to hide, no other options opened to them.

Brother Gallagher smiled patiently. "I had wronged others, including my own mother, and had to face up to what I had done before God. And the only way for me to do that was to separate myself from the world and to connect myself to God through Jesus Christ. And in so doing I knew that God forgave me and loved me."

"How exactly did you wrong your mother?" Mandy said, her voice soft but focused.

"This is not easy to talk about," he began, his face rippling with emotions. "At the time, my mother and I did not get along. She had a serious heart condition, a case of angina pectoris—hardening of the arteries. My sister had bought her a medical alert device, which she was supposed to wear at all times. Because she lived miles away, it was my job to be certain that my mother wore it at all times. Also, to check that the batteries were charged. That's where I was remiss. I had not checked for some time, and they had died, and she never knew, or didn't notice the signal. As a result, she had a heart attack and could not signal for help and fell down her cellar stairs. She died in a matter of hours." They could hear the catch of emotion in his voice. "I've never forgiven myself."

"That's understandable," Kirk said.

Mandy cleared her throat audibly. "Was one of those others you had wronged Vadima Lupescu?"

Grayson closed his eyes for too long a moment. When he opened them again, he said, "Yes, I'm sorry to say, it was."

Mandy took a deep breath of anticipation. "Can you explain how you had wronged her?"

Here it comes, thought Kirk, as Gallagher looked away to again summon his words, knowing they would be his last on this side of innocence, his eyes fixing on the crucifix under the round stained-glass window.

"I had become convinced Vadima was a witch and accused her of putting a curse on a girl I was going steady with at the time."

"Justine Zajac."

"Yes. Justine. She was my girlfriend at St. B's, and she died suddenly from an aneurysm. Everybody was shocked, including the medical people. She was simply too young and too healthy for that to happen. She played on the girls lacrosse team, so her sudden death didn't make sense.

"So, I became convinced that Vadima had put a hex on her. She was from Eastern Europe and was of Romany ancestry, so I fell for all the myths about Gypsy people. I was wrong, of course. But I was young and susceptible to rumors of demonology. Rumors of evil."

"You also spread rumors that Roma people caused the Black Death in Europe in the fourteenth century."

"Yes, and I'm ashamed of that also."

"Did you have anything to do with her death?"

He held Kirk's glare and smiled. "So that's what this is all about: Did I kill Vadima Lupescu and possibly Sylvie."

After a long, portentous moment, Kirk said, "Yes."

"No, I did not. But I'm interested in why you would suspect me."

Kirk felt his inner organs knot. He and Mandy had been humming for a confession. "On the night that Vadima Lupescu died in a fire in the treehouse, you were among the group of kids in the Bolts' backyard, right?"

"Yes."

"So, given how in your own words you had accused Vadima of putting a curse on Justine and possibly causing her death, you had a motive—revenge. You even had partaken in a little witch-effigy burning on a fire pit, correct?"

"Yes, along with a bunch of other kids."

"Right. So it's possible that after everybody else left, you came back and set the structure on fire."

"That could have been anybody, but I assure you that that wasn't me. I had gone home to bed. Unfortunately, I have no way to corroborate that, since my mother is dead and my father has little memory left. But they had confirmed my presence at home the next day when the police came by."

That meant almost nothing since no one was looking for a murderer back then. "But you had a motive."

"Yes, but that ended with the effigy burning."

"Okay," Kirk said, reaching for his trump card. "Following a toxicology screening of Sylvie Thornton, it was determined that atropine was found in her system. Atropine is found in belladonna, a plant also known as nightshade." He held up his phone with shots he had taken. "According to Saint Julian's website, you are named as the head horticulturist here, and belladonna is one of the plants growing outside. That plant is one of the most poisonous in nature and not one that is cultivated. So I want you to tell us why it grows in one of your gardens outside."

He gave that same empathetic smile that now infuriated Kirk who was convinced that a multiple killer lived under that holy-man robe.

"Yes, belladonna is a highly toxic plant to humans and not one that ordinary gardeners would cultivate. But we grow that for two reasons. One, out of tradition with medieval monasteries after which this place has been designed.

"Two, we grow it for a small pharmaceutical company in Pittsfield which synthesizes the business compounds for a variety of medicines. In return, the company pays the monastery for cultivation rights. And as is indicated in your photos, we have several warning signs on a high fence not to enter. I will be more than happy to give you contact names of people at Saban Pharmaceuticals."

Shit!

"That would be good," Mandy said, and jotted down two names. "You also claimed that you had visited your father at Bayside Nursing Home in Sandwich, Mass. But there's no record of you having signed in or signed out on the morning of November six when Sylvie was killed."

"That's probably because my sister Rosanne signed me in when we arranged to visit my father. She may have arrived before me. But I did visit him then, and she can confirm that." And he wrote down her name and contact information.

"How do you communicate with her?"

"By phone."

"But we couldn't find a record of your cellphone."

"Because I don't own one. Few brothers do because we rarely leave the monastery. If family members need to communicate with us, the monastery has a main number."

His willful cooperation put another knot in Kirk's gut.

"I don't know if you've heard, but your old friend Riley Malone is dead."

"What? When did this happen? I just talked to her a few days ago."

"She was killed last night by a hit-and-run driver."

"Oh no. Oh dear God, how horrible." And Gallagher crossed himself.

"Because of the circumstances of her death, I must ask you of your whereabouts last evening."

"I was here, of course." Then with an edge of irritation he added, "And I didn't use a monastery car in case you're interested. And you can check with Brother Matthew who is in charge of our vehicles. He's at the reception desk."

"Fine," Kirk said. He got up. "Detective Wing will keep you company."

Kirk first went to the reception desk and asked the night clerk if Brother Gallagher had left the monastery yesterday. The clerk checked a schedule. "No. He hasn't checked out since November fifth when he visited his father in Plymouth, Massachusetts, and returned the next day."

Kirk thanked him and stepped outside. He put a call in to Kevin who had been asked to check with the nursing home security cameras if there was any indication that Grayson's sister had signed in for him.

"I was going to tell you in the morning. Security cameras had recorded his arrival and departure at the times he had claimed. Also, we reached his sister Rosanne Hornyak who confirmed that she and her brother had indeed visited their father around breakfast time on the sixth and had signed him in using just his initials."

Feeling almost sick, Kirk put a call to Chad Davidson who was in bed and understandably annoyed at the call.

Kirk explained that a possible suspect grew belladonna and wanted to confirm that it might have been used to drug Sylvie Thornton.

Even annoyingly aroused from sleep, Davidson still sounded as if he were giving a guest lecture at Harvard Medical School.

"As you may know, that plant has several pharmacological compounds that are used as human meds. And, yes, atropine is one of them. Your speculation that the suspect would be your perp makes good sense. However, there were no other compounds found in the assay on the Thornton woman. Just atropine. If she had been poisoned by belladonna, toxicology would have found several tropane alkaloids including scopolamine, hyoscyamine, as well as atropine."

"So what are you saying?"

"I'm saying that Sylvie Thornton was not subdued by the belladonna plant but by the purely synthesized pharmaceutical-grade atropine that comes only from a prescribed drug."

"But according to her doctor she had not been prescribed atropine. Nor was any vial found in her house or belongings," Kirk said.

"Then someone else provided it."

Of course!

CHAPTER 54

MORGAN

Nineteen years ago, Halloween

I WAS BACK IN BED, shuddering with a toxic mix of hate and anger. I could not control my feelings, nor get comfortable as my mind raced in and out of dark places. I still felt the effects of the pot and vodka, but something in me flamed through all of that.

The room was black but for my alarm clock, which read 1:07. I got up, still in my jeans, as if prepared all along. I opened my door and stepped onto the landing as if on autopilot.

Riley, Sylvie, and Krista slept in the guest room, Richie in his, and my parents in their room. They had their own bathroom, so a night-light burned dimly in the hall bathroom—the only source of light, but for another one in the kitchen in case someone needed some warm milk to help sleep. Otherwise, the place was black and dead-silent.

We lived in a big old house, so the floorboards creaked as I padded down the stairs. I froze every few steps to take in any errant sounds. Nothing. Everybody was asleep. For a split instant, I thought I should go back to bed, that this was not a good idea, that I should sleep it off. But I didn't want sleep.

I made it to the back door through the kitchen and slipped on my hoodie from the mudroom.

It was still a foggy Halloween night, although the wind had picked up, sending a chill through me.

The outdoor lights had been turned off, so I made my way by the scant light of the neighbors' houses through the bushes. Still on autopilot, I moved across the lawn feeling my chest throb.

The fire pit still glowed with dying embers against the wind. The mesh top was still on. I removed it partway.

In a matter of seconds, I found myself at the wooden ladder.

The treehouse was dark and silent. She had fallen into a dead sleep from all the pot and vodka and my mother's sleeping pills that I had emptied into her cup. They were small and dissolved fast, undetected among the ice cubes.

Everything was as it should be. And I told myself I was doing the right thing. What Father de Souza once explained in catechism class—that there are some sins that cry out to heaven. *Peccata clamantia*. And what she was doing to my family had to be one of them. And only Good can come out of this—just as Gee Gee Gallagher had declared.

I moved back past the fire pit to the garage where I found the can of kerosene my father had bought for Lulu's lamp. It was a new can, and only a little had been used. For the fire pit I had used the Kingsford charcoal lighter on the wood that my father had bought us.

I looked up at the treehouse from the bottom of the ladder. I hadn't been up there in weeks. I knew my mom had not been up there in years, but I didn't know if my father had. But I wouldn't have put it past him, especially when the rest of us had gone to Springfield to visit my aunt one weekend. Besides Lulu, the only other person who had been up here was Richie. She'd tell him stories about life on an animal farm and give him drawing lessons. He was young. And he liked her.

I had rehearsed the moves in my head when a sniveling little voice said, "Don't do this." Jiminy fucking Cricket.

Another voice had cut in: *One word from her and your father will be arrested for pedophilia, and you would be humiliated and mocked by all the kids at St. B's. Richie would be mortified to have his father go to prison, scarring him for life since he's crazy about him. And your mother would get a divorce.* And that would be the end of the Bolt family. We would be town pariahs. I'd probably end up cutting my wrists.

Riley had been right: Vadima Lupescu was an Evil living in my house.

Feeling frightened had made me sweat. And before I chickened out, I climbed the ladder until I could peer inside, barely making out the dark lump of her in the sleeping bag.

I had crawled partway in and turned on the kerosene lantern and emptied nearly all of the contents of the can.

I still remember looking around. All was still. I muttered a little prayer and lit the match.

With a poof, flames shot up and made a blue and yellow snake across the floor to where she slept.

I scrambled down and pulled away a few yards, watching with pounding heart as the fire spread insanely fast through the interior and up the sides to the roof. I could hear the crackling of wood and the woof of dry leafless branches catching fire and rising into the thicket.

I half expected to hear a scream, but all I heard from within was what sounded like a human gasp . . . then a sickening sizzling sound of what may have been flesh.

Feeling a moment of sickness, I dashed across the lawn toward the house as the backyard lit up like a sunrise. I looked back just once in total disbelief at what I had done.

Then I turned back toward the house. And as I reached the back door ready to bolt inside, I spotted something that stopped me dead. Standing at the kitchen window against the glow of the night-light was Richie.

I cut inside, knowing the fire department would be here any minute.

"What's wrong?" I whispered.

He glared at me with a glass of milk in both of his hands. His face grimaced with horror.

"What are you doing up? Did you have a bad dream?"

He did not respond, looking catatonic.

"Hey, come on. Back to bed." I tried to nudge him back upstairs before everybody woke up. "The tree caught fire. I'm going to call the fire department."

I was beginning to panic that trucks and the police cars would pull into the backyard any moment. The whole neighborhood was lit up. I shook him by the shoulders. "Upstairs, dammit. Now."

I decided I'd have to carry him. As I stooped to cradle him, he moved. "Good, back to bed."

With both hands on his shoulders, I walked him out of the kitchen as I half pushed him toward the stairs, my heart drumming so hard I thought I would faint. Any second now someone upstairs could open one of the bedroom doors and wonder why we were heading for bed with a fire in the backyard.

But we'd made it up safely.

We reached the landing, and he froze once again. I opened the door to my room and whispered, “Inside.” But he wouldn’t move.

Fuck!

I took his arm and pulled him inside and closed the door. I pulled up the covers of my bed. “Get in and go to sleep.”

He moved to the bed in short stubby steps and muttered something.

“What?” In the firelight from the windows, I could see his mouth trembling as he found his words. “You burned a witch.”

I dug my nails into his arm before pushing him into the bed. “Yes. And you say nothing. Nothing.”

But hearing Richie whimpering from a nightmare, Sylvie had gotten up, and glancing out the window must have seen me out back.

She had photographed the whole thing.

CHAPTER 55

"WE FOUND YOUR DNA on the envelope of the tip you'd sent to the Lexington P.D.," Kirk said, having turned on the recorder. He laid out a photocopy of it: VADIMA LUPESCU WAS MURDERED. "This was from you, correct?"

Richard Bolt made a nod of resignation.

"Out loud, please," Mandy said.

"Yes. I sent that."

They had him brought into the station the next morning without resistance.

"How did you determine that?" Bolt said.

Mandy nodded at the pack of cigarettes on the table in front of him. "Nothing good about those things." And she showed him the photo of the filters of his cigarette.

He smiled. "It doesn't take much, does it?"

"No, just a few molecules of saliva."

"I should have used a self-sealing envelope."

"Yes, you should have," Kirk said. "So how did you know Vadima Lupescu was murdered?"

"Because I watched it happen."

"You watched it happen? Want to elaborate on that?"

"I had a nightmare that night and got up for a glass of milk. I was in the kitchen when I saw a figure with a can of kerosene climb the ladder of the treehouse and set it on fire while Vadima was asleep."

He stopped because he began to get emotional. Kirk slid a bottle of water to him. He nodded a thank you and took a swig. In the interim, Kirk felt his heart rate kick up as he could barely wait for Bolt to continue.

"I couldn't believe how fast the fire spread. In a matter of seconds, it flashed across the floor and must have consumed Vadima almost instantly. Then the flames rose up the sides where a shade hung on the eastern side to block the sunrise. It must have been made of some flammable material. She never had a chance." He choked up and took another maddening sip of water.

"Who was it?"

"At first I didn't know because I only saw a figure from the back in a hoodie. But then it turned to go into the house."

Again, he stopped to catch himself from losing composure.

"I knew it wasn't my mother because of vertigo and neck issues that she took melatonin for to help her sleep. Then I thought maybe my dad, except he was fond of her, you know, bought her little presents, clothes, magazines, stuff like that."

"Okay," Kirk said, wanting to reach across the table and shake it out of him.

"Grayson Gallagher. He was one of the kids who sat with the others around the fire pit and burned an effigy of Vadima. I watched them from my window."

Jesus, Brother Gee Gee. How the hell did he manage all those alibis?

"Keep going," Kirk said.

"They were convinced that she had put a curse on his girlfriend, Justine, that caused her to die. So I expected to see his face under the hood." He took another sip of water and dabbed his mouth on his sleeve.

Mandy could not hold it any longer. "Jesus Christ! Will you please tell us who it fucking was?"

"Morgan."

"What? Morgan Cassidy? Your sister?"

"Yes. I was shocked, but she said Lulu was evil, a witch who was trying to destroy our family and she had to be killed."

"And you said nothing to anybody for nineteen years?"

He nodded with a face full of contrition. "At first, I thought she really was a witch, and I swore to Morgan that I'd not say anything because she got what she deserved and nobody would know. So we made a pact that if anyone asked, Vadima had died by accident or suicide because she didn't want to be a witch anymore."

"So why did you wait almost twenty years to tell the police?"

He looked away for a moment, shaking his head in regret. "I loved my sister, and she was very good to me, sometimes better than my mother. And after the divorce and Mom died, and my father had moved away and was busy with his club and his social life. Morgan was all the family I had left.

"As I got older, I just buried that as some terrible prank she did, driven by delusions and fear for our family. But when I heard that Sylvie may have been murdered to cover the crime, I knew it was Morgan because Sylvie must have known. Maybe Morgan told her. I don't know."

"And Riley Malone."

"What about her?"

"She was killed three days ago in a hit-and-run, and there's suspicion that she was intentionally killed."

His eyebrows shot up in shock. “Riley Malone? Oh God, no.”

Kirk snapped off the recorder and turned to Mandy. “Get Kevin to send an APB for Morgan Cassidy and the York PD to retrieve Krista Saliba. She may be next.”

CHAPTER 56

MORGAN
The present

Poor Richie. He had heard all the talk about witches and secretly watched the effigy burning, and then went to bed and had nightmares that woke him up and sent him downstairs for some warm milk—what our father prescribed when he couldn't sleep. That's when he saw me through the window. I made him promise not to squeal or our family would be destroyed.

He didn't emerge from his room until the next day, afraid I'd be arrested. Throughout the police questioning he was terrified but held tight, convincing them that he slept through the whole ordeal until my parents woke him after the firefighters came. I was proud of him. Too bad he had to hold that in for all those years.

Looking back, I know it was an impulsive thing. I lay in bed that night, knowing I just couldn't take another day with her in my house. She had come between me and my father, between him and my mom, between me and the damn world. She had made life hell and I was convinced my mother knew and would file for divorce once Richie was old enough. The deed was in front of me and filled me with a frisson of dread, but I still got out of bed and did it because there was no choice. And I didn't fucking regret it.

What I regretted was Sylvie seeing me. She'd gotten up to attend to Richie and happened to look out the window. I think she suspected something because she got her new Nokia cellphone and clicked and clicked and clicked the whole affair, me going to the garage for the quart of kerosene then climbing the ladder and torching the thing with that father-fucking bitch in it.

It was a few days later at the funeral that she showed me the images. She had sworn that she'd not tell anyone, and because we were BBFs I believed her. And she promised to delete all the shots from her phone. But she wasn't as good as her word because she showed them to Riley whom she was closest to. That's the weird thing about secrets—they get hold of you and make you want to share them. She said that holding in such a huge secret like that would change how we'd all relate to each other. It would always be there, the proverbial elephant-in-the-room kind of thing. Plus, she had yielded to that Oh-wow! reaction one gets from sharing taboos. And because we were a sisterhood, Sylvie had blabbed to Riley. But she swore she had not told Krista who could never keep secrets.

It was amazing that Sylvie and I never talked about it for years. Vadima Lupescu was out of our lives, and we went on living until that big thing faded to nothing.

Then Sylvie's son died, she got divorced, and had to quit her job while living in that big old house outside of Harvard Square. Suddenly she discovered that she couldn't afford to take care of the place as she had when married to Harry. So she came to me for a handout, and when she couldn't pay me back, she threatened to release the photos to the police. She had made a bunch of copies, storing some on CDs in some bank's safety deposit box.

Over the course of three years, I'd transferred a hundred and fifty thousand dollars into a secret account of hers. And it would have gone on indefinitely until my husband found out. I did the bills, but he did the taxes; and as I continued draining investment accounts, he would have eventually caught on. And then what? "By the way, Honey, I murdered this Roma bitch nineteen years ago and I'm being blackmailed."

I was also convinced that it was Sylvie who sent that tip to the police on the Halloween anniversary, probably driven by guilt, as if she had been in complicity with me—a sister in crime.

Whatever, I had to fabricate a scapegoat. And Gee Gee Gallagher was it.

So I went to Sylvie's house early that morning, brought some Saint Julian's muffins, a bottle of Monk's Brew, and a cup of coffee that I had spiked with my husband's heart meds. He had a condition called bradycardia, which has do to with the heart's electrical system. Normal heart rate is sixty; his was around forty, which had caused him to pass out until his cardiologist put him on atropine. Coincidentally, the business chemical in that medication was synthesized from deadly nightshade, also known as *Atropa belladonna*.

I had known nothing about that until some months ago when I had visited Grayson. On a private tour of Saint Julian's famed gardens, he explained what that plant was and how he was growing it for a pharmaceutical company that processed the toxins in small amounts to treat several ailments including spastic colons, dizziness, and bradycardia. Sorry, Gee Gee. It was you or me.

Given the amount I had slipped her, it worked fast. I walked her into the backyard where I sat her down then rigged up a noose on the tree limb, pulled her to her feet, and with rubber gloves, tied up her neck and strangled her. Because she was still alive and scuffling in place, I put my full weight on her until I heard a snap. And then I was out of there.

I didn't like having to do that, but she was threatening my whole world, my whole way of life. Why couldn't she have gone to her sister for handouts? Or maybe she had, and after a few, Erin had put a stop to it.

Riley was another story. I knew the police would initially suspect her because she was so nutty religious that she'd confess that she encouraged Vadima to kill herself. But they'd eventually suspect that she was delusional and dismiss that, especially after nearly two decades.

What bothered me is that she knew I had torched the bitch, and I was certain that she was the one who had sent the tip to the police. But just to be sure, before the drugs took effect on Sylvie, I asked if she had tipped off the Lexington PD. She didn't know what I was talking about, which left Riley.

Even as a kid, Riley Malone was a flake. A superstitious nervous wreck who spent half her days in confession booths, asking forgiveness for cutting through a neighbor's yard or French kissing Timmy D. after Bible-studies class. She was the one who had convinced us that Vadima was a Gypsy witch putting hexes on people including my father. She was a basket case back then and got even nuttier the older she got. Also, she was living alone in a trailer like white trash and resented that my life was light-years above hers. So there was no way she'd not spill her guts to the authorities.

Claiming that Gee Gee couldn't travel himself, I had sent Riley a forged note from him along with Monk's Brew hoping that she'd attend the twentieth reunion of St. B's next month. Sorry, Gee Gee.

I knew she was a jogger and did her miles on her street late in the day. When I spotted her, I drove past her and circled back because there were other cars on the road. So I had to act fast. After a few rotations, the road was clear, so I came up on her from behind, did a sideswipe to avoid a telltale fender bender, pushing her face-forward into some scrub. I then jammed the car in reverse and slowly rolled over her body a couple of times, feeling the crush of her bones beneath the tires. Back on the road, I was gone. And the papers would say she was killed in a hit-and-run accident.

Before I took off, I stuffed into her jogging pants pocket a half-eaten Cranberry Almond Fruit and Nut Bar still in its Monks' Oven wrapper. Sorry again, Brother Gee Gee, but you always were holier than thou. He knew nothing about the video Sylvie had taken, so he never suspected. Same with Krista. But she must have squirmed when the police questioned her about that Halloween night. She might have even mentioned that Gee Gee had the biggest grudge against Vadima because of Justine.

Up to this point I had had complete control over the situation—even when that tip was sent to that damn Detective Jemma Jones. I first had figured that it was Sylvie who had squealed. Then Riley. Krista was out of the loop.

But at the moment I'm hearing a distant siren, which tells me there's only one person left who knew. Poor Richie, you couldn't hold back. You always did have a moral sweet spot.

The walkway around the pond is open only to authorized vehicles such as those of the DPW. And, in emergencies, police.

From the parking lot on Pond Street, I could see them approaching, no sirens but flashing blue and white lights. As they got closer, I recognized those same two obnoxious detectives, here for the big score. So much for the ingenious detection—I had kept my cellphone on for their GPS to do the work.

From the other side, a bunch of officers on foot blocked that way out, leaving me nowhere to run, and no place to go. Nor did I want to. This was my favorite place in the world.

I waved at Lucian and Wing as they approached, guns in hand like in the movies. I guzzled down the contents of my water bottle and watched a swan flap its wings, run across the water's surface, and take flight into the fiery clouds of the western sky.

CHAPTER 57

IT WAS NOVEMBER 23. And since Megan's death, Kirk and Olivia visited the gravesite at Mount Auburn on her birthday to lay flowers.

Throughout her short years, the cemetery had been a special playground for Megan—walks in her babyhood stroller, duck-waddling after water birds, mucking for frogs in Willow Pond, picnicking on the banks of Halcyon Lake, hiking the rolling leafy paths, learning how to bike and drive, bird- and fox- and coyote-watching. Days that had left them deliriously happy. And now—a dark pilgrimage to her resting place.

It was nearly closing, and the acreage was autumn-brown and deserted. Kirk meandered down the narrow paths to his usual parking spot where there sat a silver Audi. In disbelief, he got out holding a decorative wreath and headed toward the headstone and the solitary figure.

Olivia had laid an arrangement of greens, pine cones, and red ribbons at the base of the headstone.

"I thought you weren't coming back until Sunday."

"I changed my mind," she said in a flat voice.

He could see the color in her face from the Caribbean sun. This was the first time they had been here together since last November 23. "Beautiful arrangement."

She nodded at him. "Pretty wreath."

She was dressed in jeans, boots, and her lavender parka. "When did you get home?"

"Yesterday."

"Did what's his name come back with you?"

"No."

"Oh." Kirk felt as if he were entering a minefield and tried not to sound hopeful. "So, when's he coming back?"

She made a dismissive shake of her head. "Sunday I guess."

"If you don't mind me asking, did something happen down there?"

"I didn't want to miss today." Her voice cracked and tears filled her eyes.

"Then why didn't you go another time? You have most of December off."

She nodded. "Not the same."

Megan's birthday was their private holy day, one they marked on their calendar—like Easter and Christmas. November 23.

"I think she would have understood if you missed by a few days."

"Mmm. I just hoped to get away."

He wasn't sure if she meant she had gone to St. Lucia to escape this sad ritual, but discovered that she couldn't? Or something else?

"Well, it's good to see you," he said.

"She would have been sixteen years old, probably thinking about college."

Kirk nodded, his own eyes filling as he lay the wreath against the headstone.

LOVED WITH A LOVE BEYOND WORDS.

MISSED WITH A GRIEF BEYOND TEARS.

"Good to see you too."

"Nice to hear. So how was your stay down there?"

"That's not something I want to talk about."

Kirk nodded. "Of course." He was about to remind her of the time Megan found a robin fledgling in the grass when Olivia's phone chimed. She pulled it out of her pocket, and Kirk could see it was from Ted Rizzo. She rejected the call and slipped the phone back into her parka.

"I could use a glass of wine," she said. "Do you have time?"

Kirk felt his heart gulp happily. "I think I can squeeze you in."

They each kissed their fingers and touched the headstone. Then Olivia took Kirk's arm as they walked back to their cars. "So how's the case going?"

"Cases. We have our prime perpetrator on the main one. One more to go on the other. But we know that one's identity, so any day now."

"Congratulations." She gave his arm a squeeze, which set off a small warm glow in his chest. "Maybe after that's closed, you can take a break."

"Maybe," Kirk said. "By the way, Greg's is just down the street, and they still make the best pizza this side of Naples, Italy."

"Like old times."

"Yes." It was where they brought Megan after visits to the cemetery.

They were nearly at their cars when a sleek black Mercedes roadster skidded up and Ted Rizzo jumped out and stomped toward them.

"What the fuck!" he said, glaring at Olivia. "Not even a fucking note. Just take off in the middle of the fucking night?"

Kirk felt his chest swell, but he clamped down. This was Olivia's battle, and he knew she could handle it. But he'd play backup if needed. And from the looks of her, she didn't need it. She folded her arms in front of her and glared at Rizzo.

"I mean, I know you had this thing about your daughter's birthday, but you could have told me you might not be able to handle it. I mean, I booked us for a week during high season . . . and for a small fortune."

He said that to Kirk with a supplicating face as if making a common-guy appeal, forgetting that they were discussing a Thanksgiving getaway with his wife. Then to Olivia: "It wasn't like you weren't having a good time."

"I was having a good time until I realized what a world-class dickhead you are."

"Pardon me?"

She walked up to him point-blank. "I looked the other way while you played Charlie Charm with every attractive staffer and ogled every bikini that strutted by. I figured that was just boyish high spirits, like maybe the spring break you never had."

"Jesus, Livie, it's a tropical island and I was just taking in the scenery is all." Then to Kirk, with a chuffing smirk, "I mean, come on! Any red-blooded guy would understand, right? It meant nothing."

Rizzo was inviting Kirk to sympathize with his ogling other women while dating his wife. *Jesus!* But Kirk just nodded to let him continue burying himself.

"Maybe you should learn that it's not a good idea to leer at other women while on a date," Olivia said.

"Okay, I'm sorry, but that was no reason to fly home."

Olivia's face sharpened. "No, but that leggy barmaid was."

"What barmaid? What are you talking about?"

"Her name badge said Rosie."

"Yeah, so?"

"Flirting is one thing, even a hug and a kiss every time we showed up."

"I was just being sociable."

"Being sociable—like one a.m. two nights ago when you sneaked out of the apartment to go skinny-dipping with her in the pool?"

She was closing in, and Rizzo's face had morphed into a polished mackintosh. "Huh?"

Olivia extracted her phone from a pocket, clicked a few buttons, and held it up. It was a video shot from a balcony looking down on a dimly lighted swimming pool empty of people but for Rizzo and a woman in naked embrace and bobbing against each other in the shallow end.

He made a sheepish grin. "Look, what can I say? You were asleep, and I was drunk, and I went out to get some air, and she was . . . you know, I made a mistake."

"The only mistake you made was getting caught."

"Look, I'm sorry."

"Correction. You made a second mistake—bringing me with you."

"Jesus! It was nothing personal. I was blotto, okay? And, you know, I just messed up is all."

"Yeah, you messed up because I'm not one of the notches on your fucking bedpost."

Rizzo didn't quite know where to appeal, turning his head from Olivia to Kirk and back. "Look, I'm sorry," he muttered. "I don't know what to say. I'm sorry."

"Sorry doesn't cut it. You used me, Ted, and that's why I left."

"How did I use you?"

"To make you feel cool and important and accomplished. Whatever, you're forty-seven years old, three times divorced, childless, and all your friends are married with kids, and you're still playing frat boy. Maybe it's time to grow up."

"I thought we had a relationship going."

"You don't want a relationship. You just want to bed hop—or what you call your polyamory thing."

His mouth made an O of comprehension. "What? Where did you . . . ?"

"From Facebook and someone who knows—Nora Montana. Your latest ex-wife."

"Nora? What did she say?"

"She said you think with your man-gland."

"Nora's a bitch and knows shit."

"I just wish I'd gotten that message before I left." Then with her Mona Lisa smile, Olivia said. "Ted, if all you're interested in is getting laid, get yourself a sex doll."

Kirk wanted to applaud.

"Yeah, well, it'd be a lot better than you."

Still smiling, Olivia said, "Ted, are you familiar with the expression 'Go fuck yourself'?"

For a stiff moment Rizzo glowered at them trying to come up with an exit line. Then he turned and headed to his car. As he moved off, Kirk clicked on his phone and muttered into it. When Rizzo reached his car, he opened his car door and gave Olivia and Kirk the finger, and then peeled away.

Kirk pocketed his phone and smiled at Olivia. "How about that glass of wine?"

"Who was that?" she asked.

"Unfinished business."

It was getting dark and near closing. Oliva took Kirk's arm as they walked to their cars and started up. "Sorry about all that," she said.

"My pleasure."

She smiled. "He's not you."

"Aren't I lucky?"

They pulled onto Spruce Avenue as Kirk led them to the front exit at Mount Auburn Street. But as they neared it, two police vehicles were blocking the gate with their blue-and-whites flashing. And surrounded by uniforms was Ted Rizzo, his hands in cuffs.

"What the fuck is this?" he said to Kirk as he got out of his car and approached them, Olivia beside him. "A fucking ambush. What'd I do?"

Kirk shook hands with Sergeant Detective Frank Sabo who took the lead. "Mr. Rizzo, you're under arrest for breaking and entering, criminal destruction of property, and the malicious killing of an animal."

"What the fuck you talking about?"

"His cat," the sergeant said. "We have a video, which we'll be happy to show you at the station."

"You motherfucker," Rizzo said to Kirk as one officer took hold of his arm and Sabo recited Rizzo's Miranda rights.

"Nobody likes a potty-mouth," Kirk said to Rizzo who continued swearing as the officers led him to one of the squad cars. Then to Olivia: "The other perp."

Olivia looked at him in disbelief. "What?"

"He still had a key to the house and let himself in. He also knew the code to the security system because he installed it and disengaged the cameras while he took Daisy outside and mauled her with an ice pick and left her dead on the grass."

She put her hand to her mouth. "I don't believe it."

"You'll believe it when you see the video from Dave and Jessica's security cam."

As she watched the cruiser leave with Rizzo in the back seat, she said, "But why?"

"You don't like somebody, you kill his cat," Kirk said. He then thanked Sabo and the officers. They watched them leave after the first car in the direction of the Cambridge Police Station.

"That horrible creep."

"Well, we got him, case closed. By the way, there's a bottle of wine waiting for us at Greg's. Still up for it?"

"Yes, more than ever."

EPILOGUE

Two weeks later

"IT WAS TOO LATE. She controlled everything including her own death. We found her slumped over on the bench, a water bottle on the ground, and an empty vial of atropine."

"Atropine. Isn't that what she used on Sylvie Thornton?"

"Yes. It's to treat a heart condition that her husband had. Take too much, it kills."

Just yesterday they had discovered three anonymous fifty-thousand-dollar deposits in different bank accounts of Sylvie Thornton that matched withdrawals from accounts held by Morgan Cassidy. Sylvie had been blackmailing again, but this time it killed her. *Do we ever change?* Kirk wondered. In literature, characters usually ended up sadder but wiser. But the difference between life and literature was that literature had to make sense.

But maybe we do change. He smiled at Olivia, taking in the face he loved.

"I guess she knew she'd get life without chance of parole and decided that she couldn't spend the rest of her days in MCI-Concord."

"Especially given the lifestyle she was used to—a mansion by the sea, endless traveling, and privileges most people dream about."

"Right." *And I'm back with you.*

Like old times, they were at Mama Lucia's in the North End. They had ordered their favorites—Olivia, shrimp scampi and Kirk, frutti de mare. They shared a bottle of a Sangiovese varietal.

"She was the alpha of the group," Kirk said. "Like a grand puppeteer, she set up others including Sylvie Thornton, Riley Malone, Grayson Gallagher—even her own father. Thankfully, Krista Saliba was out of the loop."

"Given how clever and methodical she was, she could have made an excellent detective," Olivia said.

"Except she had a 'mind of winter.'"

"Poetry for a psychopath."

"Right."

"So, what's going to happen to Ted Rizzo?"

"With all the charges, he could get seven years. And maybe even more when he gets out, since he apparently made false promises about contract work, claiming that materials never came from vendors, yet they did, and he used them on other projects. A kind of Ponzi scheme for contractors."

"'One nail, no jail,'" Olivia said. "I still can't believe that he killed Daisy."

Kirk nodded. "I'm just glad he didn't decide to set off a gas leak."

"Me too." Olivia took a sip of wine.

"I don't know how to say this without saying this, but I missed you."

"I missed you too."

Yes!

"And how's Mandy doing?"

"She's great and is going to have a baby next July."

"That's wonderful."

"Even more wonderful, she asked me to be the baby's godfather."

"What an honor," Olivia said. She put her glass down with a clink. "So where do we go from here?"

"Well, I joined a gym and a book group."

Olivia smiled. "Good start."

"I may even take up pickleball."

She laughed. "Even better."

"And I found a marriage counselor. With your permission, we start next week."

She smiled again and took his hand. "Better still." Then she added, "And what do you say that when the snows come, we head for the White Mountains for a long weekend."

Kirk gave her hand a squeeze. "Now that sounds like a plan."

And they clinked glasses.

BOOK CLUB DISCUSSION QUESTIONS

1. Do you think the title, *Rumor of Evil*, is appropriate? How do you think it fits the story?

2. How would you characterize the working relationship between Detective Kirk Lucian and Detective Mandy Wing? How did you see it evolve from the beginning of the story to the end?

3. What did you think about the almost two-decade shift in settings?

4. How do you think the author handled the discussion of the prejudice against Roma people (Gypsies)? Realistically? With sensitivity? Do you see parallels to today's social and political issues and/or conspiracy theories?

5. Who do you think had the most compelling reason to murder Vadima? Sylvie?

6. Initially, who was your main suspect for Vadima's murder? For Sylvie's murder? Did either of these change as the story evolved?

7. Did you see evidence of a psychopathic personality in any of the characters?

8. Teenage girls set the stage for this story. How much do you think teenagers have changed over the decades? Could this happen in today's world?

9. What do you see ahead for Kirk and Olivia? Can they survive the loss of a child?

10. Which character in *Rumor of Evil* did you find the most sympathetic? The most admirable?

11. Which character did you find the least sympathetic and least admirable?

12. When the killers were revealed, were you surprised? Disappointed?

13. What are the most compelling and controversial issues of today that this novel addresses?

14. Would you like to see Kirk and Mandy return in future homicide investigations? Do you have any suggestions for them when they do?

For more information about Rumor of Evil *and author Gary Braver, visit his website at: www.garybraver.com.*